The Boiled Frog Syndrome

MARTY RUBIN

THE BOILED FROG SYNDROME

A Novel of Love, Sex and Politics

Boston • Alyson Publications, Inc.

Published as a trade paperback original
by Alyson Publications, Inc.,
40 Plympton St., Boston, Mass. 02118.

Distributed in the U.K. by GMP Publishers,
PO Box 247, London, N15 6RW, England.

First U.S. edition: September, 1987

ISBN 1-55583-108-7

To all the freedom fighters, everywhere, who oppose fascism of every variety, whether religious or otherwise, wherever and whenever it appears.

I

IT GETS COLD IN EUROPE IN WINTER

1

Whenever he awakened in Amsterdam on a cold, grey, wintry Dutch morning, Stephen Ashcroft would find himself temporarily disoriented, adrift in space and time. Huddling under the flimsy blanket in his chilly room at the Leather Eagle Hotel, he thought that he was back in the pleasant little house in Fort Lauderdale that he had shared with Troy. In a moment, he thought, he would get up and adjust the air conditioner to a more moderate level, then pull on a pair of shorts and take a stroll in the back yard. The orange, grapefruit and key lime trees would be heavy with fruit, and the bougainvillea in bloom. From the kitchen would come wafting the smell of freshly brewed coffee as his young lover, Troy, always up ahead of him, prepared breakfast. They would clasp each other tightly in a morning embrace, grateful to have survived the night, grateful for each other. In the cooler months, they would take their breakfast outdoors on the patio; in the dense heat of the South Florida summer, indoors in the dining alcove. Sometimes they held hands across the breakfast table, even after five years together.

Suddenly he realized where he was, and opened his eyes to the clean but shabby little hotel room. His face became a mask of pain and bitterness as he fought to hold back his tears. Next to him, Kiki stirred in sleep, and then, almost as though feeling Ashcroft's pain, came fully awake.

The slender brown Indonesian boy raised himself on one elbow and regarded Ashcroft compassionately.

"Oh, Stephen, Mijnheer Stephen. . ." he began to speak, then cuddled himself tightly in Ashcroft's arms. The older man, his face still a mask of pain, held Kiki to him. The boy caressed and kissed him, gazing with adoration at the strongly-chiseled features, the firm jaw, the heavy salt-and-pepper moustache, and the greying hair of the American.

"Sometimes, my friend, it is better to cry. To let your feelings out, *neen?*" Besides his native Dutch, he spoke excellent English, plus a smattering of German, French and Spanish. He worked as a go-go boy at the Viking Bar, on a small street off the Leidseplein whose name Ashcroft never could remember, although he knew where the bar was. Kiki also did a little high-class hustling to earn a few extra guilders; in Amsterdam, it was a quasi-respectable profession.

"I have no more tears left, Kiki." He had a deep baritone voice that had once been considered sensuous; now, it sounded as though it emanated from a deep, hollow space.

"You would like maybe a shot of *oude genever?*" The bottle on the dresser was still half-full.

"Oh, God, no," replied Ashcroft. "You know I'm not a morning drinker. Why don't you slip down to the bar and bring us a pot of coffee?"

"And *uitsmijter?*"

"I'm not hungry. You can order *uitsmijter* for yourself. Tell them to put it on my tab." The "tab" was a polite fiction. Dirk, the owner of the hotel, refused to accept any money from Ashcroft for food or accommodations, although occasionally he'd let Ashcroft pay for a drink at the bar just to save face.

"After all that has happened over there," Dirk had explained, "it is the very least I can do for an American brother, especially with the brave work that you are doing." In Amsterdam, the spirit of Anne Frank was never very far away.

Kiki leapt out of bed and dressed very quickly before the chill of the room could penetrate. He was about nineteen years old, with firm, slender brown limbs, a slender, well-defined torso, and lovely Oriental features with a small nose, very sensuous mouth, and those exotic almond-shaped eyes. A lock of his thick, dark hair hung boyishly over his forehead.

When he had left the room, Ashcroft got up and urinated in the sink, not daring to brave the icy, draughty hallway and the steep, winding staircase to the nearest bathroom, which was one flight up. He washed himself in the lukewarm water, and brushed his teeth. In the mirror his face looked bleak and drawn. He had aged at least five years since leaving America, although it had been only eighteen months.

With a shock he remembered that his forty-fifth birthday was only two weeks off. "What a hell of a time in a man's life," he reflected, "to be a man without a country. And I used to think that expatriates were so romantic." He rinsed his mouth and spat into the sink, again fighting back the urge to cry. "What a bunch of lousy bullshit!" he exclaimed to himself.

When Kiki returned bearing a heavily laden tray, he served Ashcroft his coffee in bed, then undressed and got back into bed to eat breakfast, the tray resting between them. He ate hungrily, with the morning appetite of youth. Ashcroft sipped his coffee.

"You must eat, Stephen," the boy said, spearing a forkful of egg, ham and bread and proffering it to the older man, who pushed it away.

"Thanks all the same, Kiki. The coffee will do just fine, thank you."

"It is a bitter thing to lose one's country," the boy said, sipping from a large glass of the fresh, delicious Dutch milk. "After all, I lost mine, too."

"Not really," replied Ashcroft. "You told me yourself that your parents fled back to the mother country after the fall of the Dutch East Indies, and you were born much later, right here in Amsterdam. Besides, you also said they were more Dutch than Indonesian."

"Yes, this is true. My father was a lawyer, and half white. But still, I feel as though I live between two worlds, not fully belonging to either. Now, if I were some blond, rosy-cheeked Dutch boy..."

Ashcroft smiled in spite of himself. "If you were a blond, rosy-cheeked Dutch boy, you very probably wouldn't be here in this bed." Indeed, every time he had tricked with someone like that, it had been too painful, as it tended to remind him of Troy.

Kiki finished his breakfast, removed the tray and Ashcroft's coffee cup, and slid back into bed. "I think we should make love to each other now," he said.

"Didn't we make love last night?"

"Yes, but you were drunk. You had obliterated your pain. Now we should make morning love." His breath was warm against the older man's ear; somehow the boy always smelled of sandalwood and spice. He was nibbling on Ashcroft's ear, his hot little tongue flicking in and out of the orifice. His slender, busy hands made a sensuous, erotic rhythm as they caressed the older man's body eagerly. With a sigh, Ashcroft surrendered to the boy's embrace.

"Just relax, Stephen," murmured Kiki. "Let me do everything." He lay on top of Ashcroft face-to-face, kissing his eyes and taking quick little nibbling, teasing bites of his earlobes with his sharp, white teeth. Sliding himself down, he then started working on Ashcroft's nipples, again with those perfect teeth teasing and nibbling. Ashcroft began to caress the boy gently, running his hands through Kiki's thick, dark hair and clinging to his shoulders. Kiki moaned with delight and, slid further down, tonguing Ashcroft's navel before finally burying his face in the older man's crotch.

Now fully aroused, Ashcroft grabbed Kiki and pulled him back to a face-to-face position. Clasping the boy in his arms, he turned Kiki over on his back and began in turn to kiss and lick and nibble at the firm, slender brown body with a passion that, when he first awakened, he could not have anticipated. When he in turn had worked his way from the boy's firm but tiny nipples, past his navel down to his crotch, he then turned the boy over onto his stomach. Before attempting to penetrate him, Ashcroft put on a condom; even here in Europe, in the waning days of the plague, it was considered good hygiene.

"Please, Mijnheer Stephen," begged the boy. "Not that way, as though you were some rough sailor I'd picked up on the docks."

Ashcroft held him tightly in his arms. "How, then, Kiki?"

"Face to face. You know the way I like it best."

Ashcroft smiled. "The good old missionary position. Okay, son, you've got it." Positioning Kiki on his back, he raised the boy's perfectly smooth, slender legs over his shoulders. Burying himself to the hilt in the sensuous warmth of the boy's body, their lips locked together as Kiki clung to his shoulders, Ashcroft was able, briefly, to lose himself in the act of love, and momentarily to forget his pain.

When they had finished their lovemaking, they lay cuddled, legs intertwined, under the covers.

"I love all men with hair on their chests," Kiki said, "but there's something special about Americans. No other men are ever *macho* in quite the same way." He reached over and turned on the radio that stood on the nightstand. A program of music was just ending and a news broadcast came on. Kiki moved to change the station.

"No!" said Ashcroft. "Leave it on!" By this time he understood enough Dutch to be able to follow the local news broadcasts, but there was nothing in the news that morning that concerned him. The Common Market was prospering, India was having another famine, and a hypersonic had crashed into a mountain in Brazil. There was no mention of the United States.

Kiki kissed him tenderly. "Stephen, Stephen," he said. "Do you think it will happen all of a sudden? Do you really think that one morning you will listen to a news broadcast and suddenly the long nightmare will be over? That you will be able to go back?"

"Do you think that's what I really think?"

"*Ja*, Stephen, in your heart you do, because Americans are all sentimentalists and romantics, and everything must come out right in the end. You believe justice will triumph and good will prevail over evil. Stephen, my beautiful hairy-chested American friend, I fear that things will not change so quickly for you. The work you are doing will go on for a very long time. I know that I myself will not see my true homeland ever again, and probably neither will you." He got out of bed and began to dress. "I must go now. Will you be at the Viking Bar this evening?"

"Perhaps," said Ashcroft. "You understand, I live from day to day."

"I understand."

"Do you have enough money, Kiki? Do you need a few guilders?"

"Don't be ridiculous. Have I ever taken money from you?"

"No, but last night you could have had that fat German traveling salesman. He'd have been good for two hundred guilders, at least."

"I can have men like that anytime I want. To be with you is an honor, a privilege. I know who you are and what it is that you do. Never would I accept money from you." He put his arms around Ashcroft's neck and kissed him. "I may be a nineteen-year-old Dutch whore," he said, "but at least I know what it is all about, the meaning of gay pride and brotherhood."

"I wish more of our own people had felt that way," said Ashcroft sadly.

When Kiki had left, his agile footsteps tripping down the narrow, winding staircase, Ashcroft considered taking a shower, but the thought of the cold, draughty bathroom one flight up did not appeal to him. "I'll go to the sauna later," he decided, and gave himself a sponge bath out of the sink, thinking wistfully of American bathrooms.

When he came downstairs to the bar, Dirk, the owner, had all his employees gathered about him for their morning staff meeting. With characteristic Dutch courtesy, he switched almost in mid-sentence from Dutch to English as Ashcroft entered the room.

"*Dank U*," said Ashcroft, smiling appreciatively, "but would you please — *alstublieft* — speak *Nederlands?* How the hell can I practice my Dutch if you people speak nothing but English to me all the time?"

That made the owner and his boys burst out laughing. Dirk, a tall, handsome leatherman in his late thirties, threw an arm around Ashcroft.

"You think, then, that you might stay here, perhaps? And become one of us?"

"You make me feel like one of you now," said Ashcroft. "This is the *warmest* country I have ever known." A blast of icy wind off the canal, as if to belie his statement, blew in underneath the ancient front door. "I don't know my plans," he added, in answer to Dirk's question. "As I told my friend Kiki just now, I live from one day to the next."

"That's all very good, mate," said Hartt, the pimply English boy who was night bartender. "We know you have your work in the Resistance cut out for you. But you might think twice about settlin' down, eh? That little Kiki thinks the world of you, y'know."

"I know. If I ever do stop in one place, this will definitely be the place. Unless I can go home, of course." He could not help but notice the quick, surreptitious exchange of looks they gave each other. He asked Gerard, the handsome French day bartender,

"Could I have some more coffee, *s'il vous plaît?*"

"Of course." He poured a cup of the lovely strong, dark Dutch coffee and, at a signal from Dirk, a shot of cognac next to it. This time, with the northern European cold of the winter day already seeping into his bones, Ashcroft did not refuse. He downed it and sipped his coffee.

"Oh, I almost forgot," said Dirk. "Ten Eyck phoned again. He wants to see you as soon as possible." It was an open secret that hotel as a message center and courier relay station for the American Resistance.

"I'm flattered," said Ashcroft. Aaron Ten Eyck was a wealthy Jewish member of Parliament, a Holocaust survivor, and a diamond merchant by trade. He was known for his international support of gay and other human rights causes, and it was at his behest that the Dutch Parliament had passed, quite unanimously, a very strong resolution condemning the internal policies of the American government and its leader, the Reverend President Peter Joshua Wickerly. When it came time for the Queen to sign the resolution, actually a mere formality in a tiny constitutional monarchy, she had chosen to do so on national television from the Hague.

"That's one news brief they won't show on the American telly," a British newsman had wisecracked.

"In this country," responded a Dutch colleague, "that bastard Wickerly would be in jail."

His coffee finished, Ashcroft bundled up with his muffler around his neck and the warm parka of his duffel coat over his head. Dirk offered to drive him to see Ten Eyck, but Ashcroft refused, saying,

"Thanks, but you've got a business to run. I know how to get there." A blast of icy wind off the North Sea enveloped him as he stepped into the street.

2

The Leather Eagle Hotel, which catered primarily to leathermen and bikers, was located on the Oude Zijde Voorburgwal, the narrow street which fronted on the canal of that name. One block away was the infamous Warmoesstraat, with its porno shops, cribs, leather bars and brothels. Ducking his head against the wind, Ashcroft crossed the little canal bridge, barely wide enough for one vehicle, and proceeded past the bars and restaurants with their windows steamed up on this winter morning, each with its rack of outside vending machines that sold hot and cold snacks and drinks. A few minutes' walk brought him onto the Damrak, the main boulevard that terminated at the Central Station, beyond which lay the broad expanse of waterfront and the busy port.

Adjoining the Central Station was the main post office. Ashcroft checked his box for mail, but there was none. In front of the railroad station was the trolley terminus. Ashcroft caught the trolley which took him out past Vondel Park to an elegant block of nineteenth-century apartment buildings. On the fifth floor of one of these, in quiet, tasteful elegance, Aaron Ten Eyck lived alone, except for a couple of servants. Ashcroft had met him once at a human rights rally, but had never been to his home.

The old man himself opened the door and welcomed Ashcroft. He was tall and very portly, with a fringe of white hair and a small white moustache and goatee, neatly trimmed. His features were fleshy and sybaritic, but the eyes were warm and kind. He wore a brocaded silk smoking jacket. Ashcroft was pleased to note that the walls were lined with well-filled bookshelves, and that the paintings were mostly originals of old Dutch masters and French impressionists. There was a reassuring quality about the room, and about Ten Eyck himself.

"I'm so glad you could come, Ashcroft. Let me have the maid fetch something warm for you."

"That would be much appreciated."

Ten Eyck chuckled sympathetically. "A little colder here than in Florida, eh?" His one affectation was his English, which was much more crisply-accented upper-class British than was usual in most of his compatriots; the bilingual Amsterdam people tend to speak English that is almost mid-Atlantic; some, even, almost American. Ashcroft had heard that following the outbreak of World War Two, Ten Eyck had fled Holland ahead of the Nazi occupation, and had spent the war in England, flying, with no small amount of distinction, for the R.A.F.

The maid brought hot chocolate and biscuits and little glasses of Curaçao. When she had left the room, her footsteps silent on the thick Oriental carpeting, she drew the sliding doors shut behind her.

Ten Eyck opened a panel on the Louis XIV cabinet that contained his computer console, revealing a state-of-the-art bug monitor and baffler. He turned it on, but there was no warning beep.

"I doubt very much," said Ashcroft, "that our Reverend President Peter Joshua Wickerly is listening."

"One never knows, does one? I shouldn't be in the least sur-prised if your C.I.A. chaps were trying to share this conversation, although I had the whole apartment swept and scanned this very morning."

The thought had occurred to Stephen also, but only as a very remote possibility. "I don't think I'm very high on any of their pri-ority lists," he said.

"Nowadays they're not very discriminating about priorities, as I'm sure you must know. Believe me, my boy, they'll hit any-one, anywhere, who is working against your Reverend President."

Ashcroft shrugged. "I can't let myself worry about things like that. I didn't when I was active in the movement at home, and I don't let it stop me now."

"You're a very brave man."

"No," replied Ashcroft. "I'm a very frightened man."

"But you act like a very brave one. What is the trick?"

Ashcroft thought deeply for a moment. "The trick," he finally decided, "is in not pretending to be without fear. Any intelligent person with an ounce of imagination knows what fear is, much more so than some insensitive clod. The trick is to look fear in the eye, acknowledge it, and then just sort of carry on anyway." Then he added, very softly and respectfully, "Isn't that what you did, sir, during the War?"

Ten Eyck smiled and nodded. "That's exactly what I did. I was flying Lancaster bombers over the Ruhr. Industrial raids, mostly. You recall, or rather you can't possibly recall, you were too young, that the Lankies were made mostly of plywood. Didn't take much shrapnel to tear them apart, and the Jerry flak was most intense. But, d'you know, I made it through one hundred and forty mis-sions without even so much as a scratch?"

"One hundred and forty bombing missions?" Ashcroft ex-claimed in amazement.

"Oh, yes, indeed. There were chaps who flew two hundred. After that, I'm afraid, the old nerves started to go and they grounded me. Spent the rest of the war shuffling bumpf behind a desk. Well, I didn't ask you here to listen to an old man's reminis-cences, did I? What do you hear from America these days?"

"All bad," said Ashcroft. "There are a lot of men dying in the camps."

"Really? I had been told they were relatively humane, not at all like the German camps during the Holocaust."

"I'm sure they're quite humane, technically speaking. Immaculately clean, adequate food and clothing, and at least minimal medical care."

"Then why are they dying? Surely not a resurgence of the AIDS epidemic of the Eighties, I trust?"

"No, very rarely that. Actually that's really not much of a medical problem anymore, although it's still very much of a political one. As soon as their program of grotesque experiments had been discontinued, the number of cases reached a plateau and then started to drop off. Unfortunately, the medical panic factor is taking much longer to eradicate. The one thing the doctors seem to have forgotten, in their mad dash to serve the present regime even if it means abandoning all common sense, is that a virus is a virus is a virus, no matter how deadly. Once everyone who was susceptible had been exposed, all we had left was the dead and the permanently immune, or, if not immune, at least very strongly resistant. Of course it was too late for us, politically; by the time Wickerly and his cohorts had attained power, we gay people had been relegated to the status of lepers, rather like the caste of Untouchables in India. But at least, Mijnheer, AIDS is not the reason so many of us are not surviving the camps."

"Then why are they dying?"

"I don't really know. Somehow, things always seem to get lost in the bureaucratic shuffle. If there's an outbreak of influenza, for example, the medicines never seem to arrive in time. Or all of a sudden the food trays give an entire camp food poisoning or dysentery. Most of our people survive it, but always a few more die. The suicide rate is high, too. You must remember that these are, for the most part, people who basically believed in America; who thought that this could never happen in our country. They just can't seem to accept the fact that it *has* happened."

"Isn't it amazing," said Ten Eyck, "how history always repeats itself? One cannot help but recall the fat, sleek, prosperous Jews of Germany, the cream of their country's arts, sciences, business and professional life. 'But we are good Germans!' they all said. 'We have nothing to fear! This madness will all pass away.'

And next thing you know, off they all went to the jolly old concentration camps."

"Yes, what happened in my country was very similar. Businessmen and professionals who'd been in the closet for years were swept up in the DIVAF program. Suddenly they were taken out of their nice, comfy homes and condos and forced to live in barracks. Army food off plastic trays. Bunks instead of waterbeds. And lovers always separated, of course." He broke off painfully.

"Did you — forgive me, dear lad — did you have a lover?"

"I still do have a lover. He's in one of the camps."

Very gently, Ten Eyck replied, "But you cannot know that, for certain."

Ashcroft smiled sadly. "Yes, I do know it for certain. He's strong and smart and resourceful. If anyone can survive the camps, he will."

"And when did you last have news of him?"

"I have a letter that he wrote less than three weeks ago and had smuggled out of the camp. It came over on the hypersonic. He's alive and, for the moment, physically well." His eyes filled with tears. "God damn it, he *must* survive!"

"Of course he must," agreed Ten Eyck. "Well, then!" His voice was suddenly crisp and military. "Enough of this sadness. Let's get down to business, shall we?"

"Yes, of course. How can I be of service to you?"

"Not to me, Stephen. To your community. And, in a sense, to the larger community."

"I'm listening, Mijnheer."

"Tell me, what does the name Yad Vashem mean to you?"

"It's in Israel. It's the museum of the Holocaust."

"Very good, young man! Not too many Gentiles, if you will forgive me, are aware of it. I'm sure that as a journalist, you can appreciate the purpose of such a museum."

"Only too well. Incredible as it may seem, even now the enemies of Israel and of the Jewish people are trying to claim that the Nazi Holocaust never really happened. We, of course, both know better. Actually, it was the most thoroughly documented cataclysm in human history."

"Of course it was. The Germans actually thought they were

doing the world a favor, and that history would one day reward them. And they were such meticulous record-keepers, so precise and meticulous about keeping documents as they are about everything else. Well, and how much do you know about Yad Vashem?"

"The Israeli government has assembled, in the museum of the Holocaust, all the evidence for posterity. Books. Photographs. Physical evidence. Newsreel footage. The pictures of the furnaces and the piled-up corpses that were taken by the Allied armies that liberated the camps. And finally, videotaped interviews with as many survivors as they could find. Of course, there are still those who will claim it was all a Jewish media hoax."

"I wish it were, Ashcroft. I really wish it were. Do you think Yad Vashem was a very good idea?"

"Of course it was. No one can guarantee that it won't happen again, but at least keeping a record for posterity is a step in the right direction."

"But it is happening again," Ten Eyck reminded him. "Isn't it?"

"Yes," agreed Ashcroft." It happened to us. To me and Troy. I got out in time, he stayed and got caught up in the DIVAF program. But what has this to do with Yad Vashem?"

Aaron Ten Eyck leaned forward in his leather armchair. "I want you to begin a similar piece of work."

"Not a museum, surely?"

"Well, not quite. Not exactly. But at least a record. Firm evidence. Documentation. Videotapes. When the madness in your country has finally settled down, the present regime will have rewritten their own version of history. We need something we can take in front of the World Court and make liars out of them."

Ashcroft thought about that for a moment. "Why me?" he finally asked.

"Because you're the most professionally qualified of all the refugees presently working in the Resistance. You were a great photographer and journalist, my boy. At least, I always thought so."

"Thank you, sir."

"The proof, as they say, is in the pudding. In a highly literate country such as England, they don't usually bother with the ungrammatical natterings of the frowsy little pencil-pushers you

Americans used to call journalists. But you were one of the few whose stories and photographs have been regularly printed in the *Guardian*, under your own by-line."

"I appreciate that recognition."

"And totally out of the closet, too! Now, that took bloody balls, I must say, to have been so open. Whenever you wrote about the affairs of the gay community, you actually stated that you were writing as a member of that community. I admire that."

"I wouldn't have had it any other way, sir. Besides, that openness very often gave me much better *entrée* to the people with whom I really wanted to speak."

Again, Ten Eyck leaned forward confidentially. Almost reverently, he asked, "How well did you know Douglas McKittrick?"

"Probably better than anyone else on his political team. I was with him when he was assassinated."

Ten Eyck was silent a moment. "I envy you the privilege of having known him. I feel that had he been allowed to live, he would one day have attained the political stature of another Disraeli or Lloyd George. And I want the full story of his brutal assassination to be part of this documentation that I have proposed. But first, are you ready to take on this work?"

"I'm not quite sure. I'd love to do it — in fact, I'd be very proud to do it; but you must understand that I am greatly depended upon for, shall we say, certain things?"

"I appreciate that, Stephen, but I know approximately what it is that you do in the Resistance. There are others who can do that sort of work quite as well. Can't you take a leave of absence for something like this?"

"I'll speak to my group leader. It may take a little time to arrange. Apart from that, I'm ready and willing."

"Splendid! Let me know when you're able to begin."

When they shook hands in parting, Ashcroft had the strange feeling that he had found a friend. His head was reeling as he walked from Ten Eyck's apartment to the trolley stop. All his life he had been an ardent reader and student of history; indeed, he had reported and photographed it while it was happening. Now, it seemed, he was to have his share in writing it.

He decided to spend the afternoon at the sauna. Although he felt sexually sated after his morning with Kiki, at least he could

get warm and clean. There was no need to actually trick with anyone if he didn't want to. Perhaps a little massage for relaxation,
and to help him sort out his thoughts.

He was shivering again by the time the trolley arrived.

3

Ashcroft loved the saunas. They were the only places in Europe
where he was able to get completely warm during the winter. His
favorite in Amsterdam was located behind the C & A Department
Store, not far from the Wells-Fargo Bar. It had a gymnasium and a
swimming pool in addition to all the usual facilities.

In the steam room, one of the younger men, a handsome
blond in his early twenties, kept staring at Ashcroft as though he
knew him. Finally, he came over and sat next to Stephen.

"*Spreekt u Engels?*" he asked. "Do you speak English?"

"*Ja*," replied Ashcroft, "although I understand a little
Nederlands."

"You must forgive me for staring at you so rudely," the young
nan said, "but you seem very familiar to me."

Ashcroft shrugged. "Perhaps we saw each other in a bar."

"No, I don't think so. Please, may I have the privilege
soaping you?" When Ashcroft did not refuse, he took the loofah
sponge and gently lathered Ashcroft's back and chest, then knelt
and applied the suds to his lower torso and thighs. When he
looked at Ashcroft, his intense blue eyes seemed to be running
him systematically through a file of dossiers. Finally he
exclaimed,

"*Ach!* I have it now! How foolish of me not to have recognized
you at once! You are Stephen Ashcroft, the writer." He extended
his hand. "My name is Hans."

Stephen accepted the young man's firm, masculine handshake. Hans took a bucket of warm water and washed the lather
off Ashcroft's body. Then he positioned himself behind the older
man and began to massage the tenseness from his back. His strong
hands felt kind and reassuring.

"Wouldn't you like to come to my room and lie down?" invited the young man, sensing Ashcroft's preference for privacy.

More out of loneliness and compassion than sexual desire, Ashcroft assented.

They smoked a joint of *kif* together. Ashcroft lay on his back in the dimly-lit cubicle, his eyes closed, the strong North African *kif* spreading through his body and giving him as much of a sense of peace and relaxation as he ever attained these days. He was vaguely aware of his companion caressing and stroking him. Hans was strong and robust, with well-defined muscles and peach-fuzz blond hair on his chest and on his legs. They made love companionably, but when they had finished, Ashcroft found to his dismay that his eyes were brimming with tears.

"You have a great sadness, my friend," said Hans. "Just like all of the American refugees."

"Yes," agreed Ashcroft. "I do."

"What is it about me that made you cry? Do I remind you of someone?"

"Yes, very much."

"I see." He bent over Ashcroft and kissed his tears. "Come, my friend, let us go have a workout in the gymnasium and then a swim in the pool. Exercise is a great remedy for sadness."

Arm-in-arm, they went to the gym. After they had pumped iron to the point of exhaustion, each one spotting the other on the heavier lifts and bench presses, they took a shower and then swam together in the pool. Ashcroft was shocked by how much the boy reminded him of Troy, except that Hans was somewhat more slender and did not have Troy's square-jawed, all-American look. His hair was longer, too.

"We will see each other again," said Hans as they were dressing. It was a statement, not a question.

"I'm sorry," replied Ashcroft, "but I never make plans for the future. I enjoyed our afternoon together, though."

"Where are you staying in Amsterdam?"

"At the Leather Eagle Hotel. But I'm not home very much."

"Look, my friend, there is something you should know." He pulled out his wallet and showed Ashcroft his police badge and identification card. "Since you are one of our more distinguished refugees, we are bound to meet eventually. That happens to be my official area of concern. You see, because I myself am gay, they thought I would be most effective in the Refugee Liaison Unit."

"I've heard of it." Nothing shocked Ashcroft anymore, not even the revelation that his companion of the afternoon was a cop. "Just what is it that your unit does?"

"Oh, we deal with any problems that arise that are outside the scope of our social services and relocation people. For example, we try to protect you from trouble. We also, unfortunately, in some cases, have to try to prevent you from getting into trouble. Tell me the truth, now. Are you in the Resistance?"

"I never heard of it," replied Ashcroft.

Hans smiled enigmatically. "We shall see." They shook hands, almost formally. "Good luck, Stephen Ashcroft."

"*Dank U.*" That's all I needed, thought Ashcroft, as he passed through the arcade that led back to the Damrak. A gay cop who's keeping his eye on the Resistance.

The late afternoon sky had darkened, portending the blizzard to follow. Ashcroft stopped at a rank of vending machines and bought a hot *brodje* and a cup of coffee.

The worst part about the Resistance work was the endless waiting, the killing of time. Sometimes days would pass during which there was no activity and no communication. Always an active individual by nature, Ashcroft could not accustom himself to days of reading, shopping, sightseeing, or just hanging out. How many times, after all, can one visit the Anne Frank House or the Rijksmuseum? This was one of those days. Not yet ready to go back to the hotel, he caught a movie. When he left the theater, the snow had started to fall.

It was almost nine o'clock by the time he got back to the Leather Eagle. Hartt, the pimply English boy, was already behind the bar for the night shift. Dirk, the owner, greeted him warmly.

"You're just barely in time for dinner, my friend. We've had *fricadellen*, and I believe there are still some left." He knew that Ashcroft loved the large, savory Dutch meatballs.

"Thank you, Dirk, but I'm not very hungry." He always felt a little guilty about the fictitious "tab" that Dirk always refused to collect.

"*Ach*, don't let me hear that!" He called to Gerard, who had finished his shift and was sitting at the end of the bar having a drink. "Go to the kitchen and tell Pieter to bring Mijnheer Ashcroft some dinner." To Ashcroft he said, "I know it is hard, my friend, but you must keep up your strength. There is so much work that lies ahead."

In a few minutes Pieter, the kitchen boy, spread a placemat in front of Ashcroft and served him a large bowl of homemade soup, with chunks of chicken and fresh vegetables in it. Then came a huge plate of *fricadellen* with noodles and gravy. Ashcroft ate desultorily, without much appetite, not wanting to hurt Dirk's feelings. He washed down his meal with several mugs of strong, dark beer.

When he had eaten as much as he could of his dinner, and Pieter had cleared his place, he remained alone at the bar, not wanting to go upstairs to his room. Outside, the snowfall had freshened into a blizzard, and there were no other customers at the bar. Drinking shot after shot of *oude genever*, each one accompanied by another mug of dark beer, Ashcroft took out Troy's last smuggled letter and read it for perhaps the hundredth time; the folded paper was starting to come apart at the creases.

My dearest Stephen: (Troy wrote.)

I have no assurances that this letter will ever reach you, so I'm going to restrict myself to information rather than endearments. Of course, the mail route has been fairly reliable up to now, and I'm told that eventually you will be contacted by someone who will take your answering letter. The ordinary mails are out of the question, as part of their technique is to allow the detainees to have mail privileges only to and from immediate next of kin, and as you know, I don't have any. Except you!

First of all, let me put your mind at ease about one thing. We are not being physically mistreated or abused in any manner, shape or form that we can detect. They are far too sophisticated for that. We receive plenty of food, not particularly appetizing from the standpoint of a gourmet such as yourself, but well-balanced and nourishing. The barracks are kept clean. We're given clothing, of a sort, when the limited wardrobe each of us was allowed to bring with him wears out; usually the issue is second-hand military coveralls or fatigue uniforms. Those of us who have funds on deposit are allowed to purchase a small weekly ration of beer and wine, but not hard liquor. We may also buy toilet articles and a limited selection of snack foods, which we gladly share with the needier detainees. The spirit of gay brotherhood in most barracks is really quite good, all things considered; we are, after all, a pretty thoroughly mixed bunch.

What we are not allowed is reading material of our own choice. The books with which the camp library is supplied tend to be of a religious nature, along with some of the more sterile so-called classics. The books that we are not allowed are basically the same ones the witch-hunters used to root out of school libraries back in the Eighties, when all of this, had we been astute enough to see it, was all getting started.

Among the banned authors are Mark Twain, J.D. Salinger, Hermann Hesse, William Faulkner, Ernest Hemingway, Arthur Conan Doyle (but not Jules Verne), and, amazingly, Charles Dickens and Sir Walter Scott. There are many others, including every author who was a known homosexual.

On the approved list, Louisa May Alcott is widely circulated, and is a "camp" favorite in both senses of the word. Some of our more flamboyant brothers dress up and play the parts of "Little Men" and "Little Women." On the other hand, Edna Ferber and Daphne DuMaurier are banned; Agatha Christie is not; Theodore Dreiser is banned; O. Henry is not. That will give you some idea of the erratic way their minds function.

Any expression of sexuality is officially prohibited, and is punishable by varying terms of solitary confinement and restricted diet. The terms range from five days for being caught masturbating to thirty days for oral or anal sex; sixty days for a second offense; ninety days for a third, and so on. There are no guards inside the camp itself, only on the barbed-wire outer perimeter, but the all-seeing eye of their closed-circuit television observes our movements at all times. However, where there is a will, there is a way; prison romances have flourished since primitive man first learned to put his fellow human beings into cages.

There is a television set in each barracks, but it is locked onto the religious channel. Occasionally they show selected G-rated movies. Radios are contraband. They play piped music, the sort one used to hear in elevators and waiting rooms.

Almost every day, one of us falls ill and is taken to the infirmary. At least, that's where we're told he's taken; once an inmate falls ill, we never see him again, and a new inmate arrives from the outside to take his place. They're still using their original DIVAF program for making sweeps and analyzing dossiers, so there's always a need for new barracks, and I suppose, new camps. There are no women's barracks in the male camps and no male barracks in the women's camps; perhaps they are afraid we'd start breeding a whole new gay population. Like all religious fanatics, their ignorance is so monumental it staggers the imagination. They can't seem to comprehend that even after they've eliminated all of us, approximately one out of every ten babies that gets born will be homosexual, and in time they will grow up, somehow discover their roots and their culture, and emerge once again as a community.

The barracks themselves are reasonably comfortable. Another Auschwitz or Dachau this certainly isn't. We live in four-man cubicles, except that since I've been elected Barracks Leader, I have a room all to myself, which is nice. There is, I think, no company quite as good as one's own. The nicest compliment I ever paid you, Stephen, at least in my own mind, was when I told you that having you for a lover was almost as wonderful as not having a lover at all! And you understood exactly what I meant, and were flattered rather than offended.

Now I'm starting to get depressed, thinking about you and the wonderful years we shared together. I'd better close at this point and go play some chess. One of the men has made a chess set out of bread dough. They don't allow real chess sets, because on the outside chess was notoriously known, whether justifiably or not, as a game for intellectuals. And talking of intellectuals, at least we gay people got off lucky; all we got was preventive detention and quarantine. I'm told that the most brilliant writers and philosophers in America are all dead. In addition to the more vocal political dissenters, everyone with an IQ of over 150 was automatically given euthanasia.

Stephen, I am so proud of you for the work that you are doing. I don't discuss it here because they probably have spies planted amongst us, but for God's sake, don't lose courage and don't stop! I don't know if it will ever bring an end to all of this, but our hearts go out to all of you Resistance groups out there. You're the only hope we have!

Take good care of yourself, and you needn't feel that you must be alone all the time because of the commitment we made to each other. Take care of your manly needs; I assure you I will understand. Love always, Troy.

Despite the solid foundation of soup and *fricadellen*, Ashcroft was starting to feel a little drunk. He folded the letter and replaced it in his pocket. Hartt brought him another round of *oude genever* and dark beer.

"That letter you've been reading over and over. Is it from your lover?"

"Yes," replied Ashcroft.

"He's in the camps, eh?"

"Yes."

"That's tough, mate."

Ashcroft shrugged resignedly. "Have you ever had a lover, Hartt?"

The pimply English boy grinned. "Not me, old chum! I guess I'm too skinny and ugly to have a lover."

"No, you're not. At least, *I* don't think so."

"Good of you to say, mate, but tell that to the lads. It's the lookers that wind up with the hot numbers."

Ashcroft downed his shot and took a few sips of beer. "Don't you believe it, Hartt. You've got something better than hot looks. You've got a hell of a personality, plus you're a very nice guy."

"You're drunk, Ashcroft." He poured two more shots. "But your line of blarney is music to me ears, which as you can see stick out like bloody jug handles."

"The better to grab you by," said Ashcroft teasingly.

"Aw, go on, now! Tell me, what did your lover look like?"

Ashcroft took out his wallet and extracted a small photo which he'd had laminated to preserve it. "This is Troy," he said, handing it across the bar.

"Oh, my! He was a looker, wasn't he?"

"Is. He's not dead, you know."

"Right. I'm sorry. He's one hell of a looker. How long were the two of you together before — before it happened?"

"Five years."

Hartt poured two more shots, "Dirk doesn't like his bartenders to drink on the job, but what the hell, it's just the two of us here. Why don't you tell me all about it, mate?"

"All right," said Ashcroft. "I will."

4

I remember the night we first met (said Ashcroft).

Several years ago, there was a leather bar in downtown Miami called the Glory Hole. It was pretty much patterned after the New York sleaze bars. It was a long, narrow bar, and at the rear was the john and also a passageway that led to an area that was equipped with a sling and various other S&M equipment.

To the left of the john, a long narrow staircase led up to a roof area where various activities also took place. A friend of mine named Greasy Grossberg, who wrote for the gay press, used to refer to that area as "The Smorgasbord Room of the Starlight Roof." He's also in Europe now, poor dude; he never could learn to keep his mouth shut.

Just as they did in New York, the management tried to keep all the dizzy little twinkies who didn't belong there out of the sling room and away from the roof by stationing a doorman at the far side of the john entrance. You either had to be someone or know someone to be admitted.

As for the bar itself: Well, what can I say? It was a typical South Florida bar. The music was much too loud, the smoke was much too thick and, since there was no dress or conduct code, there were too many Cuban cha-cha queens from a nearby disco trying to crowd our own guys off the bar stools. Don't misunderstand me, Hartt; you Brits always think we Americans are incorrigibly racist. I can assure you my prejudices against Cuban cha-cha queens were strictly social, not ethnic. We had some very decent Hispanic leather dudes who came to the Glory Hole. But by this time, the center of gravity of gay life in South Florida had already shifted from Miami to Fort Lauderdale, and whenever those of us who had fled what we jokingly called the Banana Republic came back for a drink on our old turf, we always kidded each other about having our passports in order and showing our documents at the Border Patrol checkpoint along I-95. We little realized how soon we would all need to have our passports in order. Few of us did.

Sunday evenings at the Glory Hole were almost pleasant. The owner was usually away, so the manager would turn down the jukebox and play some rather decent country and western music at a tolerable volume. The dizzy little twinkies and the Cuban cha-chas always took Sunday off to attend the tea dances, so we weren't bothered by them. Mostly it was just a sprinkling of leather dudes, bike club brothers, and levi-western types. The atmosphere was relaxed and unrestrained.

I almost didn't notice when Troy walked into the bar, because I was busy talking to someone, but it's just not possible *not* to notice him for very long. For the briefest moment there was an awed hush, a sort of hiatus in the conversation, and then everybody went back to their drinks. In a real leather bar, it's not considered good form to pounce on somebody like a hungry vulture, the way they do in the troll bars. I suppose I should have said "used to do," since there are no longer any gay bars in the United States, but I can never accustom myself to using the past tense.

How can I describe Troy without becoming hopelessly clichéd? That he was a tall, blond god dripping in leather? That he was built like a brick shithouse? That he had features Michelangelo would have wanted to sculpt? I leaned over the bar and said to Carlos, the bartender, "What would you consider the quintessential all-American wet dream?"

Glancing over at Troy, he replied without a moment's hesitation. "A tall hunky young blond, dripping in leather." Then he added, "I'll bet he goes home alone, too. Either he'll be too stuck on himself to meet anyone, or else everyone will be too awestruck to talk to him."

At the risk of being obvious or, worse than obvious, rude, I observed the young man in the mirror. Even though I was already too old and jaded to lose my equilibrium over a hot new trick, I couldn't help myself. I was fascinated, enchanted, entranced. Just the way he held himself, the way he ordered and paid for his drink, spoke volumes about him. Manners. Prep school. Old family money. A trained observer such as myself notices these things.

Suddenly our eyes met. We both smiled; I nodded, and returned to my drink. It doesn't do to be pushy. But when I looked in the mirror again, he was looking at me, too.

Carlos slid another drink in front of me which I hadn't ordered. "The all-American wet dream," he announced, "just bought you a round. Also he sent you this note."

I took it and read, "My name is Troy. Are we going to stare at each other like idiots all night, or are we going to get acquainted?"

I folded the note, stuck it in the side pocket of my leather vest, picked up my drink and walked over to him.

"My name's Stephen Ashcroft."

"Troy Anderson," he replied. His handshake was firm and manly. I noticed that he was wearing his keys and other paraphernalia on the left, just as I was, signifying his preferences; "flagging top," we call it. That didn't concern me particularly, because I've found that in real life most things are negotiable.

"I suppose you think that was pretty brazen of me," he began.

"Thank goodness somebody has the balls! Think of all the people who come in here every night..."

"...and sit and stare at each other..."

"...and then go home alone..."

"...after all the missed opportunities..."

We laughed together, and I wanted to embrace him right then and there, but one of my rules is never to get physical too soon.

"What kind of work do you do?" I asked him.

He worked for a major advertising agency in Fort Lauderdale, where he lived. At twenty-three, he was already an account executive. He was articulate, well-spoken, and obviously very bright, which turned me on even more than his sexy good looks. Even without his good looks and physique, he'd still have been a hot number; he had that certain *je ne sais quoi*.

"And you?" he asked me.

"A gentleman of the fourth estate. Or rather, a peon of the fourth estate. I'm a freelance photographer and journalist. Mostly overseas."

"Sounds exciting. Seen any combat?"

"Viet Nam. Cambodia. Central America. The Caribbean. Trying to expose the atrocities of our increasingly misguided war machine."

He stiffened slightly. "I really don't believe our foreign policy has ever been that misguided," he replied. "We do what we have to do. But let's not get into that right now. We'll save politics and religion for after we're married!"

It was just a barroom joke and we both laughed, but many a truth, as the saying goes, is spoken in jest.

"Well!" he exclaimed. "Are we going to sit here all night choking and gagging on other people's smoke, and buying drinks until we're too drunk to worry about sex, or shall we get the hell out of here now?"

"Your place or mine?" God, I hate that phrase!

"Never mind that, your car or mine?"

"Let's take both cars. Don't try to stay together on I-95. We'll meet for a nightcap in Fort Lah-de-dah, then you can follow me to my place. I kind of like to be in charge, first time around. Next time, if there is one, we can go to your place."

"That suits me," he replied. "And by the way," he added, fixing me with his piercing blue eyes, "there *will* be a next time. I've never bothered with anyone I thought would be just a one-night stand."

One of the things that made an impression on me was Troy's reaction when he first entered my apartment, or to put it more accurately, my hovel.

How do you describe a working writer's quarters? A rat's nest? A warren? A den? Certainly, the small efficiency apartment that I kept as a *pied-à-terre* in Fort Lauderdale would never have won any Gracious Living awards. The books I had accumulated over the years had long ago overflowed the bookcases and stood in piles on the floor. A clutter of manuscripts and reference papers made the actual surface of my desk indiscernible to the naked eye. The bed was a tangle of sheets and pillows, and as for cleaning the kitchen and bathroom, I've never been one to bother with picayune details like that. Sooner or later, I've always found a willing slaveboy to do the honors.

Troy, however, seemed oblivious to all the chaos and disorder. On the contrary, he seemed quite charmed, and totally without any condescension. When I had poured myself a nightcap and, at his own request, a club soda for Troy, I seated myself in the recliner. To my surprise and pleasure, Mr. All-American Wet Dream knelt at my feet. I stroked his lovely blond hair.

Gently, he took my leather boots onto his lap as he knelt before me, stroking and caressing the shiny black surfaces, then pressing his cheek against them. When he placed his mouth against each boot, he did nothing so crude as to lick and slobber over them as so many leather slaveboys do; instead, he merely pressed his lips against the leather. Symbolically, the mere gesture connoted a greater measure of subservience than a more overt action would have done.

I pointed at his keys, still hanging on his left side. With a snap of authority in my voice, I demanded, "What the hell is *that* supposed to mean, slaveboy?"

"It means," he said softly, "that you're going to catch hell tomorrow night at my place. But for tonight, I want you to be Daddy — all the way!"

"Let's get those goddamn clothes off, then," I ordered. "Now!"

Submissively, with his eyes averted, he slowly and carefully removed his clothing, folding it into a neat pile on the sofa before standing at attention in front of me, stark naked.

If he had seemed the epitome of physical perfection in the bar, he was even more so in his state of *deshabille*. He was the quintessential boyish blond college athlete, perfectly defined, but not overdeveloped. I took a sip of my drink and tried not to let myself feel overawed or intimidated. I gestured for him to sit on my lap so I could take him in my arms and kiss him, but he shook his head firmly.

"I haven't earned that privilege yet, Sir," he said. "I think across your knees would be better."

So that was what he wanted. Okay, that was fine with me too. I gave him a taste of good old bare-bottom spanking until his beautifully rounded buns were an angry red and there were tears in his eyes. Then I pushed him off my knees onto the floor, grabbed him by the hair and slapped him.

"Don't cry," I said. "I didn't give you permission to cry."

"They're my buns, Sir, and if my ass hurts from where you hit me, I'll cry if I want to!"

I slapped him again a couple of times, forehand, backhand.

"Don't make me have to really hurt you," I warned.

"Don't let your topman's mouth," he replied defiantly, "write any checks that your bottom man's ass can't cash!"

In a flash I was on him. I'm no youngster now, and I wasn't even then, but a combat journalist learns to move pretty fast. Before Joe College knew what had hit him, I had his wrists handcuffed behind his back. A set of leather restraints secured his ankles and attached with a chain to the slave collar I placed around his beautiful neck.

"Now I'm going to give you something to cry about," I said in a low, even voice as I dragged him across the worn carpet to the unmade bed. "Face down, maggot." The wrists were secured to the headboard, the ankles to the metal bedframe. "Now you're in a world of deep shit, boy!"

But it was I, not he, who finally had to call "Limits!" There was no punishment or pain, no matter how intense, that Troy would not have endured; he was self-disciplined beyond belief. As much as I reveled in his submission to me, there was, however, no way that I could have brought myself to actually harm him, and what I really wanted was to get this phase of the encounter behind us so that we could make love all night.

He grinned exultantly as I released him from restraint, leaving only the slave collar in place as he lay comfortably on his back against the pillows. At some point during the proceedings, I had shed my clothes, and I was more than ready for him.

After years of Oriental boys, Arab boys, African boys, Asian boys, Hispanic boys, and Central American Indian boys, Troy was a fantasy come to life. His blondness, his sturdiness, his rugged, manly good looks, all filled an aching void for me, a dream of something that had somehow been lacking. Although his chest was smooth, a line of curly blond hair ran from his navel down his flat, perfect stomach to where it joined his pubic hair. A trace of fine, soft golden hair graced his lower arms and his thighs. I enveloped him in my arms, gorged hungrily as though at a feast, and could not get enough.

In the morning we awoke at first light and made love again. Then, over coffee, he said as if for reassurance,

"We *are* on for tonight, aren't we? You're not going to disappoint me by turning out to be..."

"The money's on the dresser, kid," I replied. "Just leave me your beeper number. Don't call me, I'll call you."

"You son of a bitch! Just tell me where and what time."

I named a piano bar in Fort Lauderdale.

"Do we have to meet at a bar?" he asked. "I mean, now that we've already met, what's the point?"

"It's not a prerequisite," I admitted.

"Look. A bar is somewhere you go when you have no better place to spend your time and money, and no one with whom to spend them, okay?"

I shrugged. "They can be very social."

"In Fort Lah? These sleazy, stinking smoke pits?"

"Wow," I said. "You really can't stand them at all, can you? Just what is it about the bar scene that turns you off so much?"

"You mean aside from the lonely, pathetic wretches who spend every night of their lives there? And the skull-shattering volume of the music in most places, so you can't even carry on a conversation! I guess what I hate most about them is the stench. You get home from a heavy night and your hair stinks, your clothes stink, even your handkerchiefs and underwear stink. And all next day at work you're coughing up thick gobs of their air. Why do they have to be like that?"

"Because that's what most of their customers want. Don't let it get to you, kid. I've been in lots of places that smelled a lot worse. A North Korean jail, for example. Or a village in Nicaragua where *our* Contras had used *our* napalm to burn out a bunch of Indian women and kids in the name of democracy."

Troy stiffened belligerently. "Our people don't do things like that," he protested. "And if they did, I'm sure it would have been for a very good reason."

I smiled tolerantly. "You've got a lot to learn about our foreign policy," I said. "But then, you don't read about the worst parts in the newspapers, unless you subscribe to the overseas press. Anyway, I've been to lots of places that smelled a lot worse than a South Florida bar."

"Sure," he agreed, "but you were getting paid to be there, not buying overpriced drinks."

"You've made your point. Okay, then, you name it."

He gave me his personal card. "My place at seven. Cocktails, a session, and then dinner. You don't have to wear leather this time." The tone of his voice said very clearly: You'd better *not* wear leather.

His apartment on Galt Ocean Mile turned out to be, just as I had anticipated, a luxury high-rise condo. I drove my battered Ford Escort up to the supercilious eye of the security guard, who looked at me as though I were selling encyclopedias, and then called Troy on the intercom as though he couldn't quite believe that I'd actually been invited. He'd have made a great East German border guard.

Troy was wearing a cashmere sweater and skin-tight designer jeans. The cologne I recognized as Van Cleef and Arpels from Paris; I knew what it cost at the Galleria. His apartment was high-tech, but tasteful; even his computer terminal was encased in Scandinavian wood. This time, the preliminaries and amenities having been performed the night before, he grabbed me in his arms immediately and kissed me long and hard on the mouth.

When we broke for air, I looked around the condo admiringly. "You didn't get all this," I suggested, "from being a junior account executive at an advertising agency."

"No," he smiled. "I have a little income of my own. Would a martini be all right?"

"Yes," I said, "as long as it isn't a Republican martini."

"And what," he demanded with some asperity, "is a Republican martini?"

"Two-thirds gin, one-third vermouth, served lukewarm after having been diluted with too much ice. The substance is there, but not the soul."

"I suppose you'd prefer a Communist martini," he retorted, "to go with your politics. I've never had one, but I can imagine what it would taste like."

"I hope you never have to find out. But these are perfect! Where did you learn?"

He looked at me with an expression almost of disdain. "In my family we don't *learn* to make martinis. It's engraved on our genes."

"I see. Along with your polo club membership, I suppose."

"Oh, Stephen, don't try to sound so — so disadvantaged! Would you like to smoke a joint? It'll mellow you out."

"I'm sorry, Troy. It's just that whenever I enter the precincts of the rich and beautiful, it makes me think about some of the less fortunate places I've seen. Go ahead, fire up that joint."

"I keep only one ashtray in the house, and I bring it out of hiding just for prime smoke." He placed the joint in a water pipe after he'd lit it up and gotten it going.

"There's one thing I should warn you about, Troy. Grass has a strange effect on me. Three good tokes and I become totally passive; the other side of the coin, actually, from last night."

"Then I guess you'd better have at least three good tokes. Or all you want. Don't you agree, Stephen?"

"Yes, Troy, I do. And whatever happens, happens."

"I thought you'd see it my way."

And whatever happens, I thought, is what is meant to happen between us.

This time it was Troy who took the lead, once we had enjoyed our martinis and our smoke and had become completely relaxed.

There are some poor dudes who can deck themselves out in the most expensive leather gear and all the other prerequisite chains, accoutrements and paraphernalia, and still be an object of ridicule. The *persona* just isn't there. And then there are others who can wear a cashmere sweater and cologne, and be very young, and still be the hottest leather top that the wildest imagination could conceive of. True leather, I have always said, comes from within.

I want you to know that I took everything that kid could dish out and didn't even cry for mercy. Naturally, one room of that vast condo was fitted out as the apocryphal "well-equipped dungeon and play room," just the way they're described in the leather magazines. There was literally no piece of gear, equipment or paraphernalia that Troy did not own. Yet it all would have been meaningless without the perfect rapport that passed between us. Although he went far, far beyond anything I had ever experienced, even years before as a young Master in training, everything he did with me and to me was totally sensual and erotic. When I finally broke down in tears, it was partly from exhaustion and partly from the sheer bliss of perfect sexual fulfillment. Troy knew this, and this time it was he who called the limits.

In the bathroom that was larger than my apartment, there

was a Roman tub, more than ample for two. We frolicked and made love in the hot water, and then drank more martinis. It must have been after eleven when we finally sat down to dinner.

I shall never forget the delicacy of the marinated heart of artichoke salad; the perfection of the *tripe à la mode de Caen* that he'd had baking in a crock pot all day; the medley of wild rice and vegetables that he served with it; the charmingly fruity, yet mellow, Cabernet Sauvignon that he poured for me; and the dessert, a rich, perfectly aged cheddar, followed by coffee and liqueurs.

"I do hope," said Troy, with irony, "that all this hasn't been too bourgeois for your rampant sense of proletarian guilt."

"Oh, I think I can live with it. Troy, this was perfect! If you can sew as well as you cook, I'll marry you."

"I don't have to sew. I can buy tailors. For that matter, I can buy chefs, too, but I happen to enjoy messing around in the kitchen. But you can marry me anyway. What I'm really trying to say, Stephen, is that I'd like you to become my lover."

With a sudden shock I realized that he was serious.

"Troy," I said, "we've known each other only a little over twenty-four hours. I am a firm believer in long engagements. The only thing I know about you for sure is that we come from totally different worlds and from opposite ends of the political spectrum."

Troy shrugged. "All right, I'll buy that. But we can still go on seeing each other, can't we?"

"Well, of course! I'd love it! But no commitments just yet, okay? Not until we see if we wear well together."

As it turned out, we did wear very well together. Despite the disparity in our politics and our economic status, we had numerous interests in common; he was, after all, highly educated, his family had all been patrons of the arts, and he had a quick, inquisitive mind whose intellectual curiosity had not been dulled and blunted, thank goodness, by his right-wing politics.

The next time he asked me to be his lover, it was during an incredible weekend at a very exclusive resort on one of the out-islands of the Bahamas. This time I didn't dismiss it quite so lightly.

Very early on, I had tried to hold our expenses and excursions down to my own level, but Troy began to get annoyed when he wanted us to do something together that I couldn't afford. It was not that he was frivolous or extravagant about money; quite the contrary. He had simply been brought up to a degree of taste and affluence that I could not even have envisioned.

"I'm not looking for a sugar daddy, Troy," I protested.

"Then how about a sugar chicken?" he replied. "Look, Stephen, let's make a deal. Whenever you pick the restaurant or the weekend outing or whatever, it's your treat. When I pick it, it's my treat. Is that fair enough?"

That left my pride intact, so I agreed. After all, a dinner for two with wine that cost the equivalent of fifty Standard New Dollars in today's currency was about my top limit; a thousand-dollar yachting weekend was about his.

Lying on the pink sands of that deserted Bahamian beach, he asked me once again to become his lover. The sex hadn't waned, merely mellowed; we were growing closer every day.

"If I were to say yes," I said, "there's just one absolute condition I'd impose, and I'm not going to back down on that."

"I'm listening."

"I will not live in that ivory tower condo of yours. We'd have to get a place that suits both of us."

"What am I supposed to do with my condo?"

"I really don't care, Troy! Sell it, rent it, give it away! We can get a very nice house for a few hundred bones a month where our friends don't have to go through Checkpoint Charlie and where it doesn't matter if someone spills a drink on your furniture."

"Your friends might do that," he taunted. "Mine wouldn't."

"Asshole!" I grabbed him by his ankles and dragged him into the water, where we wrestled and played like little kids. Finally, exhausted, we rested on the sand before hiking back to our cottage at the resort.

By the time we got back to Fort Lauderdale, he'd convinced me to give it a try.

"Lovers?" my friend Greasy Grossberg, the writer, was quoted as having said. "Ashcroft doesn't take lovers, he just adds a slave-boy or two. And since he has absolutely no proper bourgeois values, I'm betting this rich kid won't last six months."

With his characteristic egomaniac blind side, Grossberg had a penchant for leveling accusations at others that would have been more properly directed to himself. If there was anyone in the world who epitomized the absence of bourgeois values, it was the outrageous and iconoclastic Greasy Grossberg; and as for adding slaveboys, his stable was legendary in the local leather scene.

Troy and I were destined to last a lot longer than six months. We would have lasted our entire lives, I am convinced of that, had it not been for the terrible events taking shape around us.

Would Troy and I still be together if, five years later, I had not accepted a position on Douglas McKittrick's political staff? Could we have gotten out in time, together? Could I have done anything to prevent the assassination? I still think that with the sole exception of Troy's capture by the DIVAF program, Doug's death was the worst thing that ever happened to me in my life. It hit me very hard, not only because I liked and admired him so much, but also because their blowing him away shattered whatever vestigial remnant of faith I still had in the American system and its ability to right itself and get back on the track. But I guess I'm getting ahead of my story.

5

Ashcroft lifted his head from his folded arms, on which, he suddenly realized, he'd been resting it for some time.

"Let's have another round, Hartt," he said. "On me."

"You're a bit smashed already, mate. You really don't need one, you know."

"Oh, come on. Why light a fire and then put it out?"

"Good point. Oh, what the hell, I'll have one too." He poured two more *oude genevers* and drew two more dark beers.

"You really should turn this into a piano bar, Hartt. With some glitzy pianist in preppie clothes playing old sad torch songs. Strictly for the benefit of people who are torching for their lovers. Don't you think that would be very nice?"

"This is a leather bar, mate. In case you hadn't noticed."

"Well, then, maybe we could have a naked slave in chains playing all the old sad torch songs. True love songs. The kind they don't allow anymore in America."

"They don't allow a lot of things in America anymore. Your Reverend President Wickerly sees to that."

"Well, he believes in the Word of God, with whom, I might add, he's personally in touch every day. Do you believe that, Hartt?"

"Don't be thick. If there really were any gods, they wouldn't talk to the likes of him." He started to collect the ashtrays and turn the bar stools upside down on the bar.

Ashcroft finished his drink. "Are you kicking me out of here?"

"It's almost closing time, and there's nobody else here." He flicked off all but the night lights and came around to Ashcroft's side of the bar. "Come on, mate. Upsy-daisy. I'll give you a hand." Pulling Ashcroft's arm around his shoulder, he lifted the older man to his feet with a wiry strength that was surprising.

"Where are you taking me, Hartt?"

"Well, you're too big for me to carry you to your room, so we'll just have to go along to mine, right?"

"But I'm not that drunk," Ashcroft protested. "I can make it up the stairs all right."

"Bloody likely. You'd fall asleep fully dressed, on top of the covers, with the window open, and catch your death. Don't argue, now." He half carried and half dragged the larger man down the hall to the staff quarters, which adjoined the kitchen.

"Wait!" said Ashcroft. "We've got to go back to the bar. I wanted to tell you the rest of the story."

"There'll be lots of cold winter nights, old chum." He unlocked the door to his room. It was only slightly larger than Ashcroft's, but had been made cheerful and homelike by the addition of personal items. For one thing, it was comfortably warm; Hartt had a small electric heater plugged into the wall. The sheets and pillowcases, obviously his own, were topped with a huge, warm, homemade quilt. On the wall were posters of various leather bars from all over Europe. Rather roughly, he flung Ashcroft down on the bed.

"What's going on, Hartt?"

"Come on, Ashcroft. Don't be dim. You know I've always fancied you."

"I'm too drunk. Why don't we take a raincheck?"

Suddenly Hartt was astride his chest. There was a new mastery in his eyes as he slapped Ashcroft hard across the face. "You'll bloody well do as your told, mate," he said. "Too drunk, indeed!

Don't you dare come the helpless inebriate with me, me lad! I thought spies weren't supposed to get drunk." He hit Ashcroft again, not hard enough to really hurt, but hard enough to make him feel submissive.

"I'm not a spy, Hartt. I'm in the American Resistance movement. Everybody knows that. Besides, I'm among friends here."

"To the other side, you're still a spy." He grabbed Ashcroft by the hair and pulled him up to a sitting position. "Come on, let's get that jacket and shirt off."

When he had Ashcroft stripped to the waist, he buckled a slave collar around the older man's neck and secured his wrists with leather restraints. To his own surprise, having this slender English boy dominating him gave Ashcroft a sense of pleasure and security. Still, he asked,

"Why are you doing this to me, Hartt?"

The bartender grinned happily. "Just trying to make you feel right at home. We give service to our guests; that's what the Leather Eagle's hospitality is all about." He pulled off Ashcroft's boots and then his trousers, folding them carefully so nothing would fall out. "Besides," he added, "you need a taste of discipline, old chum. You've been letting yourself get in pretty bad shape." He took out a thick leather paddle. "On your tum-tum, Ashcroft. I want to see that lovely old bum of yours sticking up in the air." With a sigh of resignation, Ashcroft obeyed. He wished he weren't so drunk.

Thwack! The first crack of the paddle made his buttocks sting from the unaccustomed pain. "Why do you say I'm in bad shape, Hartt?"

Thwack! Down came the paddle again, almost making him cry out.

"You know bloody well what I mean. Getting drunk every night. Wallowing in your maudlin self-pity." *Thwack!* came the paddle again.

"Don't you think," demanded Ashcroft, "that I really do have something to feel sorry about?"

Thwack! came the paddle. "Sure, you do. But what makes you think you're the only one?" *Thwack!* "There's hundreds of bloody Yanks in 'Dam right now, and thousands more all over Europe." *Thwack!* "Do you think you're the first and only expatriate in the history of mankind?" *Thwack*! "My parents are Jewish, in case you didn't know. On my mother's side, we came from Belgium, originally. My grandparents got out just ahead of the Nazis, but every friend and relative and family member they had all died in the concentration camps." *Thwack*! *Thwack*! "Along with millions of others, as you well know." *Thwack*! "Do you get my point, mate? Or should we bring out the old cat-o'nine-tails?"

Ashcroft was in tears, but not from the intense, searing pain of the paddle. Drunkenly, he realized how badly he'd been behaving. During the months in Amsterdam, basking in the warmth and supportiveness of his Dutch friends, he had completely relaxed the S&M discipline that had stood him in such good stead during his years as a combat journalist.

As a writer and in his personal outlook, Ashcroft had always maintained that leathersex is merely a superficial aspect of S&M discipline; true leather, he claimed, is a philosophy and a way of life that a real leatherman uses to his advantage in the business and professional world — or in combat.

"Bring out the cat, Hartt. I deserve a few good licks."

Hartt discarded the paddle, but did not reach for the whip.

"We'll put you on conditional discharge for now, old chum." He gently massaged Ashcroft's raw, searing buttocks. "Now, turn over onto your back." He began to take off all his own clothes.

Ashcroft lay on his back, his wrists still secured to the headboard. Hartt was now completely naked. The boy was attractive, with a slender, wiry musculature, fairly well defined. His skin was very white. Ashcroft ran his eyes over the boy's slim body, down his slender legs, back up to his crotch, where he was becoming tumescent. Hugely so.

"Oh, my God," said Ashcroft, staring at it.

"You've heard the expression, 'No sex please, we're British,' right?"

"I've heard it."

"Don't you believe it," said Hartt, slipping on a condom and opening a jar of lubricant. "It's just an expression."

The booze and the leather paddling finally took their toll, and Ashcroft relaxed into a state of dreamy semi-consciousness as the boy mounted him. Vaguely he was aware of Hartt's now-gentle hands caressing the hair on his chest, squeezing his nipples, and then at last, the English boy's lips were soft and sweet against his own, kissing him long and hard.

"Turn my wrists loose," said Ashcroft. "I want to hold on to you. Please."

Hartt unsnapped the buckles, and Ashcroft clung to the boy's slender shoulders and wrapped his legs ever more tightly around the slender body as the young bartender thrust and drove into him. When they soared to a magnificent climax, it was a mutual one, and the best of all the sex that Ashcroft had had that day.

In the morning, he awakened to find himself lying on his side, still impaled, the English boy inside of him, his slender arms wrapped tightly around Ashcroft. Hartt's electric heater had kept the room comfortably warm all night.

They were interrupted by Dirk, the owner, opening the door and carrying in a pot of coffee and coffee mugs on a tray.

"*Goede morgen*," he said cheerfully. "Don't let me interrupt anything! Now tell me, Ashcroft, do we or do we not give good service to our guests at the Leather Eagle?"

"The best," murmured Ashcroft dreamily, feeling the young bartender once again thrusting inside of him. "The very best."

Then, to his surprise, Dirk knelt beside the bed and kissed him. "And do you know what else, Ashcroft? One of these days I'm going to have you myself!"

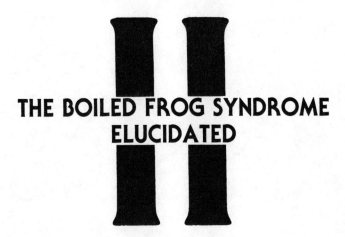

THE BOILED FROG SYNDROME
ELUCIDATED

1

Once again Ashcroft sat in Aaron Ten Eyck's spacious library, basking in the comfort and graciousness of the old man's lovely quarters.

"Well!" said Ten Eyck cheerfully as they sipped coffee. Outside, the weather was cold, but clear and sunny. "Did you arrange for a leave of absence as I requested?"

"Better than that. My superiors in the Resistance decided to call it detached service. They felt, as you do, that your project is just as important to the Movement as anything else that we do."

"Splendid, then! By the way, my Documentation Committee, which is what we've decided to call this operation, will be paying your Resistance salary from now on."

"That's very generous of you."

"Not at all! We try to avoid additional expense to the Movement because we know where the Resistance money comes from — contributions from people all over the world who believe in what you are doing; people who know that for the safety of the world, your Reverend President Wickerly must be overthrown. Pennies from school children, that sort of thing. Plus, of course, whatever your people manage to steal."

"Yes," smiled Ashcroft. "Our more radical elements back in the States do manage to knock over a bank once in a while. Or an Army installation for weapons and explosives. It took me a long time to realize they were playing hardball over there — that it wasn't just a clever exercise in gamesmanship, the way it was for me when I was a combat journalist."

"My dear boy, please don't be so modest! I should hardly call your war coverage mere gamesmanship. After all, you were getting shot at, too."

"Never in anger. I like to think they just wanted my camera."

Ten Eyck chuckled heartily. "I think you Yanks are bloody marvelous," he said. "A bit naive at times, perhaps, but marvelous. Pity you let yourselves get enslaved by that dreadful theocracy. However, to business."

Ashcroft took a sip of his coffee. "Where would you like me to begin my research for this project? Any suggestions?"

"Well, for openers, why not start where it all began? There must have been a few Americans besides yourself who were politically sagacious enough to perceive what was happening."

"There were lots of us," said Ashcroft. "But nobody was listening."

"How terribly distressing that must have been! Why *weren't* they listening?"

"Because they didn't *want* to listen. They wouldn't listen to *anything* we said. They thought it was pure paranoia. Look, we suspected very early on that AIDS, the so-called Gay Plague, was somebody's attempt at germ warfare that had gone amok. We almost had it documented, but then *they* killed a few key people. Of course, in the beginning, most people outside the gay community didn't regard AIDS as a problem; they regarded it as a solution, just as most white Americans, I'm ashamed to say, in their secret hearts regarded black poverty and sickle-cell anemia as solutions, not problems.

"We knew for a fact that our American germ warfare people had been working since the end of World War II on ethno-specific viruses that would wipe out certain populations but not touch others; I think that at one time they wanted to destroy the Chinese. Of course, none of these viruses worked outside of the laboratory, for the simple reason that in only a very few remote places on earth do you have an isolated population with a pure, unadulterated gene pool. So who knows what sort of bizarre madness could have made them think that the AIDS virus, a mutation of a Central African virus that had been endemic in the straight population for decades, would have remained confined within the gay community?

"And then there were the media. Oh, we knew also, very early on, that the Religious Right was slowly but surely taking over the media. A television station here, a newspaper there, and then slowly, gradually, the editorial slant would shift, more stories would be left out — and all the while the military-industrial complex that President Eisenhower had warned us about kept getting stronger and stronger — and more and more dangerous. But nobody would listen! The tragedy is that I think we still could have stopped them, even at that stage."

"Then why on earth didn't the people put a stop to it? Why

was there not some sort of rallying cry? Surely you still had some electoral power left, even if only at your local or municipal level."

Ashcroft was silent for a moment, and then asked, "Did you ever hear of the Boiled Frog Syndrome?"

"The Boiled Frog Syndrome? No, old chap, I can't say that I ever have. Why don't you tell me about it?"

"All right, I shall. The Boiled Frog Syndrome was first propounded to me by a renegade academic with the improbable name of Dr. Aristophanes Brent. Talk about a wild-eyed young iconoclast! This poor dude had such eminently sane, rational, common-sense ideas about practically everything that it's a miracle he wasn't locked up in some booby-hatch."

"Can you give me an example?"

"Sure I can. Take his views on medicine, for example. It had already been many years since common-sense, clinical medicine had been practiced in the United States. The profession had become a farrago of mumbo-jumbo, diet fads, absurd and needless laboratory tests, computer readouts and, worst of all, those awful and sometimes lethal — but always very expensive — medications that they loved to prescribe. As for operations, that was a farce. 'If a procedure can be done, let's do it. The insurance will pay most of the bills, and who knows, it might actually work.'

"Dr. Brent tried to point out to his fellow academicians, and to the medical profession at large, that since virtually all illnesses, with a few exceptions, are either psychosomatic or self-limiting, the best medicine is almost always the least medicine. Alleviate symptoms if indicated, comfort the patient and, most important of all, give Mother Nature a chance to take her course. No drastic intervention, no life-threatening over-treatment. Since common-sense, clinical medicine is also the least expensive kind of medicine, and since it attacks the very foundation of detached, impersonal, computerized medicine, Dr. Brent was drummed out of the groves of Academe. If the medical profession could have put him before a firing squad, they would have done so, especially since he earned his living prepping medical students to pass their State Boards, at outrageously high fees, but with a guarantee of no failure.

"It was Aristophanes Brent who, over drinks one night, explained to me the theory of the Boiled Frog Syndrome.

"If you take a frog and put him in a pot of boiling water, he will, quite naturally, try to leap out and save himself. But if you put him in a pot of cold water, and then heat the water very, very gradually, one tiny half-degree at a time, the frog will continue to sit there in that pot until he boils to death."

"Very ingenious," commented Ten Eyck. "I can see a whole plethora of analogies there."

"Exactly! Let's take another example: the automobile."

"I'm sorry, I'm afraid I don't quite follow you there."

"If we had known, when somebody first invented the automobile, that it would eventually kill and maim more people than all the wars and famines combined; that it would destroy the entire pattern of urban life in the United States, leaving nothing in its wake except ravaged downtown combat zones and sprawling, sleazy, tacky suburbs; and that it would put the entire country at the economic mercy of a tiny junta of international cartels, would we still have allowed the Age of the Automobile to proceed? Oh, I'm well aware of all the pleasure and all the social good it has accomplished as well. But at what price? For example, when I was born, Los Angeles was still a lovely paradise of a city, with a daily view of the snow-capped San Bernardino Mountains to the east. I know all about it, Mijnheer Ten Eyck; I was born and raised in Pasadena. Have you seen Southern California since they paved it all over with freeways and drowned it in smog? And had the temerity to tell us that the monstrous overdevelopment that was strangling the area and literally choking people to death was all in the name of *progress*? Once again, our old friend, the Boiled Frog Syndrome.

"It was the same with the takeover of America. They didn't take away all our freedoms and all our civil liberties in one fell swoop; they could never have gotten away with it. No, they whittled away at them one little chip at a time. And those of us who had read history, who had traveled abroad not merely as tourists but as cultural explorers and adventurers, who made it a practice to read the international press, and who spoke out against what was happening, were either ridiculed as crackpots or else despised and villified as anti-American traitors.

"That is why the country that was once the arsenal of democracy is now the bastion of religious fascism. The Boiled Frog Syndrome, Mijnheer Ten Eyck. We warned, we preached, we wrote. And nobody listened! Of course, the incredible proliferation of functional illiteracy in the United States — by design, I am convinced — certainly didn't help matters."

"Well, I daresay," said Ten Eyck, finishing his coffee, "from what little I know of life in the United States, that had I been a nice, comfortable, bourgeois American, all righteous and smug and patriotic, sitting night after night in front of his telly, barely able to read a newspaper, never reading a book, earning decent money at his job, driving his nice shiny automobile to work or to the shopping mall, knowing absolutely nothing about the rest of the world outside the United States, or at least as little as possible — I do believe, Ashcroft, that had I been such an individual, I, too, would have found you paranoid."

"Of course you would have," agreed Ashcroft. "My own lover did. And he was very well educated, compared to 99% of what they were turning out of our so-called schools by that time."

"Yes, quite so. Well, then! Where would *you* like to start?"

"I think the first person I should see is Greasy Grossberg. He was a pretty well known gay writer who saw the whole thing coming. He wasn't, like myself, an international journalist who happened to be gay. He was a local gay writer who wrote to and for the gay community. Actually, he wrote as much to shock and entertain as to inform, if not more so. Outrageous, extremely verbal and, as the Brits would say, too clever by half! But he was dedicated to the gay rights movement, and he also had the good sense and political foresight to get out in time."

"Where is this individual now?"

"Almost next door, so to speak; he lives in Luxembourg. I understand he got most of his files out with him, so I think he'd be as good a place as any to start."

"Sounds fine to me, Ashcroft. Right, then! Good luck, and call me right away if you get into any sort of trouble, or if you run short of funds. And, of course, we'll meet again after you get back and assemble your material."

They clasped hands warmly. Some day, thought Ashcroft, I'd like to hear *his* whole story.

Little did he realize the effect that Aaron Ten Eyck's strange and haunting tale would eventually have upon his life.

2

The next day after lunch, Ashcroft packed an overnight bag and, from the Central Station caught the early afternoon TGV for Luxembourg. The *trains à grande vitesse,* once a highly advanced scientific curiosity of the French national railroad, had by this time come into general use all over Europe. His journey was brief; the TGV arrived in Luxembourg within the hour.

He had always been charmed by the tiny principality, where a desk clerk might answer you in elegant French, speak perfect English to a group of British tourists, and then scream at one of his maids in strident Luxembourgeois, a dialect of German. The restaurants and pastry shops were as good as any in Europe, and all major currencies were accepted. There were even a couple of gay bars and cruising areas, happily not yet overrun, as was the rest of Europe these days, with dazed American expatriates who still didn't seem to realize what had happened to them. The weather was even colder, windier and nastier, if possible, than it had been in Amsterdam.

Greasy Grossberg lived on top of a block of elegant *fin-de-siècle* flats that had survived World War II. After being buzzed into the beautiful marble lobby, Ashcroft rode the ancient, creaking, but gorgeously filigreed elevator to the sixth floor, then climbed an ornately gilded and carpeted flight of stairs to the penthouse where Grossberg lived. To Ashcroft's amazement, if not entirely to his surprise, the door was opened by a blond German boy about sixteen years old, wearing nothing except a slave collar.

"*Wollen-sie herein kommen, bitte,* Herr Ashcroft," said the boy, smiling shyly at him.

"*Danke,*" he replied.

"Goddammit," roared Greasy Grossberg's familiar voice from the living room, "I told you to speak French or English, you putrid little Kraut maggot! You get ten strokes for that, *dummkopf!*"

"I am sorry," stumbled the boy in English, reaching for, but not quite grasping, the right words. Then his face brightened as he switched to French. "*Entrez-vous donc, s'il vous plaît.*"

"*Merci,*" said Ashcroft.

In the living room, a huge fire was roaring in the fireplace. The vast, high-ceilinged room, like Ten Eyck's, was lined with books, pictures and memorabilia. There were framed photographs of Greasy Grossberg taken during the heyday of the gay rights movement: shaking hands with President Carter, cutting the ribbon on a new Gay Community Services Center, and one with Doug McKittrick, their arms around each other's shoulders, grinning into the camera. Ashcroft looked away quickly.

Near the fire, in a capacious recliner, sprawled Greasy Grossberg himself. If he had ever had a real first name, Ashcroft had never known it. To his outraged readers, he was merely Greasy Grossberg, who for years had written his notorious column, "Gross Out With Grossberg," that had been syndicated in numerous gay publications. He had been known to brag that the high point of his literary career had occurred when his editor's ailing, aging mother, after proofreading one of his columns, had actually had to go to the bathroom and throw up. Neither money nor acclaim, he liked to boast, could ever surpass that pinnacle of achievement.

Grossberg was fat. Not so grotesquely fat that he needed special furniture or couldn't walk, just fat. His thick, greasy black hair topped a full-fleshed, jowly face. His dark, piercing eyes could explode into twinkling merriment or freeze you like shafts of ice. His lips were full and sensual. In addition to being fat, he was also large-boned and tall; he liked to think of himself as a vast Falstaffian mountain of gluttony, lust and debauchery. He was wearing a leather vest over slacks and a silk shirt, with only sandals on his large, pudgy feet. The circulation in his legs was starting to go.

"Excuse my not rising, Ashcroft," he said with his customary ironic, self-deprecating humor, "but the forklift isn't handy." He did, however, extend a huge, meaty paw which Ashcroft shook warmly.

"I see you sure as hell haven't been on short rations since you've been over here," said Ashcroft.

"What the fuck," said Grossberg, "somebody has to show these ignorant Krauts and Frogs what a nice, fat, greasy, all-American Jewish boy is supposed to look like."

"You do *that* well, at least," said Ashcroft. "Would it be an imposition to ask you to offer a thirsty fellow-American a drink?"

"It would," said Grossberg, "but if you'll settle for ordinary Scotch whiskey or whatever else you like, and not drink the last of my dwindling supply of Kentucky bourbon, I might be persuaded to oblige." He clapped his hands and again to Ashcroft's amazement, but not entirely to his surprise, another naked boy appeared, this one also about sixteen, but dark and Gallic-looking, and also wearing nothing but a slave collar. He stared at Ashcroft with naked hero-worship in his eyes.

"Good thing you keep this place heated," said Ashcroft, admiring the second boy.

"That's what *you* think," snorted Grossberg. "I don't keep the kitchen or the slave quarters heated. What'll you have?"

"Scotch and soda, no ice," said Ashcroft. "You certainly do yourself proud for young companionship."

"And so, I hear, do you, wallowing in the dens and fleshpots of Amsterdam! Oh, these two are okay, I suppose. They're called Helmut and André. Actually, I would have preferred a matched pair, but this was the best I could scrounge up in the local leather scene. San Francisco during the good old days, this place sure as hell isn't."

"Poor baby," Ashcroft commiserated. "Things are tough all over." He had a quick mental image of those two gorgeous boys, the French kid and the German, in a heavy scene with Grossberg, both of them wallowing in those huge mounds of hairy flesh. He tried to banish the thought with a shudder.

Glancing around the elegant old apartment, he inquired, "How the hell do you do it, if I may ask? Most of us try to survive on Resistance salary, or if we're not in the Resistance, on the generosity of local relief programs for the refugees."

"I got lucky," said Grossberg. "Just before the shit hit the fan, I had a couple of books that sold well in England and Europe. Of course, they froze my American rights and royalties, but who cares? They're not printing any more gay books over there anyway." He took a sip of his precious bourbon, which he drank neat. "So tell me about this project you're working on."

Ashcroft told him all about Aaron Ten Eyck and his Documentation Committee.

Grossberg was skeptical. "Hell of a lot of good it'll do," he said. "Even if you establish your documentation and prove your case, nobody's got balls enough to stand up against Wickerly and his Pentagon and his nukes. Except maybe the Soviets, and they're not about to do anything about Wickerly because he suits their propaganda purposes so well. See, now the poor, maligned little Russkies can scream about American human rights violations — how's that for the pot calling the kettle black? And as far as the World Court is concerned, the United States has never recognized its jurisdiction anyway, so it's about as impotent as an eighty-year-old drunk in a whorehouse."

"You may be right," said Ashcroft, "but still, it has to be documented, doesn't it?"

Grossberg reflected a moment. "Yes, it does. But do you really understand *why* it has to be done?"

"We're writers, Grossberg. Contemporary historians, if you like. We have a moral obligation not to let what happened over there go unrecorded, whether or not the World Court ever acts on our findings."

"You always were a dumb fucking *goyische kopp*, Ashcroft. I'll tell you why it has to be done, other than for reasons of patriotic self-flagellation and literary flatulence." As if to emphasize the latter reason, Grossberg lifted himself slightly in his chair and broke wind noisily. Again, Ashcroft shuddered.

"Fifty years from now," Grossberg continued, "or a hundred, or a hundred and fifty, there will be a country or a civilization in which the gay people think they never had it so good. And then along will come a plague, or a pestilence, or a famine, or an economic crisis, and somebody who is desperately and ruthlessly seeking power will say, 'Now, whom can we blame? And how can we blame them in the name of religion?' And as always, somebody will get the bright idea of blaming the dykes and faggots, and they'll accuse us of bringing disaster upon society by contravening the work of whatever gods or higher powers people will be believing in by then — the Great Holy Computer, I suppose, or the Trinity of the Microchip. And what do you think will happen?"

"What will happen," said Ashcroft, "is that history, the lessons of which having never been properly learned, will inevitably continue to repeat itself. Our future gay sons and daughters will continue to party and disco and do drugs, or whatever else will be the equivalent thereof a century down the road, until the religious nasties come to take them to the camps."

"Not," said Grossberg, "if your Committee does its work

properly. I don't think the world will ever be allowed to forget the Nazi Holocaust, not if *my* people have anything to say about it. The world must also never forget the take-over of the American government by Reverend President Wickerly and his Religious Right. *Now* do you understand why the work of your Documentation Committee is of such vital importance?"

"More important than even I or Ten Eyck had realized," said Ashcroft. "You lecherous old tub of lard, you've just defined my purpose for me a lot more clearly than I ever could have done!"

"That's because you're a *goyische kopp.* Now, shall we get to work? We've got a lot of ground to cover. Did you bring overnight things?"

"Yes, of course."

"Good! I'll have the boys put flannel sheets and a pile of blankets in the guest bedroom, and turn up the heat." He patted his enormous belly. "We set a pretty good table here, as you can see. We also have lots to drink. So why don't you bring out your high-density microtape recorder, and we'll have a long session before dinner." He clapped his hands again. "André! *Viens-toi! Vite! Vite!*"

The French boy scurried in, still naked except for his slave collar.

"Bring Mr. Ashcroft another drink," ordered Grossberg. "No, better yet, bring him all the fixings on a tray. Then you and that abominable piece of Heinie slaveshit close the door behind you and don't even bother us. You will serve dinner promptly at eight-thirty. Do you read me, boy?"

"*Bien entendu, mon maître,*" said the boy obediently. He continued to stare at Ashcroft adoringly. Not until Greasy Grossberg grabbed a leather riding-crop and raised it threateningly did he finally scurry off.

"Just what the hell is it you do to these little puppy-slaves, Ashcroft? I've always *liked* you well enough, for a dumb, handsome *goy,* but I've sure as hell never wanted to go to bed with you."

"Thank goodness for that," grinned Ashcroft. "Look, Greasy, they're all just star-fuckers," he went on to explain. "It's the combat journalist, freedom-fighter image, that's all! I'll bet if I were a vacuum cleaner salesman, I'd probably never even get laid."

"I don't think that's true," said Greasy Grossberg. "As much as I hate to admit it, you do have a certain *je ne sais quoi*, the sort of charisma that makes every chicken-slave in town think of you as a fantasy Daddy." He took a sip of bourbon. "Okay, I've stroked your ego enough for one day. Now, shall we get to work?"

3

For me (Grossberg began), it all started to get heavy back in 1985. That was eight years after the famous Dade County Referendum campaign, when Anita Bryant kicked our asses good. That had been our own little Stonewall Uprising, right there in South Florida, except that in 1977, unlike 1969, the whole world was watching to see what would happen.

It was then that Doug McKittrick came into his own as an acknowledged political leader and organizer, since it was he who put together the forerunners of our present-day community organizations, and it was he who, initially, funded the campaign.

Where were you in 1977? In Korea, as I recall, investigating violations, both ours and theirs, along the De-Militarized Zone — the DMZ. I remember you telling me how you had some unpleasant moments there when you got caught where you shouldn't have been, and got slapped into a North Korean jail. I also remember your delightful anecdote about how pissed off the U.N. commander was, too. As I recall your sordid little tale, he was a gay Swedish general, and he'd been enjoying leave in Tokyo, presumably wallowing in a nest of hot little Japanese boys, whom he had to abandon in order to fly back in a hurry just to spring you. Well, it could have been worse, Ashcroft; at least he *did* fly back. You weren't too much worse for wear after a week in a North Korean jail, at least nothing that some disinfectant and the Swedish general's sauna couldn't fix. I'll bet, though, that you were thankful as hell for your leather and S&M discipline, weren't you?

Anyway, while you were over there gallivanting around Southeast Asia, enjoying your little Chinese boys and Filipino boys and whatever else, probably Tibetan boys stinking of yak butter, meanwhile, back in the land of the too infrequently brave and unfortunately no longer free, we were getting our asses thoroughly kicked, or so we thought at the time.

For the sake of history, let's refresh your memory about 1977, and then move forward to 1985. Are you sure that infernal little machine of yours is working? I don't see any reels turning. They sure make them tiny and quiet these days.

In January of 1977, a small group of militant gay activists in Miami persuaded a sympathetic member of the Dade County Comission to introduce a gay rights ordinance. By a hair's breadth, it passed on the second reading and became law. Now the only way it could become nullified under Florida law was by referendum.

There was a second-rate religious folk singer by the name of Anita Bryant who was either persuaded or maneuvered by her husband, who also became her agent, into spearheading one of the filthiest campaigns in the history of American politics, under the slogan and guise of *Save Our Children.* I suppose she believed that by doing what she perceived to be "God's Work," she could also enhance her own career. Boy, was she in for a big surprise!

Besides being the most vicious referendum campaign in American history, it was also the most expensive. Actually, we outspent them slightly. The most heartening thing was the nationwide and even worldwide support that we received. Yes, Ashcroft, I was heavily involved in that campaign, and I'll remember the moments of glory and heartbreak and triumph all the rest of my life.

There was absolutely no homophobic myth, slander, or innuendo that those religious slime did not resort to. According to them, the ten percent of American voters and taxpayers who happen to be gay are each and every one, to the last faggot and dyke, convicted child molesters and practitioners of the most filthy and bizarre sexual practices, including some even too disgusting for me!

The media, as always true to their corporate puppet masters and the dictates of their major advertisers, gave us the shaft. A couple of columnists came out against repeal of the ordinance, but by far the preponderance of editorial opinion was that we should be shoved back into our closet. And they used every dirty trick in the book to do it.

I remember one full-page newspaper ad that came in from Amsterdam, paid for by the contributions of its citizens. It featured an Anne Frank theme — "From the land of Anne Frank — Don't let it happen in America," that sort of thing. It included a photograph of Anne Frank. Well, guess what our largest newspaper in South Florida did. They refused to run the ad unless we could present a signed release from Anne Frank herself, permitting us to run the photograph! That's how much world opinion meant, even back then, to the lords of our arrogant and self-censored press establishment. I mention this incident because it will become particularly relevant in the light of what happened in 1985.

The actual referendum was held in June, 1977. I forget the exact date, but we can look it up; I still have all the newspaper clippings. When all the smoke had cleared, we had lost, numerically, by about two to one. At the campaign headquarters, we cried in each other's arms. At the time, we failed to realize how much of a moral victory we had won.

The fact was that we had mobilized nearly a half a million dollars, and had polled over one hundred thousand votes, about 35% of the total, particularly in the Jewish condominium precincts where my own people, some of them Holocaust survivors, were astute enough to perceive the referendum as a civil rights issue rather than as a religious or sexual morality issue. If there was one thing that the campaign had demonstrated clearly, it was that the South Florida gay community had a hell of a lot more political clout than anyone had previously suspected.

Prior to 1977, the politicians, even the so-called liberal ones, had said, "Why should I care about gay rights? I don't even have any homosexuals in my district!" Now they suddenly realized that here was a bloc of votes and an affluent minority group that needed to be wooed. And although very few Florida politicians actually came out in favor of gay rights, nevertheless there were plenty of behind-the-scenes political alliances being forged. I'm sure Doug McKittrick must have told you lots more about that; he was always the consummate politician.

As for that horrible old sow, the religious folk singer who started the whole thing, I'm happy to say that the gay community retaliated by sending her career into oblivion. She had been under contract by the Florida citrus industry to do orange juice commercials on television; so for three years not one single gay establishment in South Florida — and elsewhere, I've been told — served orange juice. Oh, it was a time of tremendous hardship and self-sacrifice; my God, did you ever taste a Harvey Wallbanger made with pineapple juice? Or a screwdriver made with cranberry juice? But somehow, we managed to tough it out until the Orange Queen's contract was finally canceled. And that, too, was a lesson in political power for our community: gay boycotts *do work!*

Actually, the poor misguided bitch did so much to pull our community together, probably more than anyone before or since, that the following year the Gay Pride Committee wanted to make her an honorary Parade Marshal in the Gay Pride parade! I don't know what finally happened to her, but a couple of years after this fiasco, she was actually seen drinking and dancing at a mostly gay disco in Atlanta, and telling the press that she had always *loved* gay people! After that, she faded into a well-deserved oblivion. She was never *that* good a singer, anyway. *Sic transit gloria mundi!*

There was a famous old political hack who was mayor of Chicago for many, many years. Mayor Daley, as I recall. It was he who coined the famous dictum, *Power is Money and Votes.* I kept on reiterating that motto in my writing to the community, but unfortunately it always wound up being attributed to me, and Ashcroft, whatever else you may think of me, I have never been one to take credit for other people's aphorisms; not Oscar Wilde's, not Voltaire's, and certainly not Mayor Daley's.

There were other results of that spectacular campaign. Raids on gay bars and other establishments became, for at least a few halcyon years, a thing of the past. Liaisons were forged with local police departments, so that whenever there was a gay murder, the community could cooperate with the police in helping to solve it without the threat of getting fag-bashed and arrested by the cops themselves. Oh, of course there were still renegade cops who harassed gays, but at least it was no longer departmental policy.

Moving right along, folks, we now come to the year of 1985. That was the year that yours truly, fat old Greasy Grossberg, was asked to head up the publicity department of the South Florida Gay Pride Committee.

Ashcroft, you and the rest of the world may think of old

Greasy as a gluttonous, lecherous, self-indulgent slob, which I most certainly am, but please give me credit for one thing: I really do know how to do my job.

As you well know, and as everyone else knows who wasn't raised in a plastic bubble in somebody's attic, Gay Pride Day, which is the anniversary of the Stonewall Rebellion in New York in 1969, is celebrated world-wide on the last Sunday in June, except, of course, in the United States, where it has now been outlawed. In Los Angeles and San Francisco, up to half a million people used to participate, and the mayor and the city council rode in the parade. In South Florida we never did regain anywhere near the level of political energy that we'd shown in 1977, but still we always made a respectable showing. Let's face it: South Florida was always lotus land. As long as we could do lots of business, have a successful tourist season, and enjoy our perfect climate, we tended to stay out of the political mainstream.

Frankly, Ashcroft, I don't like to work. What I like to do most, other than eat, drink and have sex, is to *think*. By November of 1984, fully seven months before Gay Pride Day, I had assembled my team to do all the real work. By January we were fully operational. On my right and left hand were two top-drawer advertising agency account executives who were open on their jobs and who could use on our behalf the facilities of their respective agencies.

We then proceeded to stage a media blitz — newspapers, television, radio talk show. Suddenly all of South Florida was more aware of our community and its activities than they had been since 1977. It was the most professional public relations job, with the broadest coverage achieved, that the Gay Pride Committee could possibly have asked for.

The kick-off event of Gay Pride Week was a mammoth picnic held in a state park on the Sunday one week before the parade. What a glorious moment! I was literally tripping over reporters and TV camera crews. My biggest problem was rounding up enough presentable and articulate spokespersons to talk to them all. It was a very proud feeling when they kept congratulating my publicity team for the job we had done so well. Needless to say, I managed to blush modestly, and of course I refrained from mentioning that I, personally, had done damn little of the actual work.

And then came the debacle.

The Parade and Festival were held that year in Coconut Grove, a lovely old section south of downtown Miami, overlooking the bay. Once upon a time it had been Hippieville and Greenwich Village, with a high concentration of gays. The very first Gay Pride Parade in South Florida had taken place there. In recent years it had become urbanized, gentrified, and yuppified, with high-rise apartment buildings, high rents and high crime. Still, the Committee felt that it was a symbolic return to our roots, even though we were given an awful hassle trying to get our parade permit, since by that time Miami's city council had become totally banana. They even had a banana mayor. You'd think that getting kicked off their own island would have taught them a lesson in tolerance, but I guess human nature doesn't work that way.

Everything went off without a hitch, for once. From the parade formation site, the longest gay parade we had ever seen in South Florida made its way past cheering crowds to the Coconut Grove Exhibition Center, a vast auditorium where the Festival took place. I almost wept for joy when I saw all those thousands of beautiful gay brothers and sisters trying to get through the doors of the auditorium!

Ashcroft, I know you've spent a lot of time out of the country, so let me describe for you what a really great Gay Pride Festival is like.

There's a feeling, a spirit, a rush, that is like nothing else you will ever experience all year. For this one day, all petty differences, all political scheming and infighting, are forgotten. Gay men and lesbian women embrace each other and wish each other "Happy Gay Pride!" Even the booths and exhibits have all been put together pridefully and with a desire for excellence. At all the booths seeking funds for one righteous gay cause or another, the money flows freely. The love and the brotherhood and sisterhood are so palpable you can almost feel it with your hands.

The next day, unfortunately, everyone goes back to being their usual selves.

I went home that night in a state of euphoria. How many people had turned out for the Parade and Festival? Ten thousand? Fifteen? The media love to low-ball the estimates of the turnout at any gay event, but there were still one hell of a lot of people.

Next morning, I couldn't wait to look at the morning papers — the *Miami Herald* and the *Fort Lauderdale Sun-Sentinel*. There was nothing on the front page, but that was okay. In fact there was nothing in the main news section, but that covered national and international news. I turned to the metropolitan section. Then the business section. Then the lifestyle section. Even the classifieds.

Nothing. Not a goddamn word. Not even a picture.

At noon I rushed out and bought the afternoon papers. It was the same story: there had been no Gay Pride Parade and Festival. The thousands of people who'd been out there proclaiming their joy and their pride and their freedom simply did not exist.

I think it was at that point, Ashcroft, that I realized, beyond a shadow of a doubt, how far we had slipped down the path toward totalitarianism in America. Not that the Curtain of Silence technique hadn't been used before; it had. My parents watched it being used against the progressive labor movement in the forties and fifties, and again in the fifties at the beginning of the black civil rights movement, until that got so big it could no longer be kept hidden. It was standard practice in many cities for the news media to treat every important gay happening as a non-event, no matter how many politicians and celebrities showed up. But this time it really hit home, because it was my team and I who had been right there personally welcoming the reporters and camera crews.

Well, I need hardly tell you what I did that evening, Ashcroft; you know me too well. Normally I'm a heavy drinker, but strictly a social one; I virtually never drink just to get drunk. But that night I did. Hoo-boy, did I get drunk!

About eight o'clock that evening, good old Country Boy Joe, the news editor of the gay newspaper, called me to get my reaction. You remember him, don't you, Ashcroft? Squeaky clean, all-American good looks, North Carolina accent, and a damn good newspaperman to boot. Last I heard, the DIVAF program had caught up with him and he was in the camps. When he called me that night, I was already six drinks past the philosophical stage and I was crying into the phone, screaming about how we were living in Nazi Germany. Indeed, I felt just like my parents' old-country relatives must have felt when the Nazis were starting to seize power in Germany. I still couldn't quite believe it had happened.

Joe must have gotten really concerned about what I was going to do, because he called Janet and Susan, two ladies who'd been working on my team all year. They came over and found me sitting on the floor making speeches at the television and waving my bottle of bourbon as though I were about to throw it through the screen. They tried to persuade me to go to bed.

If there is one thing one learns from being a Jew, Ashcroft, or *should* learn, it is the lesson of political reality. Never take anything for granted, never feel too secure. Your world can tumble around your ears in an instant. I kept trying to get into my file cabinet, and Janet and Susan kept asking, "What is it, Greasy? What are you looking for?"

Finally I found it: my passport and other personal documents.

"You better keep yours handy, too!" I screamed at them. "Mark my words! You're going to need it! We all are!"

Since that night, I've developed my own theory as to what happened to our news coverage, since in other cities they still continued to cover gay community events, although on a rapidly dwindling basis. The one exception was that every time some self-proclaimed expert expressed concern on behalf of society that if you sat in the same room with a homosexual you'd die the next day of AIDS, that always got full coverage.

My theory was very simply this: somebody very high up, whether in the government, or the newspaper's corporate hierarchy, or with a lot of political clout, or perhaps a major advertiser or group of advertisers, I don't know which — had called the news editor of the largest paper and told him that if he ran even *one more* goddamn faggot story, Gay Pride or no Gay Pride, he'd be out pounding a beat in Little Havana, covering Cuban weddings and coming-out parties.

So now this editor is between a rock and a hard place. He can't run any of the reams of coverage his reporters and photographers have brought in from the Parade and Festival, and he doesn't want to get scooped by the other papers. So he calls up his buddies at all the other editorial desks in the area, explains the situation, and makes his pitch:

"You guys don't scoop me on Gay Pride and I'll owe you one. Next big story that breaks, I'll share it with you." So they *all* kill their Gay Pride stories and photo coverage.

That's just my theory, anyway. We'll never know for sure. A couple of our people tried to follow through with each of the local papers, but were dealt with very rudely by every one of them. Why should they have cared? You can force a retraction if something erroneous gets printed, but there's not a goddamn thing you can do about it if they simply decide, "All the news that fits, we print. Maybe!" The only thing that we were sure of, because it was so obvious, was that there had definitely been some sort of collusion among the four newspapers.

Let's break for dinner, Ashcroft. Talking about all this shit has got me depressed. What I need right now is a lot more bourbon and a really good dinner. Hey, you don't think I hired André just for his good looks and that big, beautiful *schvantz* of his, do you? That kid has all the makings of a four-star chef!

4

The meal, just as Ashcroft had anticipated, was on a lavish scale. Helmut and André served, no longer completely naked, but wearing leather codpieces with chrome studs.

"I'm not completely barbarian, Ashcroft," said Greasy Grossberg, "no matter what you may think. I do make them cover their genitals when they're serving at table. Okay, children, start the show."

First, by way of appetizer, came Beluga caviar on toast points garnished with just the tiniest hint of finely chopped scallions and finely grated hardboiled egg. It was accompanied by a bottle of Bouvet Brut.

"So, I'm a peasant," said Grossberg. "With wine like this, who needs real champagne?" Ashcroft agreed that the bubbly white went very nicely with the caviar.

The next course was a filet of sole poached in wine, which, when added to a roux after the fish had been removed, formed the basis of the sauce, which included tiny langoustes, mussels and shrimp.

"After all," said Grossberg, copping a feel of Helmut's firm young buttocks, "one man's *merde* is another man's *poisson*, no?" Ashcroft groaned. In addition to his other characteristics, Grossberg was famous for his outrageous puns. With the fish course, he poured from a bottle of Moselle that reminded Ashcroft of a great California chardonnay he'd once enjoyed: crisp, flinty and dry.

After a touch of sorbet to cleanse the palate, the boys carried in a huge serving platter with the *pièce de résistance*, an enormous haunch of veal, gently roasted and redolent with the aroma of herbs and spices. This was accompanied by glazed carrots, *petit pois*, and *pommes roti*.

"Y'all do yourself right proud, Greasy," said Ashcroft, as Grossberg poured from a bottle of Tavel Superieure.

"I'm so glad you're not a snob about a good rosé with veal," said Grossberg. "So many Americans used to have *attitude* when it came to rosé. Well, I guess nowadays it's back to jug wines in the White House, right?"

"If they allow any alchoholic beverages at all."

In the European manner, the salad course followed the entree, but Ashcroft, already full to bursting, declined the Belgian endive with tarragon dressing. "The only Belgian I ever liked," he said, "was Cesar Franck."

Dessert, to Ashcroft's delight, consisted of fruit and cheese — chilled sliced pears and a magnificent young Brie, at the first blush of its greatness.

"I'm so relieved," said Ashcroft, "that you didn't serve an ice cream sundae."

"Don't be silly," said Grossberg. "A fresh, runny young Brie is one hell of a lot sweeter and richer than ice cream, and it doesn't freeze your mouth."

They returned to the living room for espresso and liqueurs; Ashcroft drank Strega, Grossberg a Grand Marnier.

"My compliments," said Ashcroft. "Do you think this will hold you until bedtime?"

"Oh, I might have to fix a peanut butter sandwich, or else send out for some pizza," replied Grossberg.

"Tell me, Greasy," Ashcroft finally asked. "Aside from your gorgeous little slaveboys, whatever made you choose Luxembourg for your exile?"

"I *like* it," said Grossberg. "It *suits* me. It's tiny, it's Graustarkian, it's very civilized, and best of all I don't have a language problem. Between my high school French and my delicatessen

Yiddish, I get along just fine with the Luxembourgeois. Would you believe, the Grand Duke and Duchess have had me to the palace for cocktails?"

"You've got to be kidding! How the hell did that happen?"

"Well, they wanted to do something for the refugee community, just to show their support and to thumb their noses at Reverend President Wickerly. 'The Mouse That Roared' type of thing, you see; after all, not even Wickerly or his mad generals in the Pentagon would dare nuke a tiny, helpless, postage-stamp country like Luxembourg, and the Common Market protects it from economic sanctions. The problem was that since the United States had imposed strict travel restrictions, and since all the gay refugees went to places like London and Hamburg and Amsterdam and Copenhagen, I happened to have been almost the only American here. So instead of a mass feeding and handing out of clothing and relief checks on the lawn of the Palace, they simply made a very public showing of having me in for cocktails. Same symbolic gesture."

"I hope you wore all your leather and grossed them out."

"Oh, sure, I had André and Helmut carry me in riding on a palanquin! Come on, Ashcroft, I carried it off with real style and class. I don't know whose style and class I borrowed, but apparently I made a decent impression. Subsequently, I addressed the Grand Duke's privy council on the state of affairs in America, and since then I've been left pretty much on my own. Once in a while I pick up a modest honorarium or two for a lecture or a television appearance, but mostly I just live off my royalties, write my sleazy little novels, and enjoy the company of my two little domestic companions."

Ashcroft, stuffed with food and drink, was barely able to stifle a yawn. "I'm sorry, Greasy. It's not the company; I was never less bored in my life. But after that meal..."

"I can sympathize, Ashcroft. Even though I ate and drank twice as much as you did."

"Three times as much, but who's counting?"

"You really *are* an asshole, Ashcroft. Besides being a picky eater. Look, let's not try to do any more work tonight. We'll crash out early, get up early, and put in a good morning's work. Then you can catch the noon TGV back to Amsterdam."

"Sounds fine to me, Greasy."

Compared to his room at the Leather Eagle, Grossberg's guest bedroom was quite luxurious. The magnificent four-poster canopied bed was modest compared to Greasy's extra-king-sized one, but it was unbelieveably comfortable. No sooner had he stretched out in it, however, when there was a pounding at the door, and before he could answer it, Helmut and André came tumbling into the room, very distraught, and with fresh red welts across their buttocks. They were jabbering rapidly at him in Luxembourgeois.

"Quiet!" yelled Ashcroft. "Now tell me slowly in French or German. Very slow and clear. *Lentement, comprends? Langsam, versteist?*"

"He beat us and kicked us out," said André.

"He always beats us, but he never kicked us out before," added Helmut.

"He said that he was tired — *fatigué!* I do not believe it. That man is never too tired for sex! *Il est formidable!*

"Yes, he is that," agreed Ashcroft.

"A giant," said Helmut. "A Viking! A demi-god out of Wagner!"

"He is rather large," agreed Ashcroft. "Don't you two have a room of your own?"

"*Ja*, we do, but. . ." Two large tears suddenly welled up in the German boy's eyes.

André knelt at the side of the bed and kissed Ashcroft's hand. "The problem is, we're just not used to sleeping alone."

"Well, gee, fellas," replied Ashcroft. "I'm kind of tired, too. Couldn't you just sort of keep each other warm?"

At this they both looked as though they were about to burst out crying.

"You don't like us," said André.

"I do! I do!" protested Ashcroft. "Both of you!"

"Then I tell you what," said Helmut. "Let me bring some fresh champagne from the kitchen, and we'll have our own little party together, right here. You like?"

"I like, but what will your Master have to say about that?"

"*Ach*," said Helmut, "do not worry about that! He would kill us if we did *not* try to make your evening pleasant!"

"Besides," added André, "some day when I am your age, I will nave a *ménage* of slaves of my own. Would you deny me the privilege of telling them about the night I once spent with Stephen Ashcroft, the famous writer and Resistance fighter?"

Ashcroft sighed. Star-fuckers, he thought. But aloud he said, "What can I say? All right, boys, fetch the champagne and you may both stay here with me tonight."

It was, as Ashcroft was later to recollect fondly, an orgy of gargantuan proportions. Although the two boys wanted nothing more than to serve him, he saw to it that they, too, were well pleased. Among the other things Ashcroft enjoyed that night, it had been a long time since he had had the vicariously sensual pleasure of watching two young boys making passionate love to each other, and of being affectionately included within their sexual aura. It was both gratifying and exciting.

When all passions had finally been spent and the champagne consumed, they slept the night wrapped tightly together in each other's arms, legs intertwined. At the first light of daybreak, they awakened, and made love again. No sooner had they finished, however, when the Master's bell rang. Regretfully, the two boys kissed Ashcroft lovingly and scurried off to perform their domestic tasks. Ashcroft went blissfully back to sleep.

Shortly after eight, he was awakened by André entering with a pot of coffee and a basket of freshly-baked croissants.

"Just to sustain you until breakfast, *Monsieur*."

"But," Ashcroft protested, "for me, coffee and a croissant *is* breakfast!"

"Not in this house, *Monsieur. Le Maître* will expect you in the dining room shortly."

Shaved and bathed, Ashcroft found Greasy Grossberg at the breakfast table waiting for him.

"Did those two little bastards let you get any sleep?" he demanded. "Or did they just want to fuck all night?"

"I didn't mind. They were good company."

"Bullshit," said Grossberg. "They're both a pain in the ass."

"Yes," agreed Ashcroft with a dreamy smile. "They certainly were."

"Forget that sex stuff for right now. Have some breakfast. We've got work to do."

"I had a croissant," replied Ashcroft.

"Oh, come on, man! That's not breakfast! I've ordered André to fix us each an *omelette aux fines herbes*, with *pommes frites* on the side. And rolls with confiture. And just a few little sausages. Oh, maybe just a slice or two of ham. After all, if you're taking the noon TGV, you won't be here for lunch."

"Grossberg, you must have been bitten in the leg by a Jewish mother."

"I *am* a Jewish mother!" the fat man replied. "Now, crank up your little high-density microtape machine and we can work while we eat."

Greasy Grossberg had no startling new revelations for Ashcroft. What he did have was a collection of names, dates, places, no single one highly significant in itself, but, when taken cumulatively, tending to point indisputably to a pattern of human rights violations that could only have reflected official policy. He had a prodigious memory, augmented by his voluminous collection of files containing memos, clippings and photographs.

Ashcroft sipped cup after cup of coffee while the fat man nibbled on the remains of breakfast.

"Greasy, can you shed any new light on the Douglas McKittrick assassination?"

"You were there, Ashcroft; you almost got blown away yourself. *You* tell *me* who did it."

"The whole world knows who *did* it. And anybody with even the least amount of political smarts knows who was *behind* it. But who was *directly* responsible for it? Who gave the order? Who made the decision?"

"Who was responsible for the assassinations of both the Kennedys? Of that civil rights activist, Medgar Evers? Of Doctor Martin Luther King? Or the death within three years of some forty or so people who were even tangentially connected with the Kennedys? How many Americans ever believed the Warren Commission's report?"

"About ten percent," replied Ashcroft. "Fewer than the number who believe in Santa Claus and the Easter Bunny. God! The people back then must have been politically blind, deaf and stupid not to have realized what was happening!"

"They knew," said Grossberg. "They knew perfectly well that

the Warren Commission's report was a cover-up for what really happened. But what they just weren't able to face, and never were able to face until long after it was too late, was the utter monstrousness of *what* the Warren Commission was covering up *for!* Look, Ashcroft, this pattern of an official policy of lies and deceit didn't just start with Reverend President Wickerly. It's been going on for a lot longer than most people realize. They lied to us about Guatemala in 1954; they lied to us about Iran in 1958 when they overthrew the legitimate democratic government of Premier Mossadeqh and installed as our creature the hated Shah. They lied to us about Cuba; they lied to us for twelve years about Viet Nam. They lied to us about Chile and Nicaragua and Honduras and El Salvador. And worst of all, they taught us to believe all the lies they'd told us about ourselves."

"That's exactly what I used to tell my lover. But he would never listen."

"Well, it's all over now, Ashcroft. It's too late. There's nothing more that any of us can do except try to keep a record for posterity."

Ashcroft switched off the microtape. "I don't want to believe that," he said. "I want to go back, Greasy. Some day I damn sure want to go back."

"What the hell for? Even in the best of times, the food was always lousy, the wine undrinkable, and the sexual atmosphere repressive. They don't even know enough to use nothing but real butter in a croissant. You suddenly got a hankering for barbecue and apple pie? Or maybe a cardboard McGreaseburger served on a styrofoam bun? Count your blessings, Ashcroft. At least over here they're civilized. What the hell can you say for a country where the *vin du pays* is tap water with chunks of ice floating in it? Or worse, in places like Texas, iced tea? And where they actually drink even their best imported beer half frozen, out of a frozen glass, because they're so hooked on frozen plastic they're afraid of the real taste of anything! Do you know any other country where the word 'intellectual' is almost invariably used as a pejorative, as though we were people to be feared? Don't you remember, back when they still had Public Television, how most people used to refer to it sneeringly as 'the *educational* channel,' as though that were a term of approbrium? And pass up some of the greatest entertainment on the tube just out of sheer terror that they might inadvertently learn something! Back home they're so brainwashed that if you even dare to mention any of the civilized amenities that all the other industrial countries take for granted, like great public transport, national health care, and five-week vacations, they freak out and call you a Communist! Come on, Ashcroft, be real! Over here, André and Helmut are well past the age of consent. Back home, they'd be jailbait. You want to go back to having to live like that again, wondering when the Sex Police are gonna come pounding on your bedroom door?"

But Ashcroft could not help thinking about some of the good things, the uniquely American things that were part of his very being, and that he had missed with such desperate homesickness during his long years as an overseas correspondent.

He remembered the sun rising out of the Atlantic Ocean over the miles of beach at Cape Canaveral. The wooded hills of North Carolina. The smell of coffee and beignets at the French Market after a wild New Orleans night. Swapping friendly insults with a waitress at a truck stop in Nebraska, both of them speaking that special American language that no one else can ever quite master. Driving through the mountains of Colorado. The endless expanse of the great Southwestern deserts. The snow-capped High Sierras. The sun sinking into the Pacific Ocean off Malibu. Chinese food in San Francisco. Fried oysters and baked salmon along the waterfront in Seattle. *Chili rellenos* in Texas. Conch salad and key lime pie in Florida. The majesty of limitless space, of the big trucks rolling proudly along the Interstates from coast to coast.

Then he thought of Fort Lauderdale. Of Troy. The McKittrick assassination. The DIVAF program. The camps. He fought back his tears.

"I have to go now, Greasy," he said. "Thanks for all the help, and for the hospitality."

The two boys, Helmut and André, fetched his overnight bag. They kissed him goodbye very warmly.

"You are — *wunderbar!*" said Helmut. "It makes me feel inside of me so good to have known you."

"*Moi aussi*," said André, clinging to him. "A true honor,

Monsieur Ashcroft. Knowing you is — *comment dit-on?* — an enrichment!"

"*Au revoir*, then," said Ashcroft, hugging them both. "*Auf wiedersehen*. And thanks again to you, Greasy."

"Anytime, old buddy," said Grossberg. "For you, the pleasures of the table — and the slave quarters — are always available."

5

When the TGV from Luxembourg arrived back at Amsterdam's Central Station early that afternoon, Ashcroft had two surprises awaiting him.

The first was the weather, which had suddenly turned glorious. It was mild and sunny, a brief harbinger of the renascent spring which was just a few weeks off. Vondel Park would burst into greenery, and tulips would appear in profusion everywhere.

The second surprise was a police car parked in front of the station. Behind the wheel was Hans, the friendly young cop with whom Ashcroft had tricked at the sauna a few days before. He motioned Ashcroft over to the car.

"Hello, Stephen," he said with a broad grin. "Constable Hans von Broecklen at your service."

"Well, hello yourself. What are you doing meeting trains?"

"Oh, I like to watch people come and go. Sooner or later someone interesting turns up. In this case, you. Get in, I'll drive you home."

"Thanks, Hans, but it's such a gorgeous day. I'd really much rather walk."

"Get in, please. I need to talk to you." He opened the front door of the cruiser. Ashcroft shrugged. He threw his overnight bag onto the back seat and slid in next to Hans.

"I must say," said Ashcroft as they circled the trolley terminus and headed up the Damrak, "you really do look sensational in uniform."

The handsome young blond glanced over at Ashcroft fondly and rested his hand for just a moment on the American's thigh.

"Stephen," he said, "I'm afraid I have some rather disturbing news for you."

"Am I under arrest?"

"No, no, of course not. Well, not really. I mean, not yet."

"Hans, what are you trying to tell me?"

"Your extradition papers arrived yesterday. Your government wants you back."

"And are you going to send me back?"

"Don't be silly. Most of the charges aren't even extraditable under our laws. 'Blasphemy' is not a crime in Holland. Neither is there such a crime as 'seditious writing.' And as for 'criticism of the duly constituted government,' well, we feel that in a real democracy, that's not a crime, it's a civic duty."

"Are there any charges for which I could be extradited?"

"Unfortunately, yes. By virtue of your activity in the Resistance, you've been named as an accessory in the aiding and abetting of bank robbery, kidnapping, and commando raids against military installations."

"That's preposterous."

"Wait until you hear this one: 'Complicity in the assassination of one Douglas McKittrick,' How does that grab you?"

"It's true, actually. I was one of the people in his political circle who encouraged him to run for Governor. If he'd stayed out of the limelight the way so many people in his position usually do, he'd still be alive today."

They had arrived back at the Leather Eagle Hotel. "Mind if I come in for a drink?" asked Hans. "I have more to tell you."

"Be my guest."

When they entered the tiny lobby that led to the bar, they saw Dirk, the owner, seated on a corner stool doing his books. Although he had a small room set aside as his office, he liked to work at the bar so that he could chat with everyone. Gerard, the good-looking French boy, was behind the bar. Dirk did not seem in the least surprised at the presence of the handsome young constable.

"Hello, Hans," he said. "I figured you'd be along sooner or later, now that Ashcroft's staying here. Can I buy you a drink?" Out of deference to Ashcroft, they spoke in English.

"Thank you," said Hans. "I'll have a light lager and lime, since

I'm on duty." Ashcroft ordered a pilsner, and they excused themselves to sit at the far side of the bar, where they could talk
privately.

"So," asked Ashcroft, "where do I stand? Do I understand you
to say that the police are *not* going to act on the extradition
proceedings?"

"That is correct," said Hans. "Even on the extraditable criminal charges, we'd have to see some strong corroborating evidence,
and of course there isn't any, since this is obviously a political
case."

"So where's the problem? My Resistance work? I'm only a
writer, Hans. I know virtually nothing about the radical wing of
the Movement."

"The problem is that the extradition request was just a formality. They never expected us to extradite you. We seldom do, in
political cases; your asylum here will continue for the time being.
The problem is that when we refuse extradition, that's when their
people swing into action."

"I see. What form does this action usually take?"

"Kidnapping. Bombing. Assassination. These boys of your
government are not amateurs by any means."

"How much time do you think I have?"

"We can stall the extradition proceedings for about a month
before they ask us either to turn you over to them, or else issue
our official refusal of extradition for whatever we might consider
to be legitimate legal reasons. We have to do one or the other, unless we want to dissolve our extradition treaty with the United
States, which we don't want to do because it comes in useful in
legitimate criminal cases. After we inform them that extradition
has been refused and that you have asylum status here, then I
would strongly recommend that you not walk by yourself even in
the daytime, and that you do not go out at all after dark."

"You know I couldn't live like that," said Ashcroft.

"I didn't think you could. That means there will be some
rough action, probably, which presents another problem."

"And what is that?"

"Stephen, my friend, we will try to protect you as best we
can. But please remember that we are a tiny country of twelve
million people with a very small NATO army that doesn't even

believe in fighting. We are a very peaceful, non-violent people, as you well know. If your presence here results in any of our citizens getting hurt or killed, then we will have no choice but to ask you to leave, much as we would hate to do so. So I would suggest that you sort of stay in the attic, so to speak, like Anne Frank. Meantime, we'll keep an eye on this hotel. That's about all we can do." He snapped his fingers for Gerard. "Another round for all three of us, and please have one yourself." To Ashcroft he said, "Official business is now over. May I offer you a purely personal suggestion?"

"Of course."

"You don't have to go to the sauna, you know." The young constable smiled shyly. "I'd like to come visit you here, if I may."

"I'd like that very much," said Ashcroft.

"I'll tell you something," said Hans, sipping his lager and lime. "I've been madly in love with Dirk ever since they gave me this assignment. But he likes older leathermen like yourself. And you like little Indonesian boys, or so I've been told. And I also love older Americans like you. So I shall enjoy you as a Dirk-surrogate, and whenever we make love together, you can use me to fantasize about your American lover. That will make everybody very happy, no?"

Ashcroft chuckled. "You Dutch have a way of putting things so neatly." They finished their drinks, and Hans embraced him warmly. He also embraced Dirk on his way out.

"Goddamn cops keep getting younger every year," growled Dirk after the boy had left. "Next thing you know, they'll be recruiting them in kindergarten."

III

THE CAULDRON STARTS TO BUBBLE

1

Ashcroft was at his typewriter, writing to Greasy Grossberg to thank him for his hospitality in Luxembourg, and for his assistance to the Documentation Committee. He went on to discuss some of the things they had talked about during his brief visit.

If you think 1985 was a disastrous year for human rights, (Ashcroft wrote), 1986 was a total calamity — a real debacle. Surprisingly, it was my lover Troy who got it down on paper, and with an unintended degree of insight and perception that his own political persuasion would never have permitted.

That was the year we first got together, and as a sort of honeymoon we took our voyage of discovery in Troy's magnificent van. I persuaded him to keep a record of the trip. He did a lot better than that; he also kept a record of our reactions — particularly mine — to what transpired during the period.

Actually, I had been urging Troy to do some serious writing since we'd first started keeping company. He was quite brilliant at the kind of writing he did for his clients — ad copy, press releases, publicity campaigns. I told him he was capable of much better things.

"I'm very proud of what I'm doing!" he protested. "It's honest work, isn't it?"

"That's almost debatable," I replied. "But then, you know my opinion of the business you're in. Don't get me wrong; I'm not a job snob. Any kind of legitimate employment is honorable — even advertising, I suppose, especially since you're so good at it. All I'm saying is that you're prostituting your talent."

"What a phony, pretentious thing to say!" exclaimed Troy. "I make lots of money for my clients, don't I? I earn every cent of the excellent salary they pay me, not to mention the bonuses and perks. Just because you think every creative artist should be a left-wing social rebel starving in a garret doesn't make me a whore, Stephen. And anyway, I don't see you putting down your camera and tape recorder and writing a serious novel!"

Nevertheless, Troy did agree to keep a journal of our trip. He decided to call it, *Alexis de Tocqueville Redux — America Through the Eyes of a Foreigner.*

"Why a foreigner?" I asked him. "I was born and raised in Pasadena, California. We may be a bit trendy and upscale in Southern California, but I don't think we're all that foreign, regardless of what you think of tofu and alfalfa sprouts."

"The eyes of a foreigner," he insisted, "because you have the viewpoint and insights of a foreigner. You've spent most of your adult years outside of the country, and it gives you a perspective that's totally different from ours."

"All right," I said, "but please spare us the 'redux.' Make it *Alexis de Tocqueville Revisited*, okay?"

"Why?" he demanded. "Updike wrote a novel with 'redux' in the title."

"That's different," I explained. "Updike writes for the sort of people who read *Harper's* and *Atlantic* and *The New Yorker*. I doubt that the average American even knows who de Tocqueville was."

"But I'm not writing for the average American," Troy said. "I'm really writing for you. Besides, I'll explain all that when I write it."

So pay close attention, Greasy. What follows is Troy's own creation, not mine. You don't have to send it back to me because I've had it photocopied, but you might want to keep it in your files for whatever light it sheds on the events of that year. I hope you enjoy it, because I realize you always used to consider Troy strictly a Golden Boy, an intellectual lightweight with too much money and education and not enough street smarts. Perhaps you were partly right, or he wouldn't be where he is now.

Please give my regards to Helmut and André. Why don't the three of you come to Amsterdam some weekend, if they can ever get you to stay on your feet long enough? We could do some great partying. In brotherhood, Stephen Ashcroft.

2

Of all the hot looking older men in South Florida (Troy wrote), why did I have to connect with the most outrageously left-wing writer, intellectual, and parlor-pinko in America? I swear, if he'd been born one of the Marx Brothers, his first name would have been Karl!

Nevertheless, Stephen is one of the most incredibly attractive men I've ever known. I cannot conceive of my ever being anyone else's lover, although I suppose that if Stephen hadn't come along, eventually I would have settled down with someone else. But I know that the magic spark, the incredible dynamics of our relationship, simply would not have been there.

A moment of digression for a historical note.

In 1831–1832, Alexis de Tocqueville, a French writer and political scientist, visited America. As a result of his travels and observations, in 1835 he published his classic study, *Democracy In America*. Some of his reflections and insights would still be considered valid today. It was I who suggested, soon after Stephen and I formed our commitment to each other, that we take a long Tocqueville-style journey together, in which he could rediscover his own country.

For this purpose I went out and bought a van, the largest model they make, and with the biggest, most powerful engine. Fuel economy was not one of my considerations.

Stephen was amazed that I'd bought it stripped. I explained to him that vans were another one of my hobbies, and that I preferred to supervise the customizing myself. Every day after work I stopped by the conversion shop, one I'd dealt with before. Stephen says there's no craftsmanship or pride left in America anymore, but the men who worked in that van conversion shop were strictly old school. Everything they did was done with love and with care.

The twin captain's chairs in front were upholstered in the most outrageously expensive velour I could find. The entire interior was carpeted — sides, deck, and overhead. A tightly-hung set of electrically-operated drapes could seal off the cab from the interior. The bed was luxurious, and made up into a couch during the day. There was a holding tank for the toilet, and a self-contained ice-making refrigerator. When the conversion had been completed, the interior had all the amenities of a motor home reduced into the compact and maneuverable proportions of a large van.

For hard driving on the Interstates, I had the suspension beefed up with extra-heavy-duty shocks; and to carry the huge electrical load, an extra battery with crossover switch so I could run them in parallel or individually. To prevent too much drain on their capacity, I added a small gas-powered charging unit that could be started up when the engine wasn't running.

The windows were tinted to almost one-way visibility, for privacy. The exterior was really awesome — I had it done in my family's racing colors from back in the days when we'd had stables, accented discreetly but not gaudily in glitter-gold striping.

The first night I brought it home, we broke it in right. I stocked it with champagne, caviar, and *pâté de foie gras*, and we drove out into the Everglades and spent the night in that lovely new bed.

Stephen's lovemaking was like nothing else I had ever experienced. Although I happen to consider it to be in very bad taste to discuss private sexual matters in explicit detail, I will go so far as to say that it was not merely sexual perfection, but also the most emotionally fulfilling sex I have ever had, or ever will have. I know it was that way for Stephen, too. Polarity was of absolutely no concern to us; we were not husband and wife, we were not master and slave, we were not top and bottom. At all times, we were all things to each other. We were simply two men who loved.

After that night in the Everglades, Stephen suggested we call the van "La Belle Hélène," after Offenbach's delightful operatic satire of — you guessed it — Helen of Troy. I thought it was a nice gesture, and a neat little play on the use of my name.

Stephen had been somewhat depressed by the political news of late, and I felt the long trip would be good for him. One of the things that sent him into a blue funk was the resurgency — or as Stephen would have put it, the recrudescence — of the militant radical religious right-wing crazies. Personally, I see absolutely nothing wrong with them; they do lend a certain stability to the lower orders, and they certainly help make my own job easier. If you can tell people what to believe in, and what to think, it makes it that much easier to tell them what kind of toothpaste to buy, or to brainwash them into drinking that godawful, tasteless, over-carbonated swill known as "light" beer. But Stephen took his First Amendment issues very seriously.

It was just before we began our trip that the gangs of so-called "Christian" picketers and hooligans had finally pressured our nation's largest chain of convenience stores into removing from their shelves permanently two magazines called "Playboy" and "Penthouse." These were two rather innocuous adult magazines with a smattering of mildly sexually oriented material, but with a large and highly literate editorial content of generally excellent quality and decidedly liberal opinion. Much more Stephen's cup of tea than mine, actually. I came home to find Stephen making love to a bottle of my best Armagnac. He was really upset.

"It's a hell of a note," he said, "when these gangs of functionally illiterate religious fanatics can tell decent Americans what they're allowed to read and think."

"How do you know they're all functionally illiterate?" I said, playing devil's advocate, even though I knew that functionally illiterate is exactly what these groups are *supposed* to be.

"Well, obviously, if they weren't functionally illiterate, they'd know that whatever else those two magazines are, they're certainly not pornography. But whether they're porno or not isn't the issue. Censorship is the issue. The First Amendment is the issue." He took another large swig of Armagnac. I hate it when he gets like that, but also I love him for being so concerned. Hell, he still gets all bent out of shape about the Sacco and Vanzetti case, and that happened twenty years before he was born! It's kind of neat to have a lover with whom one quarrels only about larger issues, never about domestic problems.

"But, Stephen," I pointed out, "it *isn't* censorship! I'm not trying to rationalize or defend what those crazies did, but for one thing, you can buy these magazines at any other convenience store or newsstand. For another, this chain has a perfect right — in fact, a duty to its stockholders — to target its own market segment by selling or not selling anything they want to, and you certainly can't claim they're a chain of upscale boutiques, can you? If they want to reach the mindless morons and the TV-addicted couch potatoes, then they have the right to take anything they want off their shelves! But most important, nobody has actually suppressed these two magazines. You can still subscribe to them, can't you? You can buy them somewhere else, can't you? Let's face it, there are a couple of really filthy pieces of political smut that *you* subscribe to that are one hell of a lot more dangerous to our country than *Playboy* or *Penthouse*."

I was refering to *Soviet Life*, a beautifully-printed full-color magazine extolling the joys of life in the Soviet Union, and "World Press Review," another heavily Commie-oriented monthly that exposed its readers to the anti-American slanders of the foreign press. As soon as I'd said the words, I wished I hadn't. Stephen leaned back in his chair, took another swig of Armagnac, and smiled at me with the evil, anticipatory leer he always gets on his face when he's about to demolish somebody with his intellectual argument.

"And what," he purred, "is wrong with reading *Soviet Life*?"

"It's pure propoganda," I said. "You don't see them talking about their Gulags and their housing shortages, do you?"

"Well, of course it's propoganda," he agreed. "And what about our counterpart publication, *America*, that we publish in the Soviet Union? Do you think for one moment that when Ivan or Dmitri or Natasha — the average Soviet citizens — subscribe to *America*, they get to read about our social problems? Our ghettoes? Our slums? Our devastating crime figures? Our infant mortality rates? Our neglected senior citizens? Our collapsing infrastructure for which the maintenance funds are all drained away to feed the bloated military? Do you think we tell the Soviets all about that?"

"Well, I would certainly hope not! We want them to see the positive side of American life, not its worst aspects."

"Thank you. You've just made my point. But the real point about *Soviet Life* is this: can you honestly say that you know *more* about the Soviets and their daily lives by *not* reading *Soviet Life*? Why do you think you're doing your country a favor by knowing as little as possible about them, when they want to know as much as possible about us?"

"I never said *you* shouldn't read *Soviet Life*, Stephen. I just don't think it should be in general circulation. And as for that other Bolshie magazine of yours, *World Press Review*, that's a hatchet job from the other side if I ever saw one."

"Sure," replied Stephen, "it tells Americans everything we're not allowed to read in our own newspapers."

"Exactly!" I agreed. "If our people were meant to have such information, it would be in our own newspapers!"

"Aha!" he exclaimed. "Then you *admit* our press is heavily censored."

"No, it isn't," I replied. "You yourself told me about interviewing a New York *Times* news editor who told you, 'No, of course we don't have a government censor in our newsroom. Why should we? We all understand perfectly well what is expected of us.' That's not censorship, Stephen, that's just common sense. After all, in order for democracy to survive against the Commies, the media *should* be an instrument of national policy, shouldn't they?"

Stephen smiled at me again, that same evil leer. "Yes," he said triumphantly. "That's exactly what the Kremlin says about *Izvestia* and *Pravda*!" With dismay, I realized that he'd maneuvered me into making his point for him. Then he grabbed me by the wrist and pulled me onto his lap. I'm kind of big and heavy to sit on anybody's lap, but somehow we managed it.

"I'll give you credit for one thing, you bloody American fascist," he said. "At least you've taken my mind off the convenience stores! What do you say we go out to dinner tonight? We deserve it."

"We not only deserve it," I pointed out, "we can well afford it." I could never quite make Stephen realize how well-off we were financially, at least on my side of the family, or that our not dining out at an expensive restaurant wouldn't really do a damn thing for the starving masses in Calcutta. Lord, save me from a man with an acute social conscience!

No. I don't really mean that. I could never see myself taking as a lover some hard-boiled ad agency type with gold chains around his neck and no conscience at all. I love Stephen for his caring and his social conscience. Even though his social and political viewpoints are usually the opposite of my own.

It was even worse after we got out on the road. The first thing that really freaked Stephen out was the dreadful condition of the deteriorated Interstate system. There'd be an occasional stretch of fresh pavement, and then hundreds of miles of jarring ruts and potholes that would have torn up a smaller or less rugged vehicle.

"How did this happen?" he wanted to know. "Why build a magnificent system of roads and then let it fall completely apart?"

"It's the trucks," I explained. "They keep allowing bigger and bigger trucks, and the trucks break down the roads faster than they can be repaired."

"Wow," said Stephen. "The trucking industry sure must have a powerful lobby. But is it just the trucks, or is it also graft and shoddy workmanship by crooked contractors?"

"That too, I'm sure."

The fifty-five mile-per-hour speed limit was still officially in effect, but it was almost universally unenforced. We usually held the van to about sixty-five m.p.h., but most of the traffic drove much faster than that.

It was while we were on the road that we heard on the radio the news that the much-debated aid bill to the Contra forces in Nicaragua had been, as Stephen put it, "ramrodded through Congress."

"Sixty-five percent of Congress against it," he said, "and eighty percent of the American people against it, and still it passed. Is that what you call democracy in action?"

We alternated our overnight stops between sleeping in the van at a campground, rest area, or national park, and staying at a luxury resort motel. That night was our motel night. As soon as we'd checked into our suite and unpacked, Stephen started drinking again. The situation regarding Nicaragua had deeply upset him.

"One would think," he dictated into his recorder for an article he was starting to write, "or at least hope, that after the long generations of pain and suffering and misery and starvation and peonage that we inflicted upon those unhappy people by maintaining our puppet dictator family in power, one would have hoped that once they finally got their own government, we would finally have had enough compassion to embrace their legitimate aims and aspirations and tried to help them rebuild their shattered economy. But no, not us! Instead we gather together the dregs of former dictator Somoza's thugs and gangsters and police, impress a few hungry Indian boys into their ranks, and try to overthrow their legitimate government, one which has been recognized by almost every other Western country and all the Eastern ones. And this senile, fatuous old man in the White House has the nerve, the temerity, to insult our intelligence by calling these counter-revolutionaries 'Freedom Fighters!' It's enough to make a decent American puke!"

"Scratch one 'hope' and one 'finally,'" I interrupted. "You're being gramatically redundant. Also, it's you who are being politically fatuous. Can you honestly say that the Sandinista government *isn't* a Marxist government? Is the President wrong when he says he doesn't want Russian bases in Central America?"

"The Sandinista government may be leftist, sure, but it damn sure isn't Marxist. There's still a large private sector — starving, thanks to us — and as much press and political freedom and criticism of the government as any nation at war can reasonably allow. Troy, I was there, remember? I was there during the Somoza regime and I've been there since the Sandinistas. All they're trying to do is make things better for their people than they've ever had it before — schools, roads, hospitals, transport, communications, an infrastructure of their own. Is that so bad? And if the President doesn't want Russian bases in Central America, then why is he following a course of action in his foreign policy that makes Russian bases inevitable? What the hell other choices or options is he leaving them? Troy, if we'd only let them have their democracy, if we'd even let them have enough to eat, the whole damn country could have been one big American base!"

"I still don't see how we can possibly support a Communist government," I protested.

"Why not, if it works for them? Beside, what is a Communist government? When a government asks us for food and medicine and farm equipment and educational materials instead of guns and tanks and jet planes, why does that automatically make them a Communist government in the eyes of our administration?"

"Come on," I said. "Let's take a buddy shower. Last one in's a Libertarian!"

"Even that'd be a hell of a lot better than what we have now. We don't even have a government anymore. What we have is a goddamn monarchy!"

I could tell how upset he was, because all he wanted to do for dinner was eat in the hotel dining room. The ubiquitous steak, foil-wrapped baked potato, and salad bar. Ordinarily one of the highlights of the trip was getting out into the back country and seeking out local cuisine and local color.

But there were other times, too, of local color, and they were among the happiest highlights of our trip.

We spent a few days in New Orleans, which Stephen loved. He said it has many of the civilized aspects of a European city. The bars stay open all night, and it is almost impossible to find a bad meal. We ate French, we ate Creole, we ate Cajun and we ate Southern. We ate po' boys and muffeletas. We walked it off touring the city, and came back to our guest house in the French quarter for a romp in the hot tub before going out to dinner. We rode the St. Charles streetcar, and took a cruise on the riverboat. We held hands in Jackson Square.

After New Orleans, we visited Cajun country, of which Lafayette is the capital, so to speak. The Cajuns, in case you didn't know, are descendants of the French settlers of Acadia, on Canada's eastern shore. When the British gained sovereignty over Canada following the battle of the Plains of Abraham at Quebec City in 1759, they loaded the Acadians onto ships and transported them to the swamps and bayous of Louisiana so that they could bring in Scottish settlers to form the present-day Canadian province of Nova Scotia (Latin, obviously, for New Scotland), where all the best lox in Florida comes from. The classic American poet, Henry Wadsworth Longfellow, tells all about it in his poem "Evangeline."

Today the Acadians, or Cajuns, are still known for their rowdy, exuberant lifestyle, their struggle to retain their unique cultural heritage (a local radio station still broadcasts in French), and of course their incredible cuisine, which combines elements of genuine peasant French, American Deep South, and New Orleans Creole. As soon as we checked into our motel, Stephen asked the owner, himself an Acadian, where we could find the best Cajun cooking, and he was delighted to direct us to a local establishment nearby.

Picture a huge, gaudily-painted barn of a place, with a marquee which read, "Simply Cajun." Inside, on a small stage, was a Cajun quartet strumming and pickin' and fiddling the best Cajun country blue-grass music I'd ever heard — and not commercial, either; this was for real! The place was filled with locals of every generation, from *Grandmére et Grandpére* down to *les petits bébés*, all jumping up and down and stomping and clapping and hollering. Between numbers, the bandleader gave local announcements in English and French.

Stephen can be a bit of a culture snob at times, but to my surprise and pleasure, he really got turned on by all this Cajun ambience. "Hey," he explained, "this isn't Disney World. This is the real America that we came to see!"

Our Cajun dinners were unforgettable; we each ordered the specialty platter of the house. A bowl of rich, delicious seafood gumbo was followed by a huge platter of every kind of local seafood — fish, shrimps, oysters, crabmeat, frog's legs, seafood-stuffed bell pepper, and a huge scoop of jambalaya. The homemade bread was hot out of the oven. With our dinners we had a carafe of the house wine — there was no wine list. It was a pleasant but undistinguished California rosé which went just fine with the rich Cajun cooking. The prices were more reasonable than I would have dared to believe.

When we got back to the motel, Stephen announced, "After a Cajun dinner like that, now we're going to make love Cajun style."

"And what," I asked, "is love Cajun style?"

He replied, "Ze French, zey are a funny race. Zey fight wiz ze feet and zey fuck wiz ze face."

"Stephen!" I protested. "You're gross and vulgar!"

"*Ah, oui.* And now shall we both get gross and vulgar?"

I don't know whether or not it was authentic Cajun style sex, since I've never had sex with a real Cajun. But it was fun.

Stephen was in for a rude shock when he chatted with local residents in each state about the Central American situation. He had the true journalist's common touch, the facility of making perfect strangers from any walk of life feel so at ease with him that they would reveal their innermost feelings and private opinions. He was surprised to find that the American people had been four-to-one against aiding the Contras in Nicaragua, not from any motives of humanitarianism, but rather from good old American xenophobia — in other words, isolationism.

"What the hell do we want to help them goddamn spicks for?" demanded one gas station owner in Arizona. "They ain't never done nothin' for us except make trouble. Let the Commie bastards blow each other up!" He grinned and pointed to a sleek new high-powered rifle that rested in its rack behind the counter. "Around here, with the border so close, we have to blow up a few ourselves once in a while. Saves the U.S. Border Patrol some ammunition."

One morning we stopped at a small truck stop outside of Albuquerque. Behind the counter of the restaurant was a sign that read, "This ain't a Burger King. Around here you don't get nothing *your* way. You get it MY way, or you don't get it at all!"

The feisty little woman who ran the place delighted Stephen by serving real fresh butter with her home-made biscuits. Stephen had always hated what he called the nasty, chemical, oily taste of margarine. I never minded it because I have an important margarine account, although of course I would never have used it at home.

"I really appreciate this real butter," he told the lady.

"I'll bet your heart don't, though," she replied.

"I'll bet it does," he said. "Life's too short to settle for margarine, or to worry about cholesterol."

"Life's too short for dancin' with ugly women, my uncle always used to say." She spread out the local newspaper. "Say, what do you think about the situation in Central America?"

"I don't know," replied Stephen cheerfully. "What do *you* think?"

"I think we ought to stay home and mind our own goddamn business. First money, then military advisors, and next thing you know, for damn sure they'll be sending in American troops. I lost a kid brother in Viet Nam twenty years ago, and I say, look after our own people at home before we worry about foreigners."

Another thing that never ceased to shock Stephen was the extent to which our young people had become — well, let's just say out of kindness, *extremely limited*. At breakfast one morning, a very pretty young black waitress didn't know what "marmalade" was. The manager came to her rescue. At a steak house in Everett, Washington, much later in our trip, Stephen asked a waitress if they served any kind of imported beer.

"I'm sorry," she said, "I don't know what 'imported' means."

"My God!" he exclaimed later. "What in the hell have we raised here, with our television and our dumbed-down textbooks? A generation of retards? Foreign kids twelve years old can read, write and speak four languages fluently, and our high school graduates can't even read, write or speak English!"

"Be glad she doesn't know what imported beer is," I pointed out. "It's better for our balance of trade."

"That's not the point!" he said, raising his voice. I could see he was getting upset again. "Since starting this trip, I've talked with kids who don't know who the vice-president of the United States is; who've never heard of Woodrow Wilson, Charles Lindbergh, or Tallulah Bankhead; never even heard of, let alone read, Ernest Hemingway, William Faulkner, Truman Capote, or Tennessee Williams; have no idea of who fought whom in either of the two World Wars; and not one of them in fifty, if that many, knows where the hell Australia is — or even Portland, Oregon, for that matter!"

"Well, so what?" I responded. "Stephen, these are the people who buy the new cars and the color television sets. They're the ones who make America work! Why the hell *should* they know as much as your so-called intelligentsia? That's simply not their function."

"Oh, my God," he said, looking at me with that sad, hurt expression he sometimes gets. "You don't even think of them as people, do you? To you they're just *consumers*. Demographics. Statistics. Quarterly sales curves. Not even real flesh and blood at all!"

"Well, there are people and then there are people. There've always been different levels and classes of people, Stephen. That's the way it's been since the world began." I patted his hand reassuringly. "You'll have to admit it makes for a certain social stability, doesn't it? I mean, God help our country when even used car salesmen start speaking proper grammatical English."

"Alexis de Tocqueville," he replied, "must be turning over in his grave."

I guess the biggest highlight of our whole trip was the Gay Pride Parade and Festival in Los Angeles. We had timed our itinerary so that we would be in L.A. for that weekend. Stephen had spent so much time out of the country that he had never seen a really big Gay Pride weekend in a major city. He was so moved and overwhelmed by the experience that he wrote it up in an article for Greasy Grossberg, back home, to use as a guest column. It was the kind of vivid, heartwarming, and movingly descriptive piece that Stephen does so well.

"Fantastic," I said, after reading it. "A really nice piece of work. That should rattle a few beads back in Fort Lah-de-dah!"

"It was one hell of a weekend," he said. "A quarter of a million of us, all brothers and sisters, all in one place, all loving each other, all filled with pride. If I didn't know better, I'd say there's some hope for our country yet."

"Yes!" I exclaimed. "Not a bad weekend for having taken place in a country that you claim is teetering on the brink of fascism!"

"If you think it isn't," he replied, "don't hold your breath, kid. You ain't seen nothing yet!" As usual, he was right, of course.

The Los Angeles Gay Pride weekend was always held a week ahead of the national date, so as to run back-to-back with Gay Pride Day in San Francisco. This was held on the actual anniversary Sunday of the Stonewall Rebellion. By scheduling the two events a week apart, all interested groups and individuals could attend and participate in both occasions. It was with a renewed surge of pride that we stood on Market Street the following Sunday as San Francisco celebrated its gay heritage. Afterward we battled the crowds at the Festival in Civic Center Plaza. Although Stephen said later that it was much more political than the celebration in Los Angeles, and not quite as much fun, nevertheless he enjoyed every minute of it.

With diabolical timing, probably to prevent a nationwide rash of violent incidents at various Gay Pride Celebrations across the country, it was on the very Monday following Gay Pride Day that the United States Supreme Court announced its infamous decision in the Georgia sodomy case. For once Stephen and I were in complete agreement about the merits of the case, but whereas I passed it off as a mere piece of legal mumbo-jumbo that would have little tangible effect on our lives, Stephen, as usual, took it much more seriously. Our conversation on the subject took place as we were having a drink in the revolving cocktail lounge of the Space Needle in Seattle. We were on our way to attend Expo '86, the huge World's Fair being held that year in nearby Vancouver, Canada.

"How," demanded Stephen, "could the highest court in the land have done something so blatantly illegal and unconstitutional? They have, in effect, denied our right to exist as human beings!"

"Aren't you over-reacting just a little bit?" I suggested. "After all, all they did was to rule on the right of an individual state to have and enforce laws against certain sexual acts."

"All?" he almost screamed at me. "Is that all? Troy, can't you see what they've done? In the first place, they didn't even rule on the issue that was placed before them; they avoided it. They were asked to rule on a basic Fourth Amendment privacy issue. Unlawful search and seizure. Instead they ruled on a state's rights issue. They ruled on a sexual issue. They ruled on a Judeo-Christian morality issue. In a country which claims to have separation of church and state, but in which every taxpayer is forced to subsidize the ranting and chanting of organized religion, the Supreme Court said in effect that if any specific sexual act isn't clearly sanctioned in the Judeo-Christian bible, then it's legal in this country for any state to put you in prison for life for it! And you wonder why I'm upset!"

"But doesn't that apply to heterosexuals, too? Doesn't it make it illegal, if the individual state says so, for married couples to have oral or anal intercourse?"

"Sure," said Stephen, "but I'll give you just one little guess as to which group it'll be enforced against!"

"Look at the bright side," I persisted. "It also gives the states the right *not* to have or enforce anti-sodomy laws."

"Don't hold your breath on that one, either," said Stephen cynically. "Believe me, it'll be a hell of a lot easier for them to take away our rights in the twenty-four states where we have them, than for us to gain them in the twenty-six states where we don't."

"Stephen," I said, "let's not let a Supreme Court decision spoil our trip. After all, our van locks from the inside. Our motel room doors lock from the inside. And our house locks from the inside. Do you really think we're going to stop making love because of a Supreme Court decision?"

"Of course not. But how do you feel about being considered legally a criminal for what the breeders are granted a constitutional right to do?"

"A technicality, Stephen. It's been going on for hundreds of years. How many people did the Catholic church burn at the stake for doing exactly the same thing the Pope was doing with his acolytes and choir boys?"

"One would have hoped," said Stephen, "that in twentieth-century America, we would have evolved a little more than that from the standards of the Middle Ages."

I could tell how restless and upset he was. Normally, Stephen very seldom smoked; he knew how totally it disgusted me, and that I found it a gross sexual turnoff. It had never been a problem for him, because he wasn't addicted. But now he called over the cigarette girl and bought a package of a mild filter brand. He did, however, turn completely away from me in order to light it, and he was very careful not to blow smoke in my direction. Is there anything more aesthetically revolting than to see a handsome stud with clouds of smelly fumes belching out of his face?

"Look," he said, "I have a suggestion. We've done over twenty states already, and I've certainly gained most of the insights I needed. Why don't we go to Vancouver tomorrow, and after we've seen Expo '86, let's head for home."

"Well, if that's what you want," I grudgingly consented.

"We've been on the road over a month. You know you should be getting back to work, even though you had the time coming to you. In a cut-throat business like yours, you won't have an account left if you stay gone any longer."

"This is true."

"As for me, I've got my work cut out for me. Frankly, I'm so disgusted politically that if we weren't settled down together, I'd take another overseas assignment."

I was aghast. "Don't even think about it," I said. "I don't want a lover who sends me postcards from a distant battlefield."

"Oh, don't worry," said Stephen. "I wouldn't run out on you like that. Hell, you know I *couldn't*!" He touched my hand surreptitiously under the table. "Look," he said, as the revolving lounge came full circle.

Across the crystal-blue expanse of Puget Sound, against the

setting sun, the mountains of the Olympic Peninsula were daz-
zlingly and spectacularly silhouetted. A ferry from Bremerton
chuffed its way homeward across the Sound to the Seattle ferry
terminal. Beneath us, the evergreen hills and the downtown sky-
line of this marvelous city were spread out at our feet.

"So what great insights have you gained?" I asked him.

"Well, for one thing, the cuisine has certainly improved a hell
of a lot since I was a kid back-packing around the country. Remember that supermarket in New Mexico that had a sign, 'Fresh
Seafood Brought In Daily'? You didn't used to be able to order fresh
seafood west of Atlantic City."

"And that teriyaki steak we had in Needles! With the stuffed
mushroom caps, and the fresh broccoli served perfectly *al dente*,
and dripping with real butter."

"When I was a kid," Stephen said, "you were lucky to get
ground burro meat in Needles."

"Okay, so America's culinary sophistication has blossomed
as its political consciousness has deteriorated. Anything else?"

"Yes. The manners and the courtesy get better and better the
farther west you get from South Florida. Out here in the real U.S.
of A., *everyone* says 'Please' and 'Thank you' and 'Excuse me'."

"I hate to admit it," I agreed, "but you're absolutely right.
Anything else?"

"Yes," said Stephen. "It's still a big, beautiful country, and I
still love it."

But the following weekend was the Fourth of July, and
Stephen was in for yet another big downer. That was the year, as
you recall, when they celebrated the one hundredth anniversary of
the Statue of Liberty with a four-day bash in New York City.
Stephen started to write an article which he called, "The Shame of
Miss Liberty — A Last Hurrah on the Brink of Fascism." It began
like this:

"The glitzy extravaganza which was staged in New York this
weekend was a psychological masterpiece. Brilliantly conceived
and masterfully executed, it was perfectly programmed to make
the mindless multitudes wallow in an orgy of patriotic fervor. Extolling an idealized and romanticized version of the history of our
immigrant forebears which had absolutely no relation whatsoever
to the grim reality, it turned the nation's attention away from our

human rights violations in Central America, our economic injustices at home, and the crippling national debt caused by the scandalous waste and outright criminal fraud of our bloated military procurement."

Then he went on to rant and rave about the future economic ramifications of the national debt, and about the fact that in a Lou Harris poll, it was found that 68% of all Americans derived their greatest satisfaction in life not from money, not from food, not from sex, but from television.

"Stephen," I told him frankly, "this isn't writing. This is just plain *kvetching.*"

"Funny you should call it that," he replied, "since neither of us is Jewish."

"Understand," I went on, "I'm not criticizing this article merely because I disagree with it. On the contrary, my objections are purely literary. I hate to see such a good writer doing such bad writing."

"We can't all be lucky enough to be advertising copywriters and publicists," he replied sarcastically.

"Stephen, this just isn't you. Ordinarily, what makes your writing so devastatingly effective is the fact that you're like an ice-cold stainless steel surgical blade slicing through all the lies and the bullshit and the hypocrisy — yes, even the lies and bullshit and hypocrisy that I happen to have chosen to believe in. But this isn't that kind of writing. It's too — too whining, too angry, too petulant. It's the dissatisfaction of a middle-aged writer who has failed to fulfill his dream."

I could have bitten off my tongue as soon as I'd said it. There was a very long moment of silence during which I knew I'd finally gone too far.

"That," said Stephen, "was the cruelest thing you've ever said to me."

"I'm sorry. But when you love someone as much as I love you, sometimes you just have to say what you feel, even if it sounds a little bit cruel."

"And what," he wanted to know, "is the dream that I've failed to fulfill?"

"Nothing I haven't told you before, Stephen. Somewhere inside the rugged macho combat journalist and political writer lies a great American novel. Maybe a great American gay novel. Maybe a great global novel, I don't know. But I do know that if you wrote it, it would be a very moving, very human novel, filled with compassion and with characters who would make you laugh and cry."

"You're full of shit. I'm not Faulkner or Hemingway. Like you, I'm very good at what I do, and I'm very proud of what I do. And I've lived a life that most people could only fantasize. What the hell more am I supposed to aspire to?"

"The novel. You could at least give it a try."

"You forget I'm not rich like you. I still have to earn a living."

He didn't, of course. I would have seen to that. But he was too proud. A proud, handsome, sometimes maddening, sometimes intellectually arrogant man, but always a cut above. A man with whom I would frequently disagree, but whose principles would never make me feel ashamed. A man unlike any other I had ever met, or ever would. Stephen Ashcroft, my lover.

3

The picture appeared in glorious full color on the front page of every major newspaper in Europe. The Gay Rights faction of the Resistance movement had made a global laughing-stock of the Reverend President Peter Joshua Wickerly's American government.

Once again, they were in Ashcroft's room in the Leather Eagle Hotel. It was a cloudy, overcast afternoon. Kiki was sprawled on the bed in his tight little red briefs, watching a dubbed American western on television. Ashcroft worked at his desk, typing up a final report for his group leader to pass on up the chain of command. He was trying to ignore the television; he could never quite get used to the idea of watching Clint Eastwood riding into town and talking to people in Dutch.

Kiki watched the film delightedly, but from a series of contorted positions that reminded Ashcroft of an American teenager doing his homework while watching a rock show on the tube. At one point, Kiki's smooth, slender limbs were twisted into a full lotus position as the gunslinger battled it out on the screen.

The movie ended. Kiki clicked off the set and came over to sit on Ashcroft's lap.

"You still do not wish to tell me how this happened?" His fingers gently brushed the side of the older man's face, where there was a large, purple contusion. He also had a few other small bruises, and when he'd been typing his report, his left arm moved slowly and stiffly.

"I already told you, Kiki. I got into a little political argument in a bar. Evidently I wasn't as convincing as the other guy."

Kiki kissed him on the mouth, teasingly. "I do not believe you," he said. "I think perhaps maybe you have made a little trip to Belgium, *neen?*"

"Whatever for?" said Ashcroft. "I've already seen the *mannequin-pis*. I told you, I got this in a fight."

"I am deeply hurt, Mijnheer Stephen, that you do not trust me."

For a moment Ashcroft wondered whether or not to tell him, but then thought better of it. After all, Kiki did work at a popular disco, one which was undoubtedly infiltrated by American agents. And kids do love to brag. A few drinks, and Kiki might have said to a friend his own age, "I know the man who led the Belgium operation. We are very good friends." If such a remark were made and overheard, it could have meant the death of every man in Ashcroft's unit. He clasped the boy closely to him as he held him on his lap.

"I do trust you, Kiki. But this is war. Some things are just too confidential even for one's loved ones to know."

If he had told Kiki all about the commando operation against the American diplomatic compound just outside of Brussels, he would also have had to tell him about the young marine-of-God guard. Ashcroft was not proud of having killed someone whom he still considered to be a young American brother, but it had been unavoidable. He had killed before, in combat, but it had never become easier; it had gotten worse.

"I'm much too old for this sort of thing," he had told his group leader. "My combat days are over. Can't you find someone else?"

"I wish we could," replied Arguello. He was a huge, mean, tough Puerto Rican, a former paratrooper sergeant who had been discharged from the service when his commanding officer had found out he was gay. "The problem is, Ashcroft, we've got lots of good men, but damn few with your combat background. Besides, you've got that special kind of leadership quality. That's what makes the difference between success and failure of an operation."

"But so do you, Arguello. And you're a lot younger and stronger."

The ex-sergeant punched Ashcroft's shoulder playfully with his huge, thick fist. "Don't give me that shit, Ashcroft. You're still one hell of a man. Look, I'll supervise the operation, guard the transport, see to it that you and your guys get in and out okay. All you have to do is lead the actual raid. Trust me, man, I know how it works best."

"I could really learn to hate you Arguello, if I get killed."

The burly man ignored him and spread out a map on the table. "The diplomatic compound is on a large, wooded estate, so you'll have lots of cover. The marines-of-God guards rely mainly on their sensors to spot intruders, but we have a few little tricks of our own."

It was one of the tragedies of Reverend President Wickerly's administration that under the new regime, the character of America's most legendary and respected military organization had totally changed. The once-proud Leathernecks had been turned into a sort of elite military priesthood, conditioned to kill heretics, homosexuals, and social and political dissidents, and to do so instantly upon command, without hesitation and without qualm or regret.

The raid took place just after dawn, as the sun was about to come up. There were seven men in Ashcroft's unit. They had breached the perimeter and had almost advanced to their goal, the main front lawn of the Ambassador's mansion. One of the anti-sensors must have malfunctioned, because suddenly Ashcroft saw a young marine-of-God aiming his silenced, recoilless M-93 at young Katzman, his point man who was kneeling at the base of the flagpole.

Ashcroft crept up and took the young guard out, slashing his throat with a razor-sharp combat knife, and then, so the boy would die quickly, giving him another quick knife-blow to the heart. By this time, Katzman had finished his work at the flagpole.

"They never taught me this at N.Y.U.," he grinned when Ashcroft had regrouped his men to rendezvous with Arguello.

When the sun came up, its first rays shone upon the rainbow-striped Lambda flag, which by now was familiar to anyone who had ever attended, or even seen pictures of, a Gay Pride picnic, parade or festival. The Gay Pride banner now fluttered proudly atop the flagpole where yesterday the Stars, Cross and Stripes had flown.

That was the picture that appeared the following day all over Europe.

"It was a smashing operation," Ten Eyck had told him on the phone the next day. "The World War II anti-Nazi Resistance could not possibly have done better. Smashing, old boy, simply smashing!"

Ashcroft felt very proud, and at the same time sick at heart over the young Marine-of-God.

Kiki knelt in front of Ashcroft and was unbuttoning his Levis. The older man did not have the heart to push him away, and besides, the boy's lovemaking was like a soothing sexual balm.

"Not like that, Kiki. Let me take my clothes off." Again, the sweet, erotic, sandalwood-and-spice smell of the boy assuaged his senses, obliterating from his memory the sickly-sweet, cloying smell of the young Marine's blood gushing in torrents. But what else could he have done? he thought. Let one of his own men be killed, and the whole operation jeopardized?

He lay in Kiki's slender arms. Again, the boy touched the large, tender bruise on Ashcroft's face. Just as they had reached their rendezvous with Arguello, another Marine-of-God had come out of the woods swinging, and had nailed Ashcroft with his rifle butt. Stunned momentarily, Ashcroft had watched as Arguello himself took the man out noiselessly. There was no sound, no blood, but a moment later the man lay dead upon the ground. Arguello slapped Ashcroft back to his senses, and they ran to where their transport was waiting.

Ashcroft almost wondered whether it had been worth it, since taking enemy life was something the Resistance always tried to avoid. But when that marvelous picture appeared, he knew that the lives of the two innocent boys had been a reasonable price to pay for the courage and inspiration their daring escapade would give to freedom fighters everywhere.

"After all," he reflected, "it could have been two of us, or our whole group, and it wouldn't even have bothered them at all. God knows they've killed enough of us."

Kiki's tongue was inside his mouth, and then he bent over the older man, caressing and kissing his whole body. Slowly, the memory of the operation at dawn began to fade.

Later, after they had finished making love, Kiki said,

"There is something I do not understand about that Belgian operation."

"Why ask me? I don't know anything about it."

Kiki giggled teasingly, and then whispered in Ashcroft's ear, "But how did they get our Gay Pride flag to stay up there on top of the flagpole long enough to take a picture?"

Ashcroft finally gave up trying to pretend innocence. Kiki was just too bright a kid. "That was the easy part," he explained. "Katzman did something to jam the pulley and then cut the rope. We had someone inside the main house waiting at an upstairs window to take that picture. By the time they got that flag down, a roll of film had already been passed out of the diplomatic compound. Now, you little asshole, will you forget I told you anything about it?"

Kiki laughed delightedly. "I am so proud of you, Stephen, I promise you, I will breathe not a single word, even though at the bar tonight everyone will be talking about it."

After they had washed up, Kiki sat at Ashcroft's desk, reading everything he could get his hands on.

"You're a nosy little devil," said Ashcroft. "I really wish you wouldn't do that."

"But I love you, Stephen! I want to know everything about you and your wonderful lover." He perused the carbon copy of the letter to Greasy Grossberg. Then he asked,

"You have told me already most of it, Stephen. What happened after you and Troy returned from your long trip?"

"It was a very interesting period," replied Ashcroft. "Sort of like the calm before the storm. Why don't you run down to the bar and get us a couple of mugs and a pitcher of pilsner, and I'll tell you a little about it."

"May I order too, please, a sandwich for each of us?"

"Sure. They have some lovely Westphalian ham in the kitchen; ask Pieter to slice it right off the bone, and some off the outside and just a tiny bit of the fatty part. Lots of lettuce and mayonnaise. Put it on my tab, of course."

Kiki went to the door. Ashcroft stopped him.

"Aren't you going to put your clothes on?"

"What for? It's not cold today."

"That's not what I meant!"

"Oh, really, Stephen, don't be so stuffy! Surely they have seen naked boys at the Leather Eagle before!"

In a little while, Kiki returned carrying a tray of beer and sandwiches. To Ashcroft's amusement, he had a large kitchen towel tied around him like a diaper.

"What happened?" he grinned. "Did you suddenly get an attack of modesty?"

"*Neen*," the boy pouted. "Pieter said I looked very nice, but he didn't want me to burn myself in his kitchen!"

They settled themselves at Ashcroft's desk.

"Are you sure this isn't going to bore you?" Ashcroft asked the boy.

"*Ach*, never!" Kiki replied. "Someday I want to be a brave Resistance fighter like you. For this, I must know everything that happened over there." He munched his sandwich and took a large gulp of pilsner, as Ashcroft began.

4

It was the calm before the storm (Ashcroft related).

Our daily lives went on very much as before. There were no brown-shirted storm troopers, no goose-stepping armies, no military rule — at least, not overtly. We were still taught that we had the freest press in the world, even as the media carried less and less foreign news, and even as the journalists who covered the activities of the government and military found it increasingly difficult to keep their lines of communication open to their sources.

For example, one day I called a friend of mine in Washington, a deep-cover gay with whom I'd tricked once while attending a press convention. He worked for the Department of Defense.

"Roger," I asked him, "what's this about one of our largest defense contractors being caught with his hand in the till and losing his contracts?"

"I'm sorry, Stephen, I can't talk about that right now. I'm sure you understand."

"Of course I understand. No problem! Say no more and I'll drop the subject. Give me a call when you're free and we'll have a drink at the Press Club."

That simply meant for him to call me later from a secure phone.

Roger called that evening while Troy and I were having dinner. The story sounded big enough so that I offered to meet him next day in Washington. He met me at National Airport and drove me to the local press club.

"So what happened to Murgatroyd Missiles?" I asked, after we'd ordered our drinks. "Did they get too crooked even for military procurement?" Murgatroyd Missiles was a code name, of course.

"Don't be silly," said Roger. "*Nobody* can get *that* crooked! To the contrary, they got honest. The Board of Directors suddenly got scared of a couple of young maverick congressmen from California who were doing their own investigations, so they blew the whistle on themselves and made a clean breast of everything. You should have heard the *mea culpas* resounding through the Pentagon! The whole shtick, Stephen. Deliberate waste, extravagance, enormous cost overruns, expensive perks, limousines, country club memberships, bribes to military procurement officers — you name it."

"Well, hell, Roger, no wonder they lost their contracts!"

"But that's just the point," he replied. "They *didn't* lose them for criminal fraud and malfeasance. They could have gone on forever and nobody would have minded — except the taxpayers, and who the hell cares about them? The two mavericks from California could have been dealt with in the usual ways. No, Stephen, Murgatroyd Missiles got shitcanned for baring their breast and telling all. Confession may be good for the soul, but it plays hell with the bottom line. By the way, I'll have the documentation and figures on all of this for you in about a week."

I flew home. A week passed, and Roger didn't call. His office told me that he no longer worked there, and suggested, with some asperity, that he'd been transferred to some other department. Then a sharp female voice came on the line and demanded to know who I was, and why did I want to know about Roger? I told her my name was Leon Trotsky and that I was with the Rasputin Investigation Committee, and hung up.

Eventually I found out through mutual friends that Roger had finally surfaced in San Francisco, where he was waiting on tables in a gay restaurant. He had become monosyllabic and dull, and never spoke a word about his days in government service. I doubt that he even remembered them. I've seen what partial memory blocks can do. Their techniques were getting more sophisticated all the time.

Gradually, during this period, all of the books we'd grown up with and loved were being removed, one by one, from the school libraries. They were replaced with books that extolled the virtues of home, family, religion, and the American way of life. Even Mark Twain, the leading abolitionist and freethinker of his time, was considered far too radical for today's youth.

The pattern of commercial television subtly changed, too, week by week. Sitcoms that permitted any suggestion of alternate lifestyles were dropped from both the commercial and the cable networks. Movies were more closely edited than ever, before being shown for home viewing. As for Public Television, government sanctions were not actually imposed against the PBS network, but import restrictions were. Many people actually cried when "Masterpiece Theatre" left the air. The great documentaries about daily life in Soviet Russia and mainland China were dropped from the re-run schedules and never reshown. As a result, PBS lost most of its subscribers, and since it no longer received public funding, it was finally forced, after all its many years of public service, to shut down. After all, how long could even the most loyal subscribers continue to subsist on "Rain Forests of Central America"? The White House issued an official statement commenting on the demise of the long-beloved and deeply respected PBS network, saying:

"We see no reason why the tax dollars of an honest, decent farmer in Keokuk, Iowa, should be spent so that decadent, degenerate eggheads in New York and San Francisco can continue to watch sexual and political filth."

Because most of its retail outlets were no longer open to it, the American rock music industry was on its last legs. There was a lively trade in black-market imported rock music, much of it smuggled in from England, Canada, and even the Soviet Union, where many former American rock stars were enjoying a musical heyday.

The number of people who left the United States at this time was statistically small, but numerically significant. In Canada, there were already over one hundred thousand political expatriates and refugees who, a generation earlier, had fled from the United States during the Viet Nam War. Many of them were draft resisters who had found a new life there and had refused the amnesty offered to them during the administration of President Carter. Now the ranks of these expatriates were swelled to over two hundred thousand, as teachers and academicians found the new curricula so stringently circumscribed that they could no longer teach effectively. It was during this new exodus that I called on my friend Andrew Bahrenbohm for an interview. He had just resigned as President of Cypress-Everglades College, a small South Florida private college of unusual academic distinction quite unequaled in the state.

I had met Professor Bahrenbohm some months earlier at an ACLU fund-raising banquet, and we had instantly formed a mutual admiration society. He was a tall, aristocratic-looking gentleman of about my own age, with strongly Semitic features and just the faintest trace of the Scotch-Irish burr that marks a true Canadian accent. The son of a dry goods merchant in St. Johns, Newfoundland, he had been educated in Ontario, and liked to comment that he was "the only Jewish Newfie ever to graduate *summa cum laude* from McMaster University." Although incorrigibly heterosexual, he was a confirmed bachelor.

He received me in his office, where he was already packing his books and cleaning out his desk.

"Scotch or tea, Stephen?" he asked.

"I think both," I replied. "A cup of tea with a shot of Scotch on the side. Now, what the hell is all this about, Andrew? Why did you resign?"

"The government wanted me to turn Cypress-Everglades into an open-enrollment college."

"You've got to be kidding! Why, this school has always been strictly elitist — the only place in Florida where the best and the brightest kids can get an education not otherwise available anywhere outside of the Ivy League."

"Yes, precisely. That's why I'm leaving. I simply do not perceive it to be my function to teach remedial reading to the socially disadvantaged and the functionally illiterate. Neither will I teach them religion, which is now compulsory under the new Federal guidelines. *About* religion, yes, of course; everyone should know about the world's major religions and their influence on history. But to teach religion in an institution dedicated to wiping out myth and superstition rather than perpetuating it is, I think, blatantly ridiculous."

"Well, I agree with you, of course, Andrew. But how can they *force* you to make this an open-enrollment college?"

"Very simply a matter of money. Since we don't have a sports program or even an athletic program, other than the bare minimum necessary to fulfill the concept of *mens sana in corpore sano*, we don't get huge donations or endowments each year from the alumni. And since we don't have an ROTC program, nor would I ever permit one, I need hardly tell you how this affects our status regarding Federal funding. Our science laboratories are twenty-five years out of date. Our library is crumbling — but thank whatever gods there may be, we've never once removed a book from our shelves for political reasons. Our kids may not be athletes or trained killers but at least they know who Aeschylus and Euripides were. I'm very proud of that."

"Well, so you should be! Come on, now Andrew, there has to be someplace you could solicit funding. How about the major corporations?"

"Major corporations? You've got to be kidding! They've been part of the program right along to lower the educational standards in this country. Oh, they're great on technical and career education. But *real* education?"

"Well, gosh," I said innocently. "Have the standards really been lowered that much?"

"Don't play the clever journalist with me, Stephen," he laughed. "I've come to know you too well for that! Tell me, when was the last time you heard of a public high school that had a really good program of Latin or Greek? As though it were possible to attain an educated command of English without having had at least some exposure to the root languages from which it derives! That's like trying to learn algebra and trigonometry without ever having studied basic arithmetic. For that matter, when was the last time you met a doctor or even a lawyer who had actually studied the humanities and had a broader perspective of the world than that of the view afforded him by his own profession?"

"I can't say I ever have, truthfully. Are you saying, then, that our educational system is a total failure?"

"Oh, no! Quite to the contrary! The educational system in this country is performing an absolutely superb job of doing exactly what it was designed to do."

"And what is that?" I like to ask leading questions.

"You're a political realist, Stephen, besides being a friend. That's why you're the only journalist to whom I granted an interview. So let me put it this way. Let's assume that *you* are the economic and military oligarchy that we all know really owns and operates this country. Let's assume further that what you require is a tiny cadre of brilliantly educated men to run the corporations, plus a small army of technocrats to supervise the computers, and a vast, ignorant, functionally illiterate mass of *untermenschen* to buy the shiny new cars and the holographic color stereo television sets. What kind of an educational system would *you* have?"

"Obviously," I agreed, "I'd have exactly the kind we have right now, although I would have said *lumpenproletariat*, not *untermenschen*, Andrew; there *is* a difference. Let's not forget who once called the Jewish people *untermenschen*. But what I'd like to know is, why aren't you part of the educational establishment that teaches the small cadre of geniuses who are needed to devise the programs that can be run by any idiot with an M.B.A.?"

"Politics," he replied. "The social philosophy of this institution is hardly what would be deemed proper for the president of a large and thriving corporation. Ergo, no corporate funding."

"I see. So is this really the end for Cypress-Everglades College? At least as we've known it until now?"

"I'm afraid so, Stephen. I should imagine it will also be the end for me, too. Very possibly the next time you read about me, I'll be in jail."

"Whatever for?"

"Again, politics. Oh, don't look so shocked; this isn't something new. During Senator Joe McCarthy's political holocaust of the nineteen-fifties, they put just as many academicians in prison as they did motion picture directors and script writers."

"But," I replied innocently, "everyone knows we don't have political prisoners in America."

"You're playing games again, Stephen. No, of course we haven't had any political prisoners *per se* since the repeal of the Alien and Sedition Acts. But we've always been marvelously ingenious in this country at using our criminal statutes to put people behind bars for political reasons."

I certainly couldn't disagree with him. "So what will you do?" I asked.

"Keep my passport handy. After I get out of jail, I'll probably go back to Canada, since they'll probably try to deport me anyway. I'm sure I'll be a big hero at McGill, even if I can't ever again teach here in the States."

When we had concluded our interview, I wished him the best of luck. How prophetic his words had been I realized a few days later, when he was arrested for improper solicitation of a minor student (female) for sexual purposes, and also for misappropriation of college funds. The charges were speedily dismissed for lack of evidence, but they had already served their purpose; the mere accusations had been sufficient to discredit Dr. Bahrenbohm and destroy his career. He did indeed return to Canada, but not to McGill University in Montreal, because the new right-wing separatist regime in the Province of Quebec refused to have anything to do with him. He found his niche, however, at Simon Fraser University in Vancouver, British Columbia, where they're more of a maverick breed.

Meanwhile, the AIDS epidemic continued to rage, but with constantly decreasing severity. The original mutated African virus seemed to be losing its punch; fewer and fewer of those exposed to it contracted the disease, and those who did frequently did not acquire the full-blown syndrome. Many of those who did acquire it subsequently went into spontaneous remission, and even built up antibodies. The only thing that kept the plague going on was that new mutations of the virus kept appearing, or, as I frequently claimed in my writing, kept being introduced. Troy called it more of my political paranoia, since none of the most hard-driving and astute investigative reporters had been able to come up with a definitive solution to the mystery of the origins of this disease. Knowing a fact is one thing; proving it, another.

And then one night, shortly before I went to work for Douglas McKittrick, I had a strange phone call. A cleverly disguised voice at the other end said,

"Ribit! Ribit! This is the Boiled Frog speaking!"

I knew at once who it was. It was none other than the brilliant but erratic young genius, Dr. Aristophanes Brent, the man who had first initiated me into the philosophical consideration of the Boiled Frog Syndrome.

"I can't leave my lily pad right now," he went on, "let alone the swamp, but I have some hot information for you."

"I suppose you're in trouble with the frog catchers again."

"Oh, very much! Very much! But if you're willing to take the chance, I'd like to see you."

"Just tell me how to find your lily pad."

"That's easy! Do you remember, back in the good old days, how you used to be able to get to Washington?"

"No," I replied, "not really."

"Sure you do! Whether you wanted to be elected, or whether you wanted to be appointed, all you had to do was go to Harvard and turn left."

"Now I've got you. What time?"

"Witching hour of the third phase."

"I'll be there."

"Ribit! Ribit!" he said, and hung up.

Upon checking the lunar calendar, I saw that the moon would be in its third quarter on the following night. Witching hour was, according to Dr. Brent, at 8:00 p.m.; he claimed that a true Witches' Sabbath started at that hour, rather than midnight.

The following evening, making sure I wasn't followed, I drove out I-595 to Bonaventure, then left the freeway to follow old State Road 84 almost to the very edge of the Everglades. At Harvard Road I turned left, and proceeded south until the pavement ended. Where the road became gravel, there was a small honky-tonk redneck bar with a couple of pickup trucks in front. I was wearing levis, boots and a western hat. It was exactly eight o'clock when I arrived.

The juke box was blaring country music as I entered. A blousy old frump of a bar waitress, with a cigarette hanging out of her mouth, was cleaning the empty tables. There were a couple of (I suspected) alligator poachers at one table, and two vaguely Latin types at the bar who were probably drug smugglers.

Aristophanes Brent was waiting for me, seated at a table with a pitcher of Fuzzy Navels, the drink that had enjoyed a brief popularity a few years back. He looked wilder than ever, with his mop of black curly hair and his eyes leering and darting madly everywhere. We greeted each other with a manly embrace, which was quite acceptable in that rough-hewn milieu.

"I see you're still a madman," I commented.

"Of course! It's the only way to fly! Actually, it's you Earthlings who are quite mad. On my home planet, I am considered remarkably sane."

"'Stoph, I've never had the slightest illusion that this was your home planet. Neither has anyone else who's ever known you."

He laughed, and then became serious. "Look, Stephen, this is very important and very secret. I can't stay too long, so I'll give you the information real fast. I have bad news and good news."

"Let's have the bad news first."

He poured us each a round of Fuzzy Navels. "First, then, the suspicions you've been writing about are absolutely correct. I finally have it all documented. AIDS was definitely a germ warfare program against the gay community. And yes, as the original virus lost its punch, they kept introducing new strains. Now for the good news."

"After that, I could use some."

"The good news is that the AIDS epidemic is now officially

over. It'll take a couple of years to die out, but basically it's over. They've discontinued the program."

"But, dammit," I protested, "that's not going to do a goddamn thing for the people who already have it! They haven't found a cure, have they?"

"Well, of course not, Stephen. You know the medical profession better than that! The only thing they know how to do is isolate the virus, develop a vaccine. You know they're not capable of thinking holistically; of treating the human body as a living organism, a total entity! No, except for the lucky few who are perceptive enough to think in terms of vitamin therapy and total mental and physical health within the context of a supportive and strength-giving lifestyle, the ones who have it are goners. But at least within two years there won't be any more new cases."

I knew Brent well enough never to doubt completely anything he said, no matter how bizarre. If he couldn't document it, he didn't say it. The only exceptions were philosophical exercises in logic or fantasy.

"But why, 'Stoph? Why? Why did they start it, and why did they discontinue it?"

"They started it, obviously, in order to kill off the gay population of the United States, and eventually, they hoped, the entire world. Naturally, it spread very quickly into the mainstream population. I could have told them that. In fact, any smart nine-year-old could have told them that. But there's always some government scientist who's just dumb enough to try anything once."

"Then why did they discontinue it?"

"They discontinued the program because too many people were starting to find out about it. Too many people had to be *terminated with extreme prejudice*. It was getting very messy."

"How did you get hold of this information?"

"One of my former students had gone to work for the government. When he found out what he'd been working on, when he realized that all those cute little squiggles on his electron microscope were killing thousands of gay brothers and sisters, he very foolishly threatened to blow the whistle on the whole program. A week later they found his mangled body in the wreckage of his car. They claimed his blood alcohol level was three times the legal

definition of drunk driving. I happen to know that he was a tee-
totaler. Luckily, he'd already sent me a copy of all his documentation."

Suddenly I felt very, very frightened.

We were interrupted when one of my suspected alligator
poachers confirmed my suspicions by coming over to the table.

"You boys want to buy some nice, fresh gator tails?" His expression told me very clearly that we did.

"I don't have anyplace to cook them," said Aristophanes
Brent.

"I do," I said. "I'll take a couple."

He went out to his pickup truck where he had a cooler of ice,
and brought back a large, heavy plastic bag. "Them's the best
eatin' in the world," he told me. I gave him the ten bones he asked
for, and he went back to his table.

"What will you do with them?" Brent asked nervously, as
though they'd been radioactive.

"Troy will know what to do. He's the star chef in the family. I
would imagine he'd fry them in corn meal."

"I wish I could join you to eat them. But I'm in deep cover."

"My God! I would think so! Knowing what you do, your life's
not worth a plug nickel!"

He suddenly grinned boyishly at me. "It never was, Stephen!
Good minds have always been expendable. Look what they almost did to Galileo." Then he became serious again. "Stephen,
what in the hell am I going to *do?* Do you realize what I'm sitting
on?"

"Yes, I realize very well what you're sitting on. Do you have
the material with you?"

"No, of course not. I wanted to make sure this was a safe
meeting place, first."

"That's fine, then. First thing you do is make three copies.
You keep one, send one to your attorney for safekeeping, and then
send the other to me. I can promise you that I'll know what to do
with the material, if they don't shut me up first."

"What will you do with it?"

"I have enough clout in my business that I can leak it to the
right sources. It will definitely make headlines. In fact, it could
even bring about a change in government — the change we've

needed so badly. Fag-bashing is one thing, 'Stoph, but genocide is something else. The people won't go for it — at least I hope not."

"What do you want *me* to do?"

"I want you to fly to Geneva immediately and present your material to the World Health Organization. That way they can verify the information as soon as I leak it to the news media. That sound reasonable to you?"

"Yes! Yes, indeed! I think it's a super idea!"

I gave him the address of a mail drop I use for really top-secret stuff, and he promised to have the copies made and mailed to me immediately. We drank a couple of final Fuzzy Navels, and then said good-bye. We wished each other all the best of luck.

He left first. I drank a beer to get rid of the taste of the Fuzzy Navels, then nodded goodnight to the alligator poachers and left. The two pickup trucks were still parked outside. Whatever Aristophanes Brent had been driving, and wherever he'd had it concealed, there was no sign of him now.

The alligator meat was delicious. What we didn't use right away went in the freezer. I was correct about frying it in corn meal. Troy also served it blackened, Cajun style. He'd learned that on our trip a few years back.

I never again heard from Dr. Aristophanes Brent. He never sent me the documentation, and he never showed up in Geneva. I can only hope that he somehow survived, and that somewhere he is well and happy, although frankly I doubt it.

My throat is dry from talking, Kiki. Why don't you trot your hot little buns down to the bar and get us another pitcher of pilsner? Then afterwards, if you're ready to go to work, I'll walk with you to the bar. I never get enough exercise these days.

Except (Ashcroft thought) for that little health trip to Brussels night before last!

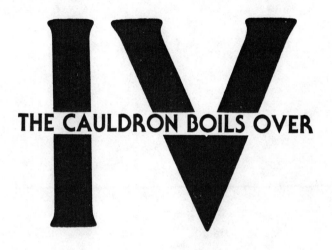

IV

THE CAULDRON BOILS OVER

"I'm terribly sorry, old boy," said Aaron Ten Eyck, "but I simply do not comprehend. I was born much too early to grasp the arcane mysteries of computer technology, and I'm afraid I'm much too long in the tooth to learn about them now. Oh, I *use* computers, of course, just as everyone else does, but I don't understand them, just as most people who drive automobiles don't really understand what makes them run."

"What is it that you don't understand, Aaron?" replied Ashcroft. They were sitting once again in his book-lined study, sipping English sherry, as the afternoon drew to a close. It had been several days since Ashcroft had returned from Luxembourg, and he had brought a sheaf of notes and other material to turn over to the elderly diamond merchant for his Documentation Committee.

"What I don't understand," said Ten Eyck, "is how a computer program, however sophisticated, can put its electronic finger on virtually every homosexual person in America and send them off to the the camps. Can you explain that?"

"Yes, very readily. The problem with the DIVAF program is that it isn't all that sophisticated. Its basic simplicity is what makes it so unbeatable. Let me give you an analogy. You use your computer in your diamond business, right?"

"Of course."

"How do you use it to keep track of your inventory?"

"Very simple, really. When a new stock of diamonds arrives, each stone is taken to the laboratory and assigned a five-digit computer number. Then it is placed in a series of very precise electronic measuring devices. These instruments, each one in its turn, measure the stone for weight, color, cut, clarity, flaws, inclusions, refraction, diffusion, and all the other grading criteria that we use to determine the value of diamonds. In the olden days it was all done by look-see, actually, but nowadays a young laboratory assistant can perform the measurements."

"What happens then?"

"The measurements are entered, along with the corresponding inventory number, into the inventory data bank. I can keep track of hundreds of stones just by calling up on the screen a program so simple to use that it takes me through the process step by step."

"Could you keep track of every diamond in Amsterdam?"

"Oh, yes, quite easily."

"With a few thousand more K's of memory, could you keep track of every diamond in Europe?"

"I can do that now, old chap, by means of a telephone modem. If, for example, a customer in London wants a stone of precise characteristics, I can tell my machine to search not only my own inventory, but that of my fellow dealers in Paris, Bucharest, Zurich, wherever diamonds are sold. Naturally, all of us are free to withhold from this computer inventory any stones we especially wish to retain for one reason or another."

"And if you had a large enough memory on your computer, could you keep track of every diamond in the world?"

"My dear boy, not only every diamond, but every ruby, opal, amethyst, zircon, sapphire, and even high quality jade. But I don't see how that pertains, Stephen. Human beings are not pieces of precious stone with clearly quantifiable characteristics."

"That's where you're mistaken, Aaron."

"All right, then, how does it work?"

"In essence, the DIVAF program is very similar to a program that the U.S. Internal Revenue Service had been using for many years to catch tax cheaters. What the IRS computer search program looked for, basically, was anomalies. For example, take the average citizen earning five hundred Standard New Dollars per week. He has a wife, two-point-eight kids, a four-year-old car, and is three weeks behind on his mortgage payment. He takes standard deductions, claims no unusual expenses or contributions, and shows no other source of income which would show up on their other little goody, the Social Security Number Computer Matching Program. The chances are he'll never be audited, because there's simply nothing to audit. And if, by chance, they do audit him, by a random selection process, there's still nothing to audit.

"On the other hand, if the same average citizen claims as a deduction the sales tax on a brand new Rolls Royce, the interest payments on a million-dollar condo, and huge medical expenses and charitable contributions, he'd better be damn well ready to stand up in tax court and account for every line of his tax return."

"I see. Quite logical, of course. How does that bring us to the DIVAF program? And by the way, what does the acronym actually stand for?"

"DIVAF stands for *Discriminant Inferential Variant Analysis Factor.* A nice sounding piece of gobbledygook which basically means, How Is Your Neighbor Different?"

"But why does that work, actually?"

"It works, Aaron, because of the enormous size and scope of the data base it has to work from. Nowadays, the government can scan through income tax records, medical records, insurance records, occupational license records, credit records, bank records and, of course, the latest census records.

"Now whether we like it or not, homosexuals do have a spiked profile pattern against which the DIVAF program can compare records. For example, going through medical records, it finds a case of rectal gonorrhea. How many straight dudes ever come down with a case of rectal gonorrhea?

"But that's just one aspect of the profile. Let's say that a scan of all the various systems shows that a Mr. Jock A. Bluecollar, living in Dubuque, has a wife, four kids, lives within his income, has never been arrested, is non-political, and used his MasterCard last week to buy a new custom bowling ball and a set of mechanic's tools. He has never charged a restaurant dinner. What odds would you give that Mr. Bluecollar is gay?"

"Extremely remote, I should say."

"Precisely. On the other hand, take Mr. Adrian Twitter. He lives in San Francisco, and the latest census records show that he shares his living space with another young man, Mr. Organdy Chiffon. He works as a floral arranger, and his roommate is a dress designer. Their large combined salaries reflect an enormous proportion of disposable income, with which they buy the most fashionable clothing, imported colognes, dinners at nice restaurants, and frequent trips. A scan of their bank records reveals that they subscribe to several gay publications and have contributed to gay rights organizations. What odds would you give that these two dudes are gay?"

"I should think it extremely improbable that they could be anything other than gay, whether or not either of them has ever had rectal gonorrhea."

"They'd be an extreme case of fitting the spiked profile pattern. What makes DIVAF so effective is that hiding in the closet offers no protection at all, because most of the items that show up on the computer scan are things that you can't hide. After all, the computer doesn't know or care who you actually go to bed with; that's totally irrelevant. Of course, most people show up somewhere in between the two extremes. It's the people who have the *highest* DIVAF profile scores who are given a personal follow-up investigation."

"And this program can actually scan every man, woman and child in the United States?"

"Yes, and very quickly, too. Didn't you just tell me that with the right programs and the right data base you could scan every single precious stone in the world? After all, you yourself don't ever actually have to read all those inventory records. Let's say you want to cull from your inventory just the stones with a yellow inclusion. The only ones you have to actually deal with are the ones named on the printout."

"But that's utterly dreadful, Stephen! I think it's appalling!"

"Yes, and with luck, maybe we can catch a fugitive programmer for our Documentation Committee. The DIVAF program violates every canon of individual privacy in the World Human Rights Charter. Not that the present U.S. government cares, of course."

"Apparently not. My, my! DIVAF indeed! What did that acronym stand for, once again?"

"Discriminant Inferential Variant Analysis Factor."

"Tell me, how long after the McKittrick assassination did the DIVAF program commence?"

"Almost immediately after, in fact just as soon as Reverend Wickerly had assumed the office of the presidency. I rather suspect that the two events were inextricably linked. The fact that the gay rights movement could actually be so well organized and could gather enough clout to be able to field a serious candidate for the office of Governor of what had by then become the country's fourth largest state just spooked the hell out of them. So, first they did the assassination, and then, as soon as Wickerly was in office, they pushed through their docile and compliant Congress the swift passage of enabling legislation that made possible the detention and quarantine of a wide variety of social undesirables. These included homosexuals, astrologers, iconoclastic writers, dissident intellectuals, and organizers of all political movements outside of the two-party mainstream. This time the Jews were spared, but only as Jews, since so many of the American Jewry seemed to fall into one or the other of the proscribed categories."

"We do rather seem to have that knack everywhere," commented Ten Eyck. "Were you living with your lover just before all this dreadful nonsense started?"

"Yes. We lived together until the very night of Doug McKittrick's assassination."

"Why don't we have some more sherry and you can start to tell me all about it. Then you can continue while I take you out for the best *rijstaffel* in Amsterdam."

2

My lover Troy Anderson and I had been living together for just five years (Ashcroft related). They had been not merely good years but great years, like five years in a row of a great vintage wine. Do you know what five years of a really good relationship is like? Let me try to describe it for you.

I've heard it said that perfect happiness is being married to your best friend. Well, Troy and I were a hell of a lot more than just bed partners. We were best buddies, intimates, confidantes and brothers to each other. Since we were both laid-back and easygoing about household matters, there was a minimum of abrasiveness and domestic conflict.

Very early on, we'd laid down a working set of ground rules in which we established the areas in which we had, so to speak, agreed to disagree. One of these was our patronage of the local watering holes.

Troy hated them with a burning passion. He hated the smoke, the noise, the unruly crowds, the loud music. Perhaps if we'd lived someplace where there were fewer transient people and visitors, and the bars had had a dress and conduct code as they did in other cities, he might not have felt so antipathetic toward them. But South Florida is tourist country. There are no rules in the bars. You can be so obnoxious that you drive off all the locals, but as long as you have the price of that first drink, you're welcome. As one bartender told Troy when he objected to some deranged animal who was bothering everyone and creating a noisy disturbance, "Don't bitch to me, man, go someplace else. It takes all kinds to make a good bar!"

To me, on the other hand, as a global journalist, the bars are more than just a place to get drunk or pick up a trick. I've been in bars, saloons, taverns, night clubs, gin mills, beer parlors, discos, dives, dope dens and just plain old neighborhood watering holes in more countries than you can mention. I've made friends in them and, more important, acquired more local knowledge and information than I could have done anywhere else.

But this didn't create any problems between us, you see. We were, after all, both grown-up adults. When I wanted to go sit in a noisy, horrible barroom for awhile, I'd simply excuse myself and go. Troy would either stay home reading or working on a new ad campaign for his company, or else go out someplace on his own — to the gym, for example, or to a flick, or to his local Log Cabin Republican Club, a political organization for conservative gays.

Which brings us to the second area in which we knew we could never be reconciled — although we would be now, if we were together again.

Troy actually believed, like Candide, that he lived in the best of all possible worlds, a world in which America could do no wrong. No matter how many tinpot dictators our government armed to oppress their own people and steal their country blind, no matter how many legitimate democratic governments we toppled, he would adamantly and intransigently proclaim, like King Canute trying to sweep back the ocean with a broom, "Well, we had to protect ourselves against the rising tide of Communism. After all, the Commies export tyranny; we export freedom."

I would listen to this bullshit, totally aghast. "Did we export freedom to Chile?" I would exclaim. "To Cambodia? To Iran when we kicked out their democratic government and installed the hated Shah? And as a result wound up with the Ayatollah? Did we export freedom to Guatemala when we overthrew Jacobo Arbenz?" I would cite example after example. "What about the Philippines under Marcos? Haiti under Duvalier? Nicaragua under the Somozas? Is that what you call 'exporting freedom'? Troy, in your own lifetime you've seen half the world fall under Communist hegemony simply because we left them no other option! We've turned allies into antagonists; we've made enemies out of friends, and all because of a psychopathic, self-defeating foreign policy conceived by ignorant, flag-waving, ugly little men who have never read history. Don't you ever stop to consider that there might be a point of view other than our own? That we might not always be absolutely right 100% of the time?"

"Well, if you feel that strongly in favor of the Commies," he'd reply irrationally, "then maybe you should go to Russia and be a journalist."

What can you reply to something like that? For an extremely bright young man, he definitely had a blind spot in that area. Or else it was I who did, for not simply accepting our government's policy and learning to live with it by saying, "Well, better we do it to them than they do it to us." But I don't believe that, Aaron; I don't believe that the ends justify the means. I believe that the means determine the ends.

As for the economic system under which we lived, I need hardly tell you the pious cant that Troy could recite for hours about the sanctity of the giant corporations. He believed in the implicit *rightness* of the work he was doing, handling larger and larger accounts and directing larger and larger ad campaigns. He truly believed that the major advertising agencies were the heroes of America, the knights in shining armor, the exponents of our culture and our way of life.

"We're the ones who make the whole system work, Stephen, however much you might choose to sneer at the marketing sector. After all," he would point out, "nothing happens until something gets sold, right?"

"And what about the vast revolutionary underclass that doesn't even have the price of a square meal? How can you say that a system works which obviously has failed to work for such a large percentage of its citizens?"

"But that's not society's problem," he would retort. "Can you deny that they have the opportunity to succeed, whether they avail themselves of it or not?"

"But it's just not that simple," I would protest. And so we went on, back and forth, back and forth.

So we agreed to disagree on politics and economics. Or as my friend Greasy Grossberg used to say, "Actually, you cannot really separate the two. To paraphrase von Clausewitz, politics is an extension of economics by other means. Or a reflection of it."

As for monogamy, or fidelity, if you will, in our relationship — well, I don't believe that Nature ever made a truly monogamous man. Troy, on the other hand, liked to say that he was pretty much a one-man dog. So our arrangement was very simple: courtesy and respect for each other's feelings. I never looked for extra-curricular activity, but on the other hand I'm not made out of rock; if on rare occasions it happened, I enjoyed it without guilt, but I never mentioned it to Troy, and he never asked. On his part, I am reasonably certain that he never tricked with anyone during the five years we were together.

Five beautiful years, Aaron. One thousand, eight hundred and twenty-five nights that we spent wrapped in each other's arms, awakening in the morning to bask in the joy of each other. If one of us had to go out of town on business, he to meet a corporate client, or I to research a story or an article or to conduct an interview, the nights on the road were pure hell. We were a perfect dyad, a part of each other.

It was about this time that I had a call from Douglas McKittrick asking me to drive down to Miami to meet with him in his office.

How much do you know about Doug McKittrick? The man, not the political figure.

Doug was that American legend come true, a self-made millionaire. He came from a highly respectable, upper-class Midwestern family. Starting with a tiny savings account during his college years, he parlayed one small but astute investment after another into a vast empire of gay bars, restaurants, health clubs, publications, boutiques and escort services. He was not merely an investor, not merely an entrepreneur; he was an absolutely brilliant business manager. Everything he touched turned into money, and it was to his everlasting credit that he poured so much of it back into the community he served.

And yet, surprisingly, business was merely a livelihood with him. His main interest in life was politics, and again, I have never known a more astute or sagacious political animal. He counted governors and congressmen among his personal friends. A king-maker, a power behind the seats of power; it was as far as anyone could go who was so openly gay, despite the fact that he had an image any good campaign manager would have lusted for: a clean-cut, middle-aged, all-American WASP, pleasant, well mannered and well spoken, the soul of a gentleman under the veneer of a politician. There was no gay rights organization, and no politi-cally progressive mainstream organization, to which he did not belong, and he sat on the board of directors of many of them. I sus-pect that his real ambition in life was to become the acknow-ledged leader of the gay rights movement in the United States, but here his gentlemanly, clean-cut image worked against him; most of the rank-and-file would have felt more comfortable with some-one who wore greasy, well-worn jeans, ate McDonald's ham-burgers, used double negatives in every sentence and never con-jugated verbs.

And here was revealed yet a third and totally different side of Doug McKittrick, a side that he kept almost completely hidden. Doug was a closet intellectual, the worst thing a politician could be in a country where any sign of discernible intellect was politi-cal suicide. You must understand, Aaron, that by this time the majority of our society was so pathologically obsessed with identifying with its own lowest elements that as a London friend of mine once put it, "America is the only country I know of where it is considered dreadfully bad manners to actually *know* any-thing." The fact remains that Doug had a superb education in the humanities, even though in his home most of the books on his shelves dealt with accountancy and business management. Per-haps he kept a small hidden library with books such as *The Essays of Montaigne* and Gibbon's *Decline and Fall of the Roman Empire*. It would not have surprised me.

His detractors considered him ruthless and cold-blooded, and I suppose he sometimes was; I also know that he was unfailingly loyal to those who were loyal to him. Greasy Grossberg once told me,

"In all the years I've known him, I have yet to undertake any community project or committee assignment in which he did not give me his absolute financial and moral support. I could also cite instances of quiet generosity that nobody has ever found out about, so I won't." This, from a man who was noted for the acidest tongue in town.

So there I sat across the desk from the man whom the political *cognoscenti* regarded as the white hope, so to speak, of the gay rights movement.

"I suppose," he began, "that you've heard rumors about me lately." This was accompanied by that engaging boyish grin of his.

"I've heard you're planning to throw your hat into the political ring. I haven't heard, as yet, which ring, but I'd hope it would be a national one."

"Sorry to disappoint you, Ashcroft. Right now our own state is in dire need of good leadership. I'm planning to run for Governor of the State of Florida."

"I see."

"You don't sound particularly enthused, Ashcroft. Would you mind telling me why not?" He knew, of course, that I would do so. A man in Doug's position was always surrounded by toadies and ass-kissers; one of the reasons he'd sent for me was that he knew I genuinely liked him and always had; that I wanted nothing from him; and that I would give him my honest opinion.

"I'm enthusiastic as hell for you personally, Doug. I'm merely questioning the strategy. A run for state-wide office is always risky. Wouldn't it be better to try for a congressional seat? It would be a national office, and yet you'd only have to win a single congressional district, ideally one in which you're already well known and liked."

"You'd be absolutely right, Ashcroft, if all I wanted to do was win myself a seat. But what for? I can *buy* a congressman — lord knows most of them are for sale! No, I want to break some new ground here. We already have a sprinkling of gay congressmen. No openly gay candidate, to my knowledge, has ever run for governor of a major state."

"This is true. How do I figure in all this?"

"Well, I want you on my staff, of course, as a speechwriter, public relations man, and general political aide. You're not working now, are you?"

"Just freelancing, as usual. I'd love to work with you, Doug; I think it would be a lot of fun. But first, may I ask you an honest question?"

"Not unless you want an honest answer."

"How far are you going to go with this? Are you a serious candidate, or is this just a political tactic to buy some clout for our community?"

"I can't answer that just yet, Ashcroft. I plan to run with it and see just how far it goes. If we're lucky and smart, maybe all the way to the primaries. Maybe all the way to the Governor's Mansion in Tallahassee. Who can say?"

"Just out of curiosity, how come you picked me and not Greasy Grossberg? I've been out of the country a lot, you know that. He knows the territory, he's worked with you since 1977, and he's also one hell of a writer."

"I thought about Greasy," said Doug, "but there are a few problems. For one thing, he drinks too damn much. Oh, I don't mean he gets drunk and makes an ass of himself; he does that very well cold sober. For another, he isn't always the most tactful man in the world; when he wants to say something, he lets the barbs fly. But the worst thing about him is his image. Again, not to disparage the man, but a three-hundred-pound leather daddy with a retinue of underage slaveboys is hardly the image I'm trying to project; in fact, it reflects all the worst stereotypes the straights and the media have about our community. I'm looking for a squeaky-clean campaign team, Ashcroft, and I'll give you credit: you wear a three-piece suit or tuxedo as well as you do your leather."

"What does the gig pay?"

"For you, seven hundred and fifty Standard New Dollars a week, plus all expenses. We're well financed, Stephen. This is the real thing."

Following the collapse of the oil cartels and the year of wild and crazy hyper-inflation that followed, new currency had been introduced. Standard New Dollars meant that domestic currency was set at par with Eurodollars, and each dollar was worth in purchasing power about the same as its 1980 equivalent, or there-abouts. Seven-fifty would be a nice chunk of weekly income to take home to my lover, who had always earned much more than I did. I accepted without even having to think about it twice, as I'm sure you would have done too, Aaron.

When I got home that night, Troy's reaction came as a some-what less than pleasant surprise. Oh, I'd known he wouldn't be totally delighted by my working for a liberal Democrat, but never-theless I'd expected him to look at it in terms of what it would mean to me — to us.

"Seven hundred and fifty bones a week, Troy," I pointed out. "I can throw five hundred into the household account, and bank the rest, along with all my writing fees and royalties."

"When the hell was money ever an issue with us, Stephen? You know I'd be perfectly happy if you'd just stay home and finally write the novel you've been dreaming about for years. You're missing the point. I think you'd be putting yourself into a lot of real physical danger. Needlessly."

"Physical danger? You mean fag-bashers? When I'd be sur-rounded most of the time by members of Doug's staff?"

"Well, not fag-bashers, exactly."

"Then what *do* you mean?"

"Take a good look at Doug McKittrick. Wealthy, educated, gentlemanly, the very best that our community has to offer. And very openly gay. How do you think the Southern rednecks are go-ing to react to that?"

"*What* Southern rednecks? Doug knows he's not going to win any of the very few remaining Southern redneck counties in our state. He's not even going to waste his time campaigning in the boondocks and the orange groves and the cattle ranches. He's go-ing after the big cities, the urban areas where the big votes are, where nobody's even *heard* a Southern accent and everybody likes to think of themselves as being politically sophisticated enough to vote for a gay candidate. Or so they tell the pollsters, at least."

"And you think that's going to stop some crazy redneck with a high-powered rifle from knocking him off, and you along with him?"

"You're being awfully paranoid, Troy. Just as you always ac-cuse me of being. Do you mean to tell me that in this glorious free democracy you're always ranting and raving about, a man can't run for office if he chooses to, without having to fear the threat of violent physical repercussions?"

"Oh, come on, Stephen, be realistic. There are lots of things in this country in which we believe in principle but which the people just aren't ready for. For example, you've told me often enough that we're the only modern industrial country in the world without a system of national health care. In principle we know we should have one, but it's just that we're a different breed in this country. We prefer to think that we don't need it; it isn't our style. Or else we're just not ready yet. Look, let me give you another example. How many of the major cities in this country have mayors who are black?"

"At least half. And some damn good ones, too."

"Okay, but what would have happened if a black politician had tried it, say, in the early 1950s?"

"He'd have been lynched, damn quick. North or South he'd have been lucky to leave the filing office alive. Okay, I see your point. Everyone who can speak coherently enough to talk to a pollster says they're for gay rights, because to do otherwise would make them look like an ignorant right-wing religious fanatic. But nobody really wants to see it happen just yet, do they?"

"Stephen, you've told me yourself that if all of the gay people in America were to suddenly vanish off the face of the earth, most of the breeders would sleep just a little bit better that night. I realize how socially acceptable Doug McKittrick is personally, but I still say that the voters are no more ready for a gay governor now than they were for a black mayor in 1950."

"You're probably right, of course. But *somebody* had to make the first move! What would have happened if Rosa Parks *hadn't* insisted on sitting down in the white section of a bus in Montgomery, Alabama?"

"Then someone else would have. Just as somebody, somewhere, will try to field a gay candidacy for governor of a major state. But not in Florida! We're a wealthy, conservative state with a lot of people who are terrified of the future. Tell Doug to run for Congress or something instead."

"I have. He feels there's a matter of principle involved here. And Troy, maybe I'm being selfish, but I don't want to talk him out of it! I want to see it happen right here in Florida, win or lose! And I want the fun and excitement of being a part of it. Come on, man, loosen up! Don't you want to be known as the lover of the man who helped Doug McKittrick become the first openly gay governor of a major state?"

"Are you kidding? For sure I'd be out of a job!"

"You might be surprised about that."

□

Doug McKittrick chose to kick off his campaign three weeks later at the Jefferson-Jackson Day Dinner. This was an annual fundraising tribal ritual of the county Democratic organization, held each February at one of the biggest resort hotels which served the worst food and provided the worst service in the annals of political fundraising dinners. Or perhaps only Democratic ones; I'd never attended a Republican one.

The Lambda Democratic Club of Fort Lauderdale, an openly gay political club, carried considerable clout in the Broward County organization, because of the money and effort that it poured into the mainstream of the party. The clout didn't help much that night, however, when we were bumped from our previously assigned ringside table by a thundering herd of television beer commercial types representing the steamfitters' or pipewelders' union or some such group. The women were all dressed absolutely incredibly, and the men all looked as though they would have been more comfortable in bowling shirts. Their leader, whose knuckles brushed the ground when he walked and who had no neck, was screaming at the County Chairman,

"Hey, we paid a t'ousint bucks fa dis table, and we ain't givin' it up fa nobody!"

The Lambda Club could, of course, have forcefully resolved the question by bidding the table up to *two* thousand, but at the behest of the County Chairman, we graciously accepted a less conspicuous table in a far corner of the vast banquet room. *Noblesse oblige*, after all.

Doug and his current lover, a glamorous young actor and model, and Troy and I were wearing tuxedos, and were the most overdressed people in the room. In fact, our whole table was by far the best-dressed that night, since all the other gay men present wore suits, and for once all our lesbian sisters at the table looked totally like perfect ladies.

"We're the only table," commented Troy, "that would have looked perfectly in place at a Republican fundraising dinner." He kicked me gently underneath the table and whispered, "You know I'm only doing this for your sake, asshole. If my parents could see me now, they'd not only turn over in their graves, they'd have to install a rotisserie."

The dinner was abominable beyond belief. I think the main course may have been rubbery game hens with waterlogged vegetables, but we never found out because not even bribes or the threat of physical abuse could persuade the fledgling waiters on duty that night to bring us any silverware. On the other hand, a group of schoolteachers at the next table had silverware but no food.

"Should we give them our food," asked Troy, "or just take their silverware?"

"Knock it off. You didn't want to actually eat here anyway, did you? We can go someplace civilized afterwards."

After awhile the waiters came around — "All finished? Thank you, sir," — and picked up our uneaten food. Then the speeches started. Most of the local politicians had such thick, heavy New Yorkese dialects that we had to struggle to keep from laughing out loud. Even worse, they were almost all less than semi-educated, resoundingly unintelligent, and just plain dull.

"It's sad," said Troy. "I could have been a really devout Democrat, once upon a time, but I was born too late."

"What do you mean?" asked Jerry Levine, the Lambda Club's chairman.

"Looking at this room," Troy explained, "it's hard to believe that this was once the party of Adlai Stevenson and Eleanor Roosevelt. The party of the intelligentsia, the intellectual elite."

"And what do you consider it now?" asked Carolyn, a militant feminist.

"The party of the *lumpenproletariat*," replied Troy." The party of the armed and militant urban ghetto guerrillas, the politically dispossessed, the idealistically impoverished, the functionally illiterate."

"That's quite an indictment," said Doug McKittrick, leaning over toward him. "Tell me, do you consider me an anomaly in the Democratic party?"

Troy grinned. "Socially, if not politically, most definitely. You're probably the only Democratic candidate for public office in this state who knows the difference between a Canaleto and a cannelloni."

"You'll have to excuse my lover, Doug," I interjected. "His heart's in the right place, but his social prejudices are all Republican."

"Social prejudices don't win elections," Doug replied. "Hardcore issues do, and this is the party that cares about issues. You may consider these people a bunch of ungrammatical ruffians in bowling shirts, but they're the ones who'll support *our* rights all the way to Washington — not the Palm Beach socialites."

"Social prejudices may not win elections," replied Troy, "but they damn sure lose them. And talking of social prejudice, you'd better watch out for that new dark star on the horizon, that crazy television evangelist — what's his name, Wickerly."

There was a hoot of derision around the table. "Are you serious?" "Save your souls for dollars!" "Come on, all ye ignorant and superstitious, send in your financial blessings and ye shall be saved!" "Be real, Troy, nobody takes that asshole seriously!"

"Well, you should," said Troy.

"I'd love to hear some of the political arguments around your breakfast table," said Doug to Troy.

"Oh, it's democracy in action," I said. "Could anything be more American than to wake up on election morning knowing that one hour after you hit the polls, your lover will be down there to cancel out your vote? But there's one thing about which I do agree with him. Don't discount Reverend Wickerly. Remember, they laughed at a funny little paperhanger from Austria with a funny little moustache."

At that point, Doug was called to the podium. He asked me to accompany him so that the party faithful could get used to seeing me around.

The Democratic incumbent governor had not considered this gathering of the top officials and club members of the state's politically most important and second most populous county to be of sufficient importance to merit his presence. When Doug stepped up to the microphone to announce his candidacy officially, he had the field to himself.

The speech we'd worked out together had been carefully programmed to stress party unity rather than special interests. He made no direct reference to the fact that he would be the party's first openly gay candidate for office, but instead spoke of representing all the various and diverse interests of the party and the state. Actually, he made such an impressive and winning figure that it wouldn't have mattered all that much what he said. In his perfect, well-modulated English, he proceeded to demolish both the incumbent governor and the leading Republican candidates. Standing there in his tuxedo, perfectly groomed, he was the quintessential WASP aristocrat that all of the New Yorkers and the "ungrammatical ruffians in bowling shirts" secretly longed, in their heart of hearts, to be. When he had finished his speech, he received a standing ovation.

When we returned to our table, Troy surprised the hell out of me by giving Doug a warm, manly embrace. There were tears in his eyes.

"Doug," he said, "if anybody can bring this party back to the standards of Eleanor Roosevelt and Adlai Stevenson, you're the man who can do it!" Later, on the campaign trail, Doug told me that of all the accolades he'd received that night, my lover's compliment had meant the most to him.

I kidded Troy about it for days. "Man, he sure turned you around," I laughed.

"Maybe I'm just an impressionable kid," replied Troy, "or maybe I'm looking for a hero to worship. You know yourself, the easiest person to sell a bill of goods to is some advertising huckster who does it for a living. But you'll damn sure see a Doug McKittrick bumper sticker on my car from now on!"

The next few months were as crazy as only an election campaign can be. Doug and I lived in planes, on buses, and in his limousine traveling in motorcades. Once he got going, he was unstoppable. No longer the sage political dilettante, he had the gut instinct of a true political campaigner.

He was attacked, of course. At first the major newspapers of the state tried using their age-old ploy, the Curtain of Silence.

Then, when it became apparent that Doug was not merely a maverick, not just a dark horse, but a serious contender for the State of Florida's highest office, the press lords leapt in like hungry jackals and hyenas foraging for carrion.

Although nothing could change the official editorial stance of the major papers, Doug's charisma worked magic with reporters. When a newspaper in the Tampa-St. Pete area published a scathing editorial attack which questioned not only the constitutional right, but the moral fitness of any gay person to hold public office, and denounced him personally in the most homophobic terms, Doug turned the attack to his advantage by holding a press conference. As always, he was generous with refreshments. There was a lavish table of hors d'oeuvres and an open bar; hard booze for the old-time newspapermen and soft drinks and Perrier for the new breed. When everyone was settled comfortably, he held up the editorial and asked them what they thought about it.

"I think it stinks," said a man from Orlando. "I promise you'll never see filth like that in my paper."

"What do you think, Gonzales?" Henry Gonzales was the dean of the political press corps, a scholarly, white-haired, erudite man who worked for the Miami Herald.

"Come on, Doug," replied Gonzales. "Do I have to spell it out for you? I'm not saying you'll get our endorsement, and I'm not saying you won't. We might blast you for your liberal social philosophy, and we might blast you because you've never held elected office before. But as long as I'm chief of our political desk, I guarantee you we'll never attack you on a gutter level!" A murmur of assent went around the room. Then, with a twinkle in his eye, Doug put the frosting on the cake by adding,

"Whatever makes these idiots think that being called a multi-millionaire faggot is supposed to be an *insult?* Hey, I love it! And I want you all to *think* about it next time your kid needs three thousand bucks' worth of orthodontic work!" They ate it up.

The Reverend Peter Joshua Wickerly had not yet declared his partisan intentions; he was ready to run for any office for any party when the right time came. But he put in an appearance in Florida on behalf of the incumbent governor. Doug handled his attacks with equanimity. When Wickerly raved about the accursed sodomite who was running for office, Doug discussed fiscal sanity in the state's budget. When Wickerly talked about the Word of God, Doug quoted Biblical passages about good government and the obligations of rulers. At no time did he dignify the deranged rantings of the evangelist with a direct answer, but he did allow me to do so.

At a press conference in Tampa, one reporter quoted Reverend Wickerly as having stated unequivocally that homosexuality was against God's word. What did I have to say to that?

I replied, "That is his personal, subjective, religious belief, and for him to believe this, however irrational or illogical, is his right. What is not his right, however, is to try to impose his own personal religious convictions on anyone else."

"He also claims that the United States is a Christian country. Do you disagree with that?"

I pointed at a Jewish reporter from Miami Beach. "Horowitz, do you believe this is a Christian country?"

"Sure as hell better not be," he replied, "unless they've rewritten the Constitution since I was Bar-Mitzvah."

"Does Doug McKittrick believe in God?" I was asked, and suddenly realized that we'd never discussed it. I'd always assumed that he didn't.

"Mr. McKittrick," I replied, "or should I say, Future Governor McKittrick, is a deeply spiritual man, but he does not discuss the exact nature of his beliefs. I can assure you, however, that he does believe very deeply in the promise of America, but for all of its citizens, including minorities and groups with special areas of civil rights difficulties."

"Do you believe in God, Ashcroft?"

"I believe that if there were a god, he, she, or it would not reject ten percent of his, her, or its children, including some of the best and brightest. I also believe very deeply that the incumbent governor's use of Reverend Wickerly in his campaign makes him morally unfit to hold the office."

"You guys sure tell it like it is, don't you?"

"We do. Our entire campaign staff, from Mr. McKittrick on down to the gals who stuff envelopes, are absolutely *up to here* with lying, equivocating political hacks who wouldn't say shit if they had a mouthful. We want to see a Democratic party in the tradition of Harry S. Truman, who not only called a spade a spade, but, if he felt like it, a goddamn shovel. You may not agree with everything we have to say, but there is no issue affecting our country and our state on which you will not know exactly where we stand."

It had been many years since any candidate or his aides had spoken to the media as forthrightly as that.

One of the nicest things that came out of the campaign was that my lover Troy came out on his job. We had about three million in campaign funds to spend on radio and television commercials and newspaper ads, and we needed a top-flight agency with state-of-the-art production facilities.

"Doug," I asked my candidate, "would it be considered either nepotism or just plain unethical if we were to give Troy's agency this contract?"

"I think it would be great," he replied. "Let the business community know that voting gay, supporting gay, and buying gay can mean big, big bucks. Besides, they're a damn good agency and they've done political work before. Have them submit bids and proposals."

Troy asked his boss if he wanted the account, or if he felt it might tarnish the firm's image with the large corporate accounts.

"All's fair in love, business, politics and war, Anderson. May I ask how come you are in a position to bring this account into the firm?"

"Yes, sir, you may. Number one, Mr. McKittrick appreciates a really good agency such as ours. Number two, his chief aide, Stephen Ashcroft, happens to have been my lover for the past five years. If Doug McKittrick is elected, we stand to be getting a lot of state business over the next four years, including tourist development and business development campaigns."

His boss, a wealthy Palm Beach socialite, commented, "I don't like subterfuge and duplicity, Anderson. Next time I give a cocktail party, would you kindly give me enough credit to bring your friend Mr. Ashcroft instead of some young lady you've dredged out of the typing pool? And by the way, considering the magnitude of this account, I think a very smart cocktail party for Mr. McKittrick might also be in order. Does he also have a — friend?"

"He has lots of friends," replied Troy. "But only one lover."

It happened very gradually at first, but on every level, the McKittrick magic began to take hold. At a luncheon meeting of the ultra-prestigious Tiger Bay Club in Miami, of which he was already a member, Doug addressed a packed house of bankers, politicians and top-level businessmen on the subject of fiscal responsibility and how he would restructure the state's tax policies. At the conclusion, a leading banker came up to me with his checkbook in his hand.

"By, God, Ashcroft, that man could turn the State of Florida into a profit-making organization! I don't care about all the other nonsense; I'm supporting him from now on purely as a matter of financial self-interest!"

We had started in February. By May it was quite apparent that Doug was trailing his opponent by only two-to-one, and moving up fast. By August the polls showed him behind by only twenty percent. Everywhere he went, he impressed the average voters, as well as the Tiger Bay businessmen, with his superb command of business and finance. "A Business Governor for a Business State," was one of the slogans that we used.

And then, three weeks before the September primary, we managed to uncover the nice, juicy little revelation that Reverend Peter Joshua Wickerly's religious movement was secretly funding the incumbent governor's campaign very heavily, far in excess of what the law intended, even though it had been done very cleverly and legally. The voters were utterly appalled, even the ones who weren't especially anti-religious. At one point Doug edged slightly ahead in the polls. It appeared that we might actually have an openly gay candidate in the general election.

That was when they struck. There was simply no way that *they* could have allowed Douglas McKittrick to become Governor of Florida, any more than *they* could have allowed John F. Kennedy to bring about world peace, or Robert Kennedy to control "the mob," or Martin Luther King to bring social, economic and political equality to blacks. If the maverick voters of the Great State of Florida, or at least the Democratic ones, had temporarily lost their senses, then it was up to *them* to shock the state and the nation back to a sense of political reality.

The last big political rally before the primary election was held in Orlando, the most centrally-located major city in the state. Supporters had traveled from as far away as Pensacola in Florida's still-Southern, redneck Panhandle; from Tallahassee, the state capital; from Jacksonville, in what we snidely referred to as Baja Georgia; and of course from the four Gold Coast counties: Palm Beach, Broward, Dade and Monroe, which included, respectively, West Palm Beach, Fort Lauderdale and Hollywood, Miami and Miami Beach, and Key West. These four counties had by far the heaviest concentrations of Jews, Democrats, and gays. The enormous Hispanic population of Dade County was the only substantial voting bloc that was strongly anti-McKittrick, but it didn't really matter that much because, being deeply religious and ultra-conservative, they were predominantly Republican, and wouldn't be voting in the Democratic primary anyway.

The Citrus Bowl was filled to absolute capacity. It was a very high-spirited and happy crowd, waving campaign flags and singing campaign songs, and generally just having a party. We've always been the party that knows how to party; I suppose at a Republican rally, everyone would have spoken in quiet, well-modulated voices, or else been praying. Also, at one of their rallies, the crowd would have been mostly older and WASP, whereas our crowd that night was heavily gay, Jewish, black, blue-collar and young.

An army of local police, county sheriffs, state police, and state security agents were on hand to keep order. Although there were lots of joints being passed around, and more than a few bottles, they had enough sense not to antagonize a crowd that was so obviously good-natured. Besides, there was always the possibility that after the general election, Governor-Elect McKittrick would be their boss.

Aaron, it was the proudest moment of my life as I sat on that platform next to Doug McKittrick. It was the culmination of everything I had worked for, traveled for, written about, and believed in. Never mind the Kennedys and Dr. King; here was grassroots democracy in America being vindicated at last. When Doug stepped up to the podium, I could have wept for joy.

Doug had never looked better. Although the heat in Orlando that night was in the mid-nineties, he looked as though he had just stepped out of a shower into his air-conditioned bedroom. He wore a very expensive, but very light-weight fawn-colored suit, with a slightly darker striped silk shirt and a perfectly knotted tie.

Greasy Grossberg once said to me, "I've never understood how these upper-class WASPS never seem to sweat. Hell, they don't even *perspire!*"

Perfectly in command, radiating both confidence and serenity, Douglas McKittrick began to address the crowd.

That was when the crazed, wild-eyed man in clerical garb somehow managed to break through the cordon of police that surrounded the speakers' platform. Screaming "Filthy sodomite! Queer son of Satan!" he pulled out an enormous pistol that looked like a World War II Luger and pumped three shots into Douglas McKittrick at close range before they grabbed him and disarmed him, as pandemonium and chaos began to break loose in the stadium.

Two state security agents grabbed me by the arms. "Come on, Ashcroft, let's get out of here!" one said, and the other yelled in my ear, "Move quick, man! We'll get you to safety!"

There were exactly three things that saved my life in the next few seconds: street-smarts, combat-trained reflexes, and a sharp, clear sense of historical recollection.

First of all, frozen in my field of vision like a freeze-frame was a picture of that crazy preacher, surrounded by security agents, taking dead aim at Doug from point-blank range. There was absolutely no doubt whatsoever in my mind that the two agents on either side of him had deliberately waited the crucial second or so until he had squeezed off his shots before they grabbed him and disarmed him.

"Move, Ashcroft! *Now!*"

I remember as a kid watching on television as John F. Kennedy's motorcade had suddenly, inexplicably, detoured from its previously chosen route around Dealey Plaza in Dallas to bring the car bearing the President and Governor Connally within crossfire range of the grassy knoll and the Texas Book Depository, long since demolished. Later, the Warren Commission would try to establish the lone-assassin, single-bullet theory, which so few people believed. Then I recalled his brother, Robert F. Kennedy, being led by security agents "for reasons of safety" away from the regular exits of the of the Ambassador Hotel in Los Angeles and down through the kitchen, where *they* had their fanatical recruit, Sirhan Sirhan, waiting for him.

I thought about Martin Luther King being led onto the balcony of his motel room in Nashville, within range of where James Earl Ray was waiting with his high-powered rifle.

All of this flashed through my mind in an eyeblink. It didn't make me think, it made me react.

Somehow I managed to wrest myself free of the two security agents who had hold of me, next to where Doug was lying on the platform in a pool of blood as the paramedics tried to force their way through the crowd. In one swift motion, I kneed one of the agents in the groin, cold-cocked the other one with a well-aimed right to the jaw, and jumped off the platform into the crowd which was trying to shove its way forward. Nobody tried to stop me as I fought my way to the nearest exit tunnel of the stadium; it had all happened too fast. Outside the Citrus Bowl, a rank of cabs was waiting. I jumped into one of them.

"Where to, Mister?"

"Away from here! Fast!" Luck was still with me, but I wondered how many of Doug's staff were still alive, or still would be ten minutes from now.

"What the hell's going on in there?" asked the driver, a beefy transplanted New Jerseyite, from his accent.

"Somebody just shot McKittrick."

"Oh, yeah? Well, that's good news. I always hated that fucking faggot."

I kept my mouth shut. "Drive to the airport," I said.

From the airport I called Troy at home. Because of my work, my phone had had a bug-scrambler for years. "Meet me at the old place," I told Troy. "Bring the metal box. Bring cash. And make sure you're not followed."

Also because of my work, I had kept the tiny apartment where Troy and I had spent our first night together. The cost was negligible, and it gave me a private office and den where I could be as messy as I wished, and where I could bring people for interviews whom I might not have wanted, for one reason or another, to bring to our home.

There was a flight just leaving Fort Lauderdale. I booked a ticket under an assumed name and paid cash for it. Since this fitted the airlines' hijacker profile — single male, traveling alone, no luggage, one-way ticket for cash — I was afraid I might be detained by airport security, but as usual they were half asleep. In a few minutes I was airborne.

Troy was waiting for me at the old place. There were tears in his eyes. "I saw it on television," he said. "What in the hell happened?"

"You were right. Politically I'm the smart one, but this time you were right. There was no way *they* would have allowed it."

"What are you going to do?"

"I've got to get out of the country. Did you bring the metal box?"

"Of course." The box contained my passport and other personal papers, the rest of my credit cards, and some cash. Troy had also brought me another few hundred Standard New Dollars, every cent that he kept on hand in actual cash in our household fund.

"Troy," I said. "Where is *your* passport?"

"I never renewed it," he admitted.

"Oh, God! I *told* you and *told* you! In a world like ours, you have to sleep with it under your pillow! How quickly can you get one?"

"I suppose it only takes a couple of weeks, Stephen, but are you sure you aren't over-reacting?"

"Yes! I'm damn sure! Don't forget, I'm not just Doug's speechwriter and political aide, I've been a thorn in *their* flesh for years with my writing and my exposés. You saw what happened tonight. Don't you realize they've just declared war against us? Or do you really think it will all just blow over?"

Troy took me in his arms. I guess I was pretty hysterical by then; the shock of what had happened in Orlando was just setting in.

"Yes, Stephen, I do think it will all blow over. Get out of the country if it will make you feel better. Take a few weeks away from all of this. I'll even join you for a vacation. But please, don't tell me we have to flee our country like the European refugees fleeing Hitler."

There was no arguing with him. Instead, I begged.

"Please, Troy, trust my judgment. Come with me."

"Are you serious? Are you saying we should give up everything we've been working for? Our home? Our careers? Just when we've both been doing so well? Stephen, I know you're upset, but you're talking crazy. In a few weeks you'll be home again, or else I'll meet you on some tropical beach. You'll see."

I just couldn't make him realize that it was all over, finished, kaput; our house, our careers, everything. The best move we could make right now was to flee, but Troy refused to budge.

"Look," he argued, "if they wanted you as desperately as you seem to think, they'd never have let you get out of the stadium alive, would they?"

"They never wanted me desperately," I explained. "They just wanted to nail as many of us as they conveniently could. Besides, they know I'm someone they can pretty well put their finger on whenever they want to. As long as I'm in the country, that is."

"Where are you going, by the way?" Troy asked. "Or is it better that I don't know?"

"I'm not even sure how I'm going to get out of the country. Normally, the Canadian border is always wide open. But in my case, even if I were to slide through Canadian customs and immigration, the Mounties would be waiting for me."

"The Royal Canadian Mounted Police? But they're like our CIA, among other things. What the hell do they have to do with it?"

"When Martin Luther King was shot, they captured his assassin in London, England. He was traveling on a Canadian passport — an all-American hillbilly who'd never even been to Canada in his life! What do the Queen's Cowboys have to do with it? Troy, everyone's known for years that the Mounties and the CIA literally pick each other's fleas!"

"How about Mexico?"

"Too well infiltrated. They could nail me too easily down there."

In the end, the simplest way proved the best. Just before dawn, Troy drove me to Port Everglades, from which the daily cruise ship leaves for a gambling junket to Freeport in the Bahamas, returning late the same night. When the ship docked in Freeport, I joined a party of vacationers in a cab to the casino and shopping area. Then I took another cab to the airport, caught a flight to Nassau, and from there to London, where I stayed with friends and wrote a series of articles about the McKittrick campaign and the assassination.

Eventually I was contacted by the Resistance movement and asked to work out of Amsterdam, so I caught the boat-train and the Sealink to Holland. And here I am.

3

They were enjoying an enormous *rijstaffel* dinner in an ancient, quietly elegant country inn just outside the city. There were beamed ceilings, private booths, and a roaring fire in the fireplace.

"What happened to the chap who shot Douglas McKittrick?" asked Aaron Ten Eyck. "Did they ever find out who he was?"

"We were told he was an evangelist from Pensacola with a history of religious delusions and personal violence," said Ashcroft. "They put him in Chattahoochie State Hospital, where he was conveniently blown away, just like Lee Harvey Oswald."

"What happened then, Stephen? How did Reverend Wickerly become president of the United States? It wasn't a presidential election year."

"No, it wasn't. But *they* couldn't wait. You have to remember that although the Democratic voters of Florida were showing some common sense, all across most of the rest of the country, the religious radical right was winning one local election and referendum after another. The mountain and desert states all went radical right very early on. California remained divided.

"You must also remember," Ashcroft continued, "that compared to the other Western democracies, the United States has always been much more conservative, much farther to the right, even though we'd always liked to think of ourselves as resoundingly centrist. It was a perfect time for *them* to consolidate their power."

"Stephen, forgive me for being so politically naive about the United States, but just who or what is this mysterious *they* to whom you keep referring?"

"I wish I could give you a clear-cut, well-defined answer," said Ashcroft, "but I can't. You see, the power structure in the United

States was never totally monolithic. There was, of course, the military/industrial complex about which President Eisenhower warned us; toward the end of his second term, having accomplished as much as one man could possibly hope to achieve in his lifetime, and knowing he was dying of cancer, he kept having these embarrassing fits and seizures of political honesty.

"There was also the Religious Right, which, like the poor, had always been with us, subverting our educational system and trying to impose their theology on a country whose constitution specifically forbade it.

"And then, of course, there was that entity we loosely referred to as The Mob. By that time, it owned half of Congress, not to mention a very sizeable portion of our gross national product.

"There was never a tightly-knit organization like that of the Kremlin. It was simply a matter of the most powerful people in America interacting in matters of mutual self-interest. A mad general in the Pentagon wants a billion dollars' worth of left-handed electronic widgets, worth maybe a few thousand dollars at consumer retail price, so a mob leader orders a few of his wholly-owned congressmen to vote for the appropriation. The contractor chosen to supply the widgets is a company owned by the general and his Mafia buddies. Or, let's say the Mob wants a Caribbean island opened up for its resorts and casinos, so the military stages a *coup d'état* and opens it up for them. And all the while the well-funded and well-organized religious radical right keeps the vast majority of the people mindless, ignorant and passive."

"But Stephen," protested the old man, "while all of this was going on, where were the writers, the thinkers, the articulate liberals, the intelligentsia?"

"Where were they?" Stephen laughed bitterly. "They were busy drinking their chilled California chablis at cocktail parties and laughing their heads off at all of the above. After all, it can't happen here, can it? Even a man as knowledgeable as Jerry Levine, the chairman of the Lambda Democratic Club, had assured me some years before that the religious radical right would not only founder in its own morass of lost credibility, but that it would self-destruct by 1988. It didn't, of course; it just gained more and more strength. Evil *never* self-destructs, Aaron; it always has to be destroyed, as you well know.

"So when the power structure decided that the time had come to dump the facade of democratic institutions that had kept so many well-meaning people blinded to the slow but steady growth of totalitarianism in the United States, they were able to accomplish the final take-over with Machiavellian brilliance and simplicity. I'll come to the actual mechanics of it in a moment.

"I had already fled the country, as I told you, the morning after the night of the McKittrick assassination, but I had a very dear lady friend who kept me well informed.

"Maxine Rosenberg, *née* Bernstein, was a social worker and community activist who managed to escape the Wickerly holocaust by reason of a rather unusual course that her life had taken. Herself a lesbian, she had nevertheless wanted to experience the joys of motherhood and of parenting, so she married Alex Rosenberg, also young, gay, Jewish, and an activist."

"Was that really so unusual?" interjected Ten Eyck. "Surely, such marriages must take place all the time."

"You're quite right," replied Ashcroft. "They do. But what was so unusual in this case was that unlike the usual marriage between a lesbian and gay male, this was much more than just a *marriage de convenance* for purposes of deep cover or in order to have children. They were a great couple and absolutely adored each other. Of course, they accorded each other the privilege of outside same-sex relationships, but I suspect that in their case this privilege was honored more by neglect than by observance. They had two lovely, intelligent kids, a boy and a girl; they each had their career — Alex was a college instructor — and they had their activist activities within the gay community, so I rather suspect they pretty much had everything they wanted at home.

"When the DIVAF program started, Maxine and Alex didn't even raise a ripple on the curve, despite the fact that they were both openly gay activists. Eventually, the government's internal intelligence operatives, or as they came to be called, Wickerly's Warriors, brought in a back-up program for their DIVAF program. It was a dossier-matching program specifically designed to pick up the people like the Rosenbergs whom the DIVAF had missed because of their seemingly-straight lifestyle.

"But Maxine and Alex were nobody's fools. They kept their passports in order and their money off-shore. By the time Wickerly's Warriors came for them, they had already fled to Israel, which under that country's Law of Return had absolutely no problem about admitting them as citizens. Both were demonstrably and provably of Hebrew racial ancestry, neither had a Gentile mother, and neither had ever abandoned the practice of Judaism. They had both attended Congregation Etz Chaim, the Metropolitan Community Synagogue in North Miami Beach, which was South Florida's gay synagogue."

"Well!" said Ten Eyck. "That's a happy ending, for once. What finally became of them?"

"I'm still in touch with them, and they're still in Israel. Maxine is still a social worker; Alex is still a college instructor; and the kids are growing up to be real Sabras. But they haven't abandoned their gay roots, either; they've started a gay and lesbian reading and cultural group in Tel Aviv.

"After I fled the country, Maxine kept me pretty much *au courant* about what happened between that time and the final take-over. Could we have a little more coffee, please?"

4

"SEX! BOOZE! DRUGS! VIOLENCE! ROCK AND ROLL!" screamed the banner headline over Greasy Grossberg's column, followed by a more subdued subhead: "Adventures of a Fat Jewish Lesbian in Tallahassee." That was the way Greasy liked to write his articles, (Ashcroft related to Ten Eyck). Grab them by the balls first, and then, after you have their attention, sock it to them. Tasteful, sedate journalism was never his forte.

During the better days of the gay rights movement in Florida, a consortium of gay organizations around the state had attempted to maintain a full-time, salaried lobbyist in Tallahassee, the state capital. Underpaid and underfunded, the luckless volunteer usually wound up staying in Tallahassee only as long as his or her dedicated spouse, parent or lover could afford to foot the bills. I remember one night when I was attempting to solicit funds for the umbrella organization that actually hired and paid the lobbyist. It was at a restaurant and bar in Plantation, just outside of Fort

Lauderdale, and I'd been invited up to the mike to say a few words for the cause.

When I had finished, a rather belligerent and slightly drunk lesbian grabbed me as I made the rounds of the patrons collecting donations.

"What the fuck," she wanted to know, "did the Florida Task Force ever do for me?"

"What the fuck," I responded, with my usual tact that Troy used to give me hell for, "did you *expect* them to do for you? Wash your goddamn windows? Mow your lawn? If it weren't for our political activists, you wouldn't even be sitting here, you stupid bulldyke, because no gay establishment would even be able to get a liquor license!"

During the time the lobbying office was kept open in Tallahassee, before it finally had to be abandoned for sheer lack of support, Maxine Rosenberg was the chosen martyr for almost a year. Eventually the cost of flying home every weekend to be with her husband and kids became astronomical, and Alex finally rebelled at having to be both breadwinner and house-husband five days a week. But during the time she was our lobbyist, Maxine gave a speech one night at a benefit dinner in which she described, with wry and mordant humor, her exploits and adventures in Tallahassee, which is not one of our nation's most enlightened and sophisticated state capitals. Greasy Grossberg had taken it all down on his tape recorder, including the episode in which she had kept an appointment at the office of a fat, ancient, wattled obscenity from one of the redneck, boondock, Panhandle counties.

"Whah, Honey," this stalwart legislator had said when she had introduced herself, "yew CAIN'T be no gawdamn Lezz-bin! Y'all look jest lak a *woman!*"

When the article appeared, Maxine had rushed up to Greasy at an AIDS benefit cocktail party and, right there on the speaker's platform, kissed him right on the mouth.

"You wonderful, wonderful man!" she exclaimed. "Not only did your column bring in hundreds of dollars, but now my mother *finally* knows what it is I actually *do* for a living!" And before he could recover himself, she kissed him on the mouth again.

Greasy had fumed and sputtered. "It kissed me. It kissed me!

A female! Right on the mouth! Gaaahhh! Get me the disinfectant! Help! Medics! Help! I'm going to turn into a *fish!*"

Maxine regarded him for a moment and then said, right over the mike, "Now I know, Greasy, how come the hottest thing you've ever had between your legs is your motorcycle!" The crowd roared.

It was she who kept me posted almost daily on the events that transpired during the brief period between the McKittrick assassination and, following the accession of the Wickerly government, the start of the DIVAF program. We used a series of mail drops, since it was very important to the Wickerly forces not to let the world-wide press become aware of what was happening until after the political *coup d'état* had been successfully completed. The problem, unfortunately, was that just as it had happened during the rise of Hitler's Third Reich, everyone was very much aware of what was happening, but too few people were sufficiently alarmed or concerned.

The bar raids had begun almost immediately after the assassination; as some writers put it, before Doug's body had even had time to cool. The first bar to be hit in Fort Lauderdale was the Western Saddles, a primarily levi-leather bar that had a huge patio where, as the night progressed, the various activities began to get more and more open. It was even wilder on Jock Strap Night, a mid-week business booster during which the patrons got half-price drinks for stripping down to the legal minimum. The *bare* minimum, one might say.

"It was strictly a men's bar," Maxine wrote to me, "so I wasn't there, but Greasy Grossberg was. The management used to give him free or half-priced drinks just to keep his clothes *on.*

"One can't really call it a raid," she went on. "It was more like a military attack. The guys got hit by an army. Even if they'd been organized, ready and willing, there wouldn't have been the opportunity to pull another Stonewall Rebellion. Some undercover vice had infiltrated the place; a couple of the younger ones even stripped, hoping to entrap people.

"When the raid started, they busted the door security first, then let their buddies in. A lot of the guys got hurt, because the cops were swinging their clubs pretty freely. It was a miracle there were no really serious injuries. They filled up the paddy wagons and took over a hundred people down to the main jail on Broward Boulevard.

"The ones who'd merely been present were charged with various misdemeanors and released on their own recognizance. The ones who'd been leaving at the time the raid started got busted for drunk driving before they could even get to their cars. Those who'd been smoking pot or having sex were booked and thrown into the main holding tank, where most of them were either beaten, gang-raped, or both. It was almost three days before they could all be bailed out, due to the deliberate snail's-pace procedure in bonding out each prisoner. The names and addresses of everyone caught on the premises were given out to the straight press. Just like the good old pre-Stonewall days, right?"

The morning after the raid, Maxine, Greasy, and Jerry Levine, the chairman of the Lambda Democratic Club, along with several other community leaders, went storming downtown to see Barry Coltrane, the Chief of Police. He was an affable Yuppie type, fairly young for his position, and typical of the New Breed of cop — intelligent, well-educated, and, on the surface at least, approachable.

"What the hell is going on, Barry?" screamed Greasy Grossberg, as the others tried to restrain him. "We've had real great liaison with your department for almost ten years, and now — *this!*"

The Chief of Police tamped tobacco in his pipe but did not light it. There was a large sign behind his desk that thanked everyone for not smoking. He cleared his throat and then spoke.

"I really appreciate the liaison we've had with your community in the past," he intoned, in almost a preppie drawl. "It's made our job a lot easier. We've solved a lot of cases that we wouldn't even have been able to touch without your help. Believe me, I'm just as sorry about last night as you people are."

"Then why did it happen?" demanded Maxine. "Who told you to do it?"

"I'm sorry," he replied. "I'm not going to put my neck on the line by answering that. Let's just say it was citizen pressure."

"Aw, come on, Barry," said Jerry Levine. "What kind of citizen pressure could get you to use all that manpower to raid a gay bar? Those people weren't hurting anybody. They were in what is technically a private club, having fun behind closed doors. Are the streets of our city so safe and crime-free that you can use your facilities for this kind of thing?"

The Chief stood up and laid his pipe on his desk, its bowl resting in an unused ashtray. He put up his hands in front of himself, palms out, as though to ward off any further questions.

"Look, I told you I was sorry, and that's all I'm prepared to say at this time. You can go see the Mayor, if you want to, but I don't think it'll do you any good. However, there is one thing I'd like you to know."

His listeners faced him expectantly.

"I was under strict orders not to let you people into my office. My instructions were to keep you waiting on those hard benches outside until you got frustrated and left."

"Then why didn't you?" asked Jerry.

"I know you folks too well, after all these years. You wouldn't have left, or if you had, you'd have come back with a hundred pickets carrying signs and staged a sit-in. Then I'd have had to bust them, too. On second thought, I really wish you would go see the Mayor. After all, he does owe you."

The Honorable Deke Breyer did indeed owe the community. The gay vote had put him into office, and the gay vote had re-elected him. Young, handsome, very straight and well-married, he had even appeared at gay functions such as picnics and benefit dinners. When questioned by his opponents as to why he had done so, he had replied, with irrefutable logic, "Because they're voters and taxpayers." However, it had been at least three years since he had done this, and some of his political positions had been noticeably less liberal of late. It was common knowledge that he aspired to higher office.

Like Chief Coltrane, he immediately admitted the delegation to his office, although with considerable reluctance.

"Look," he said, "we city officials have to take orders too, you know. I'm just as unhappy about last night as you are."

"And from whom," demanded Maxine, "did you get your orders to have Coltrane and his storm troopers raid a gay bar and beat up on the customers?"

"Let's be realistic," said the Mayor. "You like the new downtown library?"

"Well, sure," said Jerry. "We backed you on that one, too."

"You like the way they painted the New River Tunnel? You like the new municipal art gallery? You like the new Center for the Performing Arts? You like the way we keep the beaches clean and our streets fixed and the garbage picked up and our services better and cheaper than any big Northern city?"

"Yes, of course, Deke. What are you getting at?"

"What I'm getting at," said the Mayor, "is federal revenue sharing. It's like the old folk story about the Seminole Indian and his dog. The dog was hungry and the Indian didn't have anything to feed him, so he cut off the dog's tail and fed it to him. That's how our tax system works. They cut off a big chunk of you, and if you're a good boy, they might even let you have some of it back."

"I take it, Deke," said Greasy ominously, "that you've been a very good boy lately."

The Mayor shrugged. "Sometimes you don't always get to do what you want to do. As I said, I'm very unhappy about what happened at Western Saddles last night. But I'd be one hell of a lot unhappier if our municipal bonds went into default."

The pattern was starting to emerge, but it wasn't until the news began to filter in from all over the country that Maxine and the other community leaders realized in shock and horror what was really happening. The bar raid in Fort Lauderdale had merely been one in a coordinated pattern of dozens of such raids, carried out in identical fashion, all across the country.

But that was just the beginning (Ashcroft continued). Maxine wrote to me later,

"We didn't realize it at first, but from then on it was open war. Gay bars were routinely raided, and the patrons beaten up by the police, until, one by one, the bars were forced to close due to lack of business. It was very common for gays to be busted for drunk driving while walking to their cars. Anybody who was open at his or her job was summarily fired with no recourse, except in the handful of states which had not yet repealed their gay rights laws. An Executive Order from the White House arbitrarily labeled all gay organizations subversive, just as they'd done with so many progressive organizations back in the nineteen-fifties. This gave the Attorney General the authority to seize the records and assets of all the gay organizations, and to order them disbanded. The message was now loud and clear: stay in the closet, don't go to meetings or bars, and maybe you won't get hurt."

You asked me earlier how the Reverend President Wickerly actually assumed the office of the presidency.

It had been carefully orchestrated for a long time so that the people would be prepared and receptive. The constant brush-fire wars that the United States couldn't seem to avoid, and the threat of major war. A series of simulated terrorist attacks on U.S. installations. Some fiddling with the crime statistics to make it appear as though we were virtually on the brink of urban revolution by the underclasses. Some more fiddling with the economic figures to indicate that a severe recession was imminent. The solution to all of the foregoing problems was obvious: only a strong hand at the helm, unfettered by a dissident Congress, could save the country.

First, the Vice President mysteriously died in a plane crash, and the President, claiming that he was seeking a better political balance of power in the Executive Branch, appointed Peter Joshua Wickerly to the office. Nobody thought Congress would confirm him, but few people realized then how compliant Congress had become; by this time, they knew pretty well what they had to do to keep their seats. They either voted very willingly for his confirmation, or they gave in to pressure of one sort or another. Upon his confirmation, Wickerly changed the title of the office to "Reverend Vice President."

Shortly thereafter, the President, acting under orders from the people who jerked his strings, claimed severe ill-health and resigned in favor of the Reverend Vice President, who in turn appointed the most reactionary, right-wing Senator then in office, a Southern Baptist and homophobic fag-basher, to be his Vice President.

Please bear in mind, Aaron, that this was not the first time in recent years that the United States had had both a President and a Vice President, neither of whom had been elected to the office. Richard "Tricky Dicky" Nixon had lost his elected Vice President, Spiro Agnew, who had gotten caught cheating on his federal income taxes, and had appointed a bland, innocuous senator from Michigan, Gerald Ford, as his new Vice President. When Nixon was forced to resign (or else be impeached) following the Watergate scandal, Ford in turn appointed Nelson Rockefeller as his Vice President. So the precedent had already been set, and it was quite legal. Only in terms of political reality could one really call it a *coup d'état*.

As soon as he had taken the oath of office, the Reverend President Wickerly went on the air on all channels with a three-hour extravaganza of the same tired old religious and patriotic rhetoric that the masses had grown to know and love. Make America great again. Stem the Red Tide of Communism. Restore God and family values. The educated and functionally literate minority, the few who still knew how to read and think, went to the john and vomited. The rest of the country, the lobotomized couch potatoes, just lapped it all up. The cauldron had really bubbled over now, and it was too late for the frog to get out.

"If we thought we'd seen censorship and repression during the Eighties," Maxine wrote, "that was nothing compared to what went down after Wickerly took office."

In a poignant letter after it was all over, Maxine recalled to me the story of *Kristallnacht* in Nazi Germany, the Night of Broken Glass, and its American counterpart that followed.

"On the night of November 9th, 1938," she wrote, "the Nazis finally went totally berserk and trashed the entire Jewish community. About 7,500 Jewish businesses were smashed and gutted, and 177 synagogues burned down or otherwise demolished. By the morning of November 10th, ninety-one Jews had been killed, thousands more seriously injured, and most of the rest had been at least beaten, humiliated and terrorized. Throughout all of this, the civilian police, on orders from Adolf Hitler, stood by and allowed the slaughter to proceed.

"Our own *Kristallnacht* in America was much worse, Stephen. Words cannot begin to describe the violence and the terror.

"On a night just ten months after Douglas McKittrick's assassination, mobs of religious fanatics attacked the gay communities from Portland, Maine to San Diego, California. The cities that had identifiable gay ghettos were especially hard hit — the Castro, the Montrose, P'town, West Hollywood, Greenwich Village.

"It was a Sunday, and their preachers had spent the day getting them all hyped up. Gay businesses were trashed. Gay men and women were killed, beaten and mutilated. Pickup trucks loaded with rednecks and bearing the kind of bumper stickers we always used to see only in places like Mississippi and Alabama — *Kill A Queer For Jesus Christ* — roamed the streets looking for victims. And, just as in Nazi Germany, the police stood by and did nothing.

"When morning came, seven hundred and sixty-three gay men and women had been brutally killed. Eleven thousand more of us had been beated or otherwise injured. These figures probably include quite a few straights who either looked suspicious or else just got caught in the wrong place at the wrong time, such as a disco. There was not a gay business that had survived until now that was left standing, anywhere in the United States. Every one of our newspapers and other periodicals — the few that were still publishing — had been destroyed.

"Not one single victim was ever able to recover from their insurance, if they still had any, on the grounds that violence, civil insurrections, and Acts of God were covered by the exclusion clauses of all standard insurance policies. As for the twenty million of us, approximately, who survived, all we could do was lick our wounds and slink back into the closet; this time, it seemed, for keeps."

Then they started the DIVAF program.

5

They were still in the restaurant, although the waiter had already cleared their plates. Ashcroft's eyes were glazed over with pain at the thought of his lover, Troy, behind barbed wire. Aaron Ten Eyck signaled the waiter and ordered Ashcroft a double shot of green Chartreuse.

"He was one of the first ones they caught," Ashcroft said. "He had a spiked profile that went right through the top of the curve. A wealthy gay Yuppie — what else could you expect?"

"I'd suggest you drink that," said Aaron Ten Eyck. "It'll either kill you or cure you." He squeezed Ashcroft's arm affectionately. "Some day it will all end well, dear lad. You'll see."

Ashcroft suddenly realized how fond he had become of the old man. He sipped the potent green liqueur. "Some day, Aaron, I'd love to hear *your* story. If I may, that is."

The elderly merchant was pensive for a moment. "All right, Stephen," he finally said. "I've never told it to anyone before, but perhaps it's time I did. How about dinner at my home one day next week?"

"I'd like that very much."

Ten Eyck paid the check. "Well, past my bedtime, I fear. I'll drive you home, or wherever else you'd like to go."

"Drop me at the Leidseplein," requested Ashcroft. "I think I'll go to the Viking Bar for a while."

It was, Ashcroft thought, characteristic of Ten Eyck that he drove a luxurious but unostentatious Volvo, and that he drove himself without a chauffeur.

The Viking Bar was packed and smoky, filled with a mixed crowd of hustlers, locals, travelers and disco types. As soon as Kiki saw Ashcroft walk in, his face brightened, and he rushed over to greet him at the bar.

"I have to go on stage now, Stephen, but afterward I will join you for a drink. There is someone I want to introduce to you."

"That sounds ominous. Have you taken some fat German traveling salesman as your new lover?"

Kiki grinned boyishly. "You'll see."

When he had danced his number, stripping down to his G-string as he did so, and had collected all the guilders, marks, francs and pounds that the audience threw at his feet, he rejoined Ashcroft at the bar. With him, to Ashcroft's enormous suprise, was a slender, angelic-looking blond boy who looked about fourteen years old.

"Stephen, this is Anton, my new friend. Anton, this is my American friend Stephen, whom I have told you all about."

"I am honored, Mijnheer," said the boy admiringly, giving him a formal, grown-up handshake. "Of all of our American refugees, you are very greatly loved and respected."

He really can't be over fourteen, thought Ashcroft, not with that cherubic face that doesn't even show peach-fuzz yet. His English was not quite as good as Kiki's, but still much better than Ashcroft's Dutch.

"Anton, why don't you go dance for a while. Stephen and I wish to talk." With a bright, happy smile, the boy obeyed and went off to the dance floor.

"He's adorable," said Ashcroft. "Yours?"

"It is a problem, Stephen. I think I am in love with you, and Anton thinks he is in love with me."

"Why is that a problem, Kiki? I'm not jealous. You know I have a lover of my own, and that we still hope to be together again some day. Why shouldn't you have someone of your own, too?"

"Stephen, he is not for me! Not as a lover, anyway. Oh, I do love him, yes, but not in the way I love you! I love him as a little brother, a dear friend. And there is one other thing that I enjoy with him that I have never been allowed to enjoy with you. Just in regards to the sex part, I mean."

Ashcroft was startled. "What on earth might that be, Kiki? I thought it was strictly no-limits with us."

"That's because you are so blind, Stephen! You may not have realized it, but to you I am just your little Oriental boy, your young androgynous sex toy whom you take just as you would take a woman from the cribs. But to Anton I am much more than that. To him I am his *man!* Can you understand that, Stephen?"

"Yes, Kiki, of course I can. But I don't think you're being quite fair! You of all people should know that I'm not hung up on sexual role-playing. Why should you think that we couldn't be anything to each other sexually that we want to be?"

"You say that now, Stephen, but you never gave that impression before. It was always, 'Turn over, Kiki,' 'Get your legs in the air, Kiki,' 'Bend over the washstand, Kiki.' Admit it, Stephen; you've never treated me like a real man. Anton does, and it's delightful! I love it! I love being the husband in the family for a change."

"Then what's the problem? You and Anton become lovers, and live happily ever after."

"But I'm still in love with you, Stephen! I enjoy your loving. I would like to wake up every morning in your arms. But I would also like to wake up every morning with Anton in mine."

Like most men his age, Ashcroft sometimes found it difficult to take seriously enough the romantic problems of the very young. He always had the feeling that a teenage boy's heart is extremely elastic, and even if stretched almost to the breaking point, snaps resiliently back just as quickly as a new interest appears on the scene.

He doesn't know what a real problem is, thought Ashcroft. Even though his parents are dead, he's never missed a meal in his life. He's never had to dodge bullets, or live in fear of the police of his own country, or had a lover in a detention camp.

Aloud he said to Kiki, "It would seem there is only one solution to your problem."

"And what is that, my friend?"

"Obviously, a *ménage à trois*. That way Anton would have you, and you would have me, and I would have both of you." As he said it, he was half-joking, not quite sure how Kiki would react. The boy looked dubious.

"I don't know, Stephen. I'm not sure how Anton would take to the idea. He's very young, you know, not quite sixteen."

Still only half-serious, Ashcroft said "Well, there's only way to find out, isn't there?"

When Anton returned to the bar, Kiki spoke to him in Dutch. Ashcroft understood that he was telling the younger boy that they were both invited back to Stephen's hotel for a nightcap, and that Stephen was not just a trick but a very dear friend.

Anton's reaction surprised both of them. He threw his arms around Ashcroft's neck, climbed onto his lap, and kissed him long and hard on the mouth. His breath, thought Ashcroft, was sweet as only that of a young boy can be. Finally, pulling back from the kiss but still nestled in Ashcroft's lap, he said,

"If you are a dear friend of my Kiki, then I love you, too!" To Kiki he said in Dutch that of course they should spend the night together with Ashcroft.

They took a cab back to the Leather Eagle Hotel, where Hartt was just closing the bar. The slender English bartender rolled his eyes heavenward as Ashcroft walked in with Kiki and the younger boy.

"Blimey, it's kindergarten time again! I say, Ashcroft, why the hell don't you just decorate your room with nursery rhyme pictures and alphabet blocks, you bloody paedophile!"

"Oh, stuff it, Hartt, before I decide never to let you rape me again. How about a nightcap before we go up?"

"You'd better take the whole bloody bottle, although I really should send up a tray of nice hot cocoa and some jam tarts. Here, now, hold on a minute." He took down a set of room keys. "You'd better not try to use your own little cubbyhole or you won't have room to do anything. Take the VIP room; it has everything you'll need for a pleasant evening."

Ashcroft squeezed his hand as he took the keys. "Thanks, Hartt. You're a real pal."

Compared to Ashcroft's room, the VIP room was luxurious. For one thing, it had its own bathroom, with plumbing that worked. The bedroom was wallpapered in imitation white brick, with a huge butcher-block bed. Since this was, after all, a leather hotel, there was a sling and various other built-in paraphernalia for dungeon sex. Ashcroft didn't think they'd be using any of that.

There was also a small refrigerator that the hotel kept stocked with an assortment of beer, sodas and mixers. Ashcroft drank his *oude genever*, Kiki sipped a beer, and young Anton drank a lemon squash.

There was a brand new aura of masculinity, almost of authority, emanating from Kiki as he sat sprawled in his chair. Ashcroft felt it almost tangibly, and found it very exciting. He didn't know what was going to happen next, but he had every expectation of enjoying it.

With a snap of his fingers, Kiki pointed Anton in the direction of Ashcroft's feet. Obediently, the cherubic, rosy-cheeked blond Dutch boy knelt in front of the older man and gently, almost reverently, removed his boots. Ashcroft caressed the kid's head, playing with his golden blond hair as the boy rested his cheek against Ashcroft's leg. Then Kiki got up from his chair, came over to the two of them, and drew them both to their feet. Embracing them lovingly, he kissed each of them in turn.

"Let's get undressed," he said, and the two boys proceeded to help Ashcroft remove his clothing. Before they could do anything, Anton whispered something to Kiki in Dutch. Kiki grinned broadly and said to Ashcroft,

"He was too shy to ask, but he wants us all to take a shower together." By way of explanation, he added, "He's very fastidious, Stephen. He likes to take a bath or a shower *before* and *after*."

There was plenty of room in the huge shower stall for the three of them. The water was more of a trickle than a flow, and barely warm enough, but better than nothing. Once again Ashcroft thought wistfully of American plumbing.

Ashcroft stood to one side for a moment and watched as the two boys soaped each other, the lather glistening on their smooth, hairless bodies. Both of their cocks were erect. Kiki raised Anton's arms and gently soaped his armpits, then pulled him into an embrace as he lathered the younger boy's behind.

When they had finished soaping each other, they pulled Ashcroft underneath the shower and began to soap him too, Anton in front, Kiki in back. He could feel his own cock stiffen and rise.

Slowly, sensuously, Anton soaped his chest, his stomach, his thighs. At the same time, Kiki was soaping Ashcroft's buttocks, gently inserting a couple of fingers and making certain the orifice was smooth with lather. Ashcroft almost went out of his mind as Kiki gently but firmly massaged his prostate as Anton continued to fondle him also.

Kiki's slender brown arms were firmly around Ashcroft, playing with his nipples, squeezing them to the point of pain. Then he continued to manipulate Ashcroft as they stood beneath the warm running water, while the young blond boy's hands worked pure magic, bringing Ashcroft closer, ever closer.

Great ripples and waves of sensation exploded through every inch of Ashcroft's body. His knees went weak and he felt himself leaning back into Kiki's arms as the boy, braced against the shower wall, supported him. He heard Kiki's delighted little yelps of pleasure and felt himself squeezed ever tighter in those slender but strong brown arms as the Indonesian boy burst forth against his thighs. At the same time Anton was stroking himself to completion.

Exhausted, they clung to each other under the stream of water, now growing ever cooler.

"Let's get out of here before we freeze," said Ashcroft. They stood on the wet tiles of the bathroom floor and toweled each other dry. The towels in the VIP room were much larger and thicker than the threadbare ones in his own room.

For a moment Anton had tears in his eyes as he turned to Kiki and said something Dutch, but they were the brief and fleeting tears of childhood. Kiki translated,

"He says you remind him of his Papi, his Daddy. When he was little, his father used to carry him to bed and tuck him in."

"Go turn down the bed," said Ashcroft. He wrapped the boy in a towel and picked him up in his arms. Anton clung to him, kissing him passionately on the mouth as Ashcroft carried him to the bed.

"We'll put him in between us," said Kiki. "That way he'll have both of us to cuddle with."

They dozed for a while and then awakened and made love again. In the dim light of the room, Ashcroft watched as his little Kiki rolled on a condom and made manly love to Anton, the younger boy's legs wrapped around Kiki's torso, his arms clinging to Kiki's shoulders, their lips pressed tightly against each other. Just before they reached their completion, Anton stretched out one arm and guided Ashcroft's hand toward his groin. The older man took the sweet young boycock with pleasure, stroking him eagerly as Kiki thrust and drove him to a roaring climax.

Afterwards, they sat up in bed and talked while sipping a final nightcap.

Anton's parents had died only six months apart when he was eleven, and he had left the dairy farm that they had managed and come to Amsterdam to live with his uncle and aunt. Although he still attended school during the day, they completely disapproved of his evening life as a go-go boy and occasional hustler. Their family ties made them feel obligated to let him continue to live with them, but still, it was not a happy life.

Kiki's parents had died in a plane crash. In a few more months he would be coming into his inheritance, which, although modest, would enable him to travel and study. He dreamed of being an artist. Ashcroft didn't care to talk much about himself, as Kiki had already told Anton all about him and his life as a refugee and expatriate. However, he did tell them about his night at Greasy Grossberg's penthouse in Luxembourg. The boys listened eagerly, and screamed delightedly when he described the obese, hard-drinking writer and his two slaveboys.

After that, they were silent and serious for a moment, until Kiki spoke up.

"Listen, both of you," he said. "I think I have an idea. Not something for tonight or tomorrow night, but for all three of us to consider for the future."

"I'm listening," said Ashcroft.

"All right, then, consider this. Anton lives with his aunt and uncle. They don't treat him badly, but they are old-fashioned and religious and would be just as happy if he lived somewhere else. I, as you know, have no place of my own; I just house-sit for whichever one of my benefactors is traveling abroad at the moment, or else I rent a cheap little room. And you, Stephen, a man like you, living in this shabby little hotel when you have stayed in palaces! No, this cannot be. We must make other arrangements."

"What are you suggesting, Kiki?" asked Ashcroft.

"Surely, between the three of us, we could have a place of our own. We could fix it up the way we like, and keep it warm enough so you would not feel our Dutch winters, and we would cook good Dutch and Indonesian meals for you, and once in a while if we weren't very hungry, we would let you fix American food for us. And at night we would all sleep together."

"Well," said Ashcroft after a moment's silence, "it's something to consider." He did not mention that he was living under threat of extradition — or, worse, retaliation of a kind that would put these two children into danger.

Anton piped up in his halting English. "I think it is a wonderful idea. That way I would have a lover *and* once again a Papi." He kissed them each in turn.

"We'll give it some thought," said Ashcroft.

"Okay," said Kiki, "and while you're thinking about it, I will be looking around for a nice little flat for the three of us."

Yeah, sure, thought Ashcroft skeptically. And the three of us will live happily ever after, until somehow Troy gets out of the camp and joins us and then all four of us will live happily ever after. That's only in storybooks, you foolish children, only in storybooks.

But oh, how he wished that it could have happened!

DID THE BOILED FROG SYNDROME
START HERE?

"I daresay," said Aaron Ten Eyck, "that there's been quite a bit of speculation about me."

Once again, they were sitting, relaxed, in Aaron's spacious library. They had dined on an enormous roast goose stuffed with a prune and apricot stuffing that Ashcroft had felt certain he wouldn't like, but which turned out to be delicious. Accompanying the goose were rich noodles and gravy, and sweet-and-sour red cabbage, German style.

"You mean," replied Ashcroft, "are you or aren't you?"

"Yes, precisely."

"Well, you are somewhat of a mystery man, you know."

"Mystery man? Dear me, do they think me some sort of Count Dracula, then?"

"Not quite that, Aaron. Everyone knows that you're an extremely popular and well-liked member of the Royal Dutch Parliament and that you are also a rather prosperous diamond merchant. But your name has never been linked with anyone, male or female. Frankly, your mysterious life had titillated the scandalmongers and gossip columnists on a global scale for many years. I read a big spread about you in *People* magazine many years ago, never dreaming that one day we'd become such good friends. The piece was called 'Mystery Mogul of Amsterdam.'"

Aaron shook his head in dismay. "I'm afraid I shall never quite understand the vicarious thrill that people derive from burrowing and grubbing about into the private lives of others. Does it never occur to them that behind my so-called mysterious life there is very simply no mystery at all?"

"All right, then," said Ashcroft, "appease my own prurient curiosity. *Are* you or *aren't* you, or am I being impertinent to ask?"

Aaron chuckled. "It's not quite that simple, my boy."

"Let me ask you one question. Has there ever been one great love in your life?"

The old man did not answer at first. Finally he said,

"Why don't I put this decanter of excellent English port on the table between us, so you can help yourself at will? Then I think it is time that I finally told someone the story that I have kept buried for over fifty years. I ask only one condition of you, however."

"Not to publish?"

"Precisely. At least not until after I am gone. When I am dead and buried, you may put my story into verse, novel, screenplay, epic poem, television episode, or whatever you choose. But until then, mum's the word, right?"

"You have my word, Aaron." He took a sip of his port as the strange narrative commenced.

You must remember, (Aaron Ten Eyck began), that we Dutch Jews are a very special breed.

When the Jews of Spain were expelled from that country in 1492, the very day before Christopher Columbus was to have set sail on his voyage of discovery, they left behind them their homes, their possessions, in some cases their wealth, but in every case a life and cultural heritage that had endured for hundreds of years as part of the very fabric of the country, until the forces of the Inquisition put an end to all that.

Thus began the second Diaspora, the second great dispersion that took our people to the ghettos of Venice, the forests of Germany and Austria, and eventually to the mud villages and *stetls* of Russia and Poland. My ancestors did not follow that dispersion. They settled right here in Amsterdam, and somehow endured. During the times of Catholic persecution, they simply kept a low profile and managed to survive.

With the end of Spanish imperialism in Europe in 1587 (although Spain's hegemony over her New World dominions did not completely and finally end until 1821), we began to enjoy a measure of freedom that we had not known before, especially after the advent of the Kingdom of the Netherlands. Eventually we prospered, gained wealth and influence, and sometimes even intermarried.

My upbringing was fairly typical of that of a Jewish boy of wealth and position at that time. My family was one of the leading diamond families in this city. Another was the Cardozos. It had been more or less understood that when the time came, I would marry Rebecca Cardozo, a girl of about my own age. There was no formal betrothal, just an understanding. Our families had been close to each other for generations; Rebecca and I had gone to school together and were very close friends. We read books together, played chess together, and frolicked together at family picnics. We were never sweethearts, never lovers; we just had a tremendous liking and friendship for each other. And that, I think, is frequently a far better basis for marriage than the sort of passion that poets write about.

In those days, I simply did not think about my sexuality. It was never a part of my life. I knew that when the time came, I would be able to arouse my feelings sufficiently to do my husbandly duties for Rebecca Cardozo. Since we both envisioned a happy and lifelong marriage based upon affection and companionship rather than grand passion, I foresaw no difficulty in that regard. Aside from that, I vaguely knew all about every single aspect of human sexuality, but only from books and conversation. As the war clouds gathered over Europe, I remained a virgin.

My days were quite fully taken up with going to college, along with the bare minimum of Talmudic study expected of a member of the Jewish community. In addition, I was commencing my apprenticeship in my father's diamond business.

In early 1939, with the blessing of my parents, I joined the Royal Dutch Air Force as a flying cadet, but no sooner had I received my commission and my wings when war broke out at the beginning of September. Despite everyone's assurances that the Low Countries were safe and that Hitler's armies could never defeat the Maginot Line, I chose to resign for the purpose of joining the R.A.F. in England.

In the early days of the war, there was no problem in getting out ahead of the Nazis; one simply packed one's bags and went. The problem was to convince people of the *necessity* of getting out at all! Even my father, who should have known better, managed to convince himself that the mighty German armies would never attack tiny Holland, and even if they did — well, as the Yanks say, money talks, and even the Germans respect good diamonds. Of course the Germans never bothered to defeat the Maginot Line; they simply flanked it, and overran the Low Countries.

My father eventually got out with the clothes on his back (into which he had sewn a few choice diamonds), and he and my mother made their way to Lisbon in neutral Portugal and from there to Argentina, where, with the assistance of the large Jewish community already there, he established his business and eventually prospered. The Cardozo family also escaped to Argentina, and after the war I was able to correspond with Rebecca, who had married very well into a prominent Argentine Jewish family.

In England, I did indeed join the Royal Air Force, but to my great dismay I was rejected as a fighter pilot. I'm afraid I was simply too large and tall to fit into the cockpit of a Spitfire or a Hurricane. I was assigned to a bomber squadron based at an enormous flying base near the Dover coast. There were also several fighter squadrons at the same station.

With the fall of France and the heroic evacuation of the British troops from Dunkirk, it was now apparent that the war was going to be with us for a good long while. Knowing that my family was safely out of Holland, I simply dug in for the duration and prepared to face death with honor every single day. One did what one had to do; indeed, what one was brought up to do. At the back of one's mind, one could be vaguely aware that we had all been duped and betrayed by the politicians, and that the whole sorry mess need never have happened at all, but that could not be allowed to deter one from trying to do one's part in coping with the dreadful situation presently at hand.

We were in a sorry mess, I can assure you. Had Hitler's astrologers not dissuaded him from invading England following the Dunkirk evacuation, we should very probably have been completely overrun. We stood almost totally alone against the Hun, with the exception of the overseas dominions, Canada and Australia and New Zealand, which were, of course, heavily commited and involved. The United States was still neutral and would remain so until the Japanese bombed Pearl Harbor in December of 1941, but at least they were finally starting to send us supplies and aircraft.

Wartime England was hardly the place one would have wished to visit on a Cook's tour. The Blitz had started, with nightly or almost nightly air raids by the Jerries against our blacked-out cities. Everything was tightly rationed, and almost every conceivable commodity soon became very scarce. Yet there was a spirit of defiance, of bravado, of *camaraderie*, as fighting men from all over the Nazi-occupied areas of Europe arrived on our tight little isle — Free Dutch, Free French, Free Polish, and so on. Many were flyers who promptly joined the beleaguered R.A.F. We were, in fact, the valiant little band about whom Winston

Churchill said, "Never have so many owed so much to so few." I don't quite know whether we were terribly brave, or simply desperate. To a man, we all knew what would happen to us if England fell.

So there I was at the age of twenty, commanding a bomber crew, never knowing how long the war would last or whether I was fated to survive another week. It was under these conditions that a young Jewish fighter pilot from Canada entered my life, and from then on nothing was ever quite the same for me, not ever again.

2

While all this was going on (as Ashcroft was later to reconstruct the tale from Ten Eyck's recorded narrative plus the copies of letters, diaries and photographs that he also turned over to him), during the grimmest years of the Great Depression a young Jewish boy named Herschel Cohen was growing up in Toronto, Canada.

He was a strikingly handsome kid with strong, dark-complected features and thick, curly black hair. Both brainy and athletic, he excelled equally at sports and scholastics. He had the usual hobbies of a middle-class Jewish kid back in the nineteen-thirties: books, stamps, chess, model airplanes and politics. He also had a pair of very loving parents. But by far the greatest joy in his life was his brother Joey.

The two boys could not have been more different. Although Joey was older by exactly one year, it became apparent very early on that it was Herschel who was the strong one, the leader. Joey was tall for his age, blond, and thin almost to the point of emaciation. He was studious, shy and scholarly and afraid of physical violence; even when Herschel was nine and Joey was ten, if they were being picked on by a gang of Gentile boys, it was Herschel who had to do the fighting, wading in with his little fists flying to send the *shaygetzes* scurrying back to their own neighborhood with bloody noses and more than one or two black eyes. Then he would put his arm around the taller Joey's shoulders and lead the crying boy home, remonstrating,

"You've gotta learn to *fight*, Joey! The *goyim* will *kill* you if you let them!"

"I'm sorry, Heschy," Joey would blubber as Herschel gave him his handkerchief. "I guess I'm just not a fighter."

"You sure ain't," Herschel would reply, as he squeezed his brother's shoulder even more tightly. Herschel saw the world as a hostile place in which it was his duty to fight Gentiles, run off stray dogs, and watch out for traffic in order to make life more bearable for his beloved Joey.

Their parents were of old-world immigrant stock who, at the turn of the century, had fled the savagery of the pogroms of Czarist Russia. Both their families had lived in the White Russian Pale, an area where Jewish settlement was permitted.

Malka Cohen (née Davidovitch) still recalled her final memories of Mother Russia. As a little girl, perhaps five or maybe even seven, she was standing on the upper deck of a river steamer holding tightly to the hands of her mother and older sister, as the Captain bellowed for the gangplank to be raised and the riverboat slipped its moorings in the very nick of time. From the high upper deck, they watched in horror as the band of drunken Cossacks on horseback, sabers drawn, swept through the little village, killing, looting, pillaging, and setting fire to the Jewish homes.

The steamer took them to Gomel, a larger city where they lived for a while. Here they had more to fear from the Czar's secret police than from bands of drunken Cossacks. Malka's father was dead, but her mother somehow managed to provide for her and her sister until the two oldest sisters, who had already emigrated to America, were able to send for them.

She met David Cohen in Brooklyn in 1916, at a dance hosted by one of the Jewish fraternal organizations. Although not handsome and dashing, there was an air of competence, almost of serenity, about him. He had fled from a *stetl* not far from Malka's native village which she had watched the Cossacks burn. Arriving in New York penniless and without a word of English, he had quickly studied the language, gone to night school, and worked in the sweatshops of the garment industry for six dollars a week. Determined to rise in his new country, he had learned the trade of cutter, and then, eventually, become shop foreman. When he and

Malka met and fell in love, he was earning a fabulous twenty-three dollars a week, and thus was well able to support a family.

A cousin had earlier moved to Toronto and opened a factory in that city's thriving garment industry. When the First World War ended in 1918, needing a reliable family member to help him with his expansion of the business, he offered David Cohen a partnership. David and Malka, who was pregnant with her first child, moved to Toronto in 1919. Yussel (later Anglicized to Joey) was born in that year, and Herschel in 1920.

In their very modest way, they prospered. There was never quite enough money for a new car, but there was always a good second-hand one for picnics and family outings, although during the week David Cohen rode the streetcar each day, just as his employees did, to the factory in an ancient loft building at the corner of Spadina and Adelaide Streets, then the center of the city's "schmatteh" business.

There was always money for books — the walls of the living-room and dining-room were lined with them. There was also enough money for theater, opera, ballet, although usually in the balcony rather than the orchestra section. And of course they ate very well; Malka prided herself on setting a lavish table. Such were the priorities of a typical lower-middle-class family of Jewish intelligentsia of that era: food first, culture second, and *goyische* foolishness at the end of the list. Once or twice a year they took the train for the day-long trip to New York to visit their relatives.

They spoke Yiddish to each other, but always English in front of the boys, whom they wanted to grow up as thoroughly assimilated, Anglicized Canadians, but aware of their unique Jewish cultural heritage. They sent both boys to *cheder* after school three times a week to learn to read and write proper Yiddish and even a little Hebrew, and to learn Jewish history. Joey loved it; Herschel hated it. It interfered with his baseball in the spring, hockey in the winter, and football in the fall.

Malka and David never ceased to be amazed at the devotion of their sons to each other.

"You'd think just once," David said over a midnight bowl of borsht after working late at the shop, "just once they'd maybe have a quarrel? Even a fight?"

"*Ess und gedank,*" said Malka. "Eat and be thankful."

"They act more like sweethearts than brothers," said David, shaking his head. "A couple of *faegelehs* in this family I don't need."

"Bite your tongue," said Malka. "They need each other. Yussel needs someone to lean on, and Herschel needs someone to protect. Don't worry, they'll grow out of it."

But they didn't. They still slept together in the double bed that they had shared since they'd outgrown their cribs. To sleep apart, unable to cuddle in each other's arms, would have been quite unthinkable. David protested that they were getting too big to share their bed; Joey would be Bar-Mitzvah in a few months, and boys that age should have their own beds. But when Malka suggested it, Joey burst into tears and left the room, and Herschel's reaction was spontaneous and indignant.

"Mamma, he's my *brother*, for gosh sake! We've been sleeping together since we were little kids! If we had twin beds, Mamma, neither one of us could *sleep* that far away from each other!" And then, when Malka looked at him sharply, he said, "Don't even think what I think you're thinking, Mamma. We ain't gonna fool around like the Gentile kids do, okay? Besides, our room's not big enough for twin beds."

"So what's wrong with bunk beds?" she suggested.

He replied with a withering glance and went off to reassure his brother.

Thus, they continued to sleep together, with Joey, afraid of the dark and of nightmares, cuddled securely in the arms of his younger, stronger brother.

But eventually they did fool around.

It was the night of Joey's Bar-Mitzvah, one of the few occasions in traditional Jewish life when it is acceptable to get a bit smashed. Traditionally, Jews are not supposed to be drunkards. From a very early age, they drink at the table with family, they take a shot of *schnapps* on a cold winter morning, and of course there is wine at the dinner table. But getting drunk is frowned upon. "*Shikur vi a goy,*" goes the Yiddish expression; "Drunk like a Gentile."

A Bar-Mitzvah, however, is one of the exceptions, like the Feast of Purim. The house was filled with relatives, friends and well-wishers, and the whiskey, beer and champagne flowed freely. Even David Cohen was drunk, for perhaps the third time in his life, the two previous occasions having been his own Bar-Mitzvah and his wedding night.

Suddenly, both Malka and Herschel observed the Bar-Mitzvah Boy sitting in a chair with his eyes closed; he had gone dead-white and he was perspiring. They both rushed over to him.

"*Yusseleh, Yusseleh, vus gibst mit dir?*" screamed his mother.

"I'm okay, Mamma," the boy replied. "I just felt a little dizzy for a second, that's all."

"Maybe I should take you upstairs to bed," said Malka.

"I'll take him," said Herschel, very firmly. "You take care of our guests, Mamma, I'll take care of my brother. Don't worry, I'll holler if there's anything wrong and we need you." He pulled Joey to his feet and supported him with Joey's arm around his shoulder, and managed to make a reasonably dignified exit from the party without creating a scene.

"My big brother's a little bit *shikur*, that's all," he told the nearest guests, making a joke out of it. "I'm gonna put him to bed."

But as soon as they were out of sight of the merrymakers, Herschel picked up his taller, slenderer brother over his shoulders and carried him quickly up the stairs. Once they were in their room, he laid Joey on the bed, then closed the door and locked it.

"What's wrong, man?" he asked anxiously. "You didn't have nothin' to drink, I watched you. You're not drunk."

"I know," said Joey. "Grab a towel from the dresser, will you? I'm sweating like hell."

Tenderly, Herschel undressed him and got him into his pajamas. The boy was soaked in perspiration, but at the same time shivering and cold.

"Get under the covers, Joey. I'll turn up the heat. When you're feeling better I'll go back downstairs."

"Please don't leave me, Heschy."

"Okay, I won't." He sat on the bed holding his brother's hand and occasionally wiping his forehead with the towel. "The party was getting ready to break up, anyway."

After awhile, the sound of the guests leaving died away. In a few minutes Malka knocked on the door.

"Pretend you're sleeping peacefully," ordered Herschel. "I've gotta let her look at you, but I don't want her making a big fuss." He opened the door. "It's okay, Mamma. He just had a shot of *schnapps* too many."

Their father stood behind her in the doorway, his face worried. "Are you *sure*, Heschy? We should call a doctor, maybe?"

"No! Just leave him alone! In the morning he'll be fine! I'm taking care of him, okay?"

"Well, all right," said Malka. "Please don't let him be sick in bed. You want I should bring you a basin in case he can't make it to the bathroom?"

"Mamma, will you two *please* get *out* of here? You'll wake him up!"

When they had gone, Herschel again locked the bedroom door, slipped off his clothes and started to put on his pajamas.

"Please don't wear those tonight," said Joey. "I want us to sleep bare-ass together, like we do in the summer."

"But Joey, this isn't summer, it's winter."

"It's warm enough in here. Okay, Heschy?" Still weak, he slipped out of his own pajamas.

Herschel got into bed and put his arms around his brother, who clung to him, shivering, although it was hot under the covers.

"Heschy, I'm scared. Hold me tight."

"I've got you, babe." He squeezed his brother so hard he was afraid something must break.

"Something's wrong, Heschy. I'm real scared. That wasn't just some ordinary dizzy spell."

"What the hell was it? Are you sick?"

"I don't know, man. All of a sudden it just felt like everything was draining out of me inside."

"You'll be okay, Joey." His lips brushed the older boy's forehead as his hands caressed the smooth, cool flesh. Something, a violent new passion, was raging inside of him.

After a few minutes, Joey stopped shivering, but he still clung to Herschel tightly. His hand began to caress his brother's body, already sturdy and well-developed. His lips were against Herschel's ear. He spoke very softly.

"Heschy?"

"Yeah, babe?"

"You know how the Gentile kids fool around with each other?"

Herschel knew exactly how the Gentile kids fooled around with each other. For the past six months, ever since he'd had his first wet dream while sleeping in his brother's arms, he'd done quite a bit of fooling around himself, and not just with Gentile kids, either. He could have given his older brother a long list of their own buddies, nice Jewish kids, who liked to fool around.

"I know all about that, Joey. What are you trying to tell me?" he said, feeling his brother's smooth, naked body pressed tightly against his own. His cock was raging.

His brother's hand slipped farther down and encircled Herschel's large, stiff organ. "I want you to bum-fuck me, Heschy. I've never fooled around with anyone before, and you know I couldn't do it with anyone except you."

"You really want me to stick it in your ass, Joey?" He knew that he could never refuse anything his brother needed of him.

"Please, Heschy, I need you real bad. I want to feel you inside of me." He raised his head slightly and for the first time, their lips met in more than a fleeting, affectionate way. Electric currents surged between them as their tongues entered each other's mouth, their hands feverishly caressed each other. Then Joey turned over onto his side with his back to Herschel.

"I'll try not to hurt you too much, babe," said Herschel. He took some hair dressing from the nightstand and gently lubricated them both. "Okay, here I come."

There was a muffled sob from the older boy as Herschel entered him, and then a sigh of fulfillment.

"Oh, my God, Heschy, that feels great! Don't stop, man, please, just don't stop!"

Herschel rolled Joey over onto his stomach and lay on top of him, his arms and legs wrapped around him as he pumped himself into his beloved brother. "Joey, I can't hold it much longer. Joey, get ready. Joey! JOEY! YEAHHHH! Joey! Oh, shit, they're right next door. I hope they didn't hear us."

"They're sound asleep. I could hear them snoring while you were fucking me. And anyway, I don't care who knows! Heschy, listen, I know you'll think I'm nuts, but I've got this funny feeling we don't have a hell of a lot of time. So just in case something happens, let's make the most of the time we have, okay?"

"Nothing's going to happen to you, babe. I won't let it. I never have, have I?"

Whatever was wrong with his brother, Herschel determined, he'd fight it off just as he fought off the Gentile kids and the stray dogs. Nothing would ever take Joey away from him.

From that night on, they made love every night, sometimes twice a night, sometimes in the morning before getting up to go to school. Joey seemed to thrive on it. At times some color came back into his cheeks, as though he were drawing strength and sustenance from his brother's lovemaking.

When summer came, they went off to camp together, where they shared a tent and found a whole new world of opportunity to make love — outdoors in the woods, in a rowboat drifting on a lonely Northern Ontario lake, or in the hayloft of an abandoned barn. The camp counselors gave them many demerits for spending so much time off by themselves, but they didn't care.

The episode of the night of Joey's Bar-Mitzvah was not the last, by any means. Numerous others followed. There was no doubt that he was getting steadily weaker as his strength and vitality failed. Malka took him from doctor to doctor, from clinic to clinic, but none of them could find anything organically wrong.

"He's just not a very strong boy," said one doctor. "All you can do is keep him well nourished and try not to let him catch cold."

They prescribed a glass of sherry in the morning, a bottle or two of stout or cream porter in the evening, and lots of red meat at dinner, along with plenty of fresh vegetables.

"They're trying to turn my son into a *shikur*," complained David Cohen. "Booze, booze, booze, morning, noon and night. And red meat! With the price of meat nowadays I'll be bankrupt. How much is prime rib roast these days, Malka?"

"Thirty-five cents a pound. Oh, David, we can afford it, you know that! I just don't understand — one boy so strong and healthy, the other so — so *schvach* all the time."

"He doesn't get it from *my* side of the family," said David. "Herschel takes after me. You've got that White Russian blood in you, Malka; thin and blond and weak. Somebody in your family let a *shaygetz* in the house one night." She through a dishtowel at him, and then they hugged and kissed. They were still in love.

There were days when Joey was too weak to go to school. Herschel would come home from class, throw his books aside, and go racing up the stairs.

"Heschy! You don't even say hello to your mother?"

"Hello, Mamma. How is he?"

She shrugged. "The same. No strength. Go, go ahead, go to him; he's been waiting for you."

Herschel would sit on the edge of the bed holding Joey's hand and tell him everything that had happened at school that day. When dinner time came, Malka would fix a tray.

"I'll take it up to him, Mamma. Please. You get dinner ready for Pop. I'll look after Joey."

If Joey was having a very bad day and was too weak to sit up to eat, Herschel would cradle his brother's head in the crook of his arm and feed him, one bite at a time.

"I don't want any more, Heschy. Please. I'm not hungry."

"You've gotta eat, babe! You've gotta get your strength back! I want to see you try out for the hockey team, okay?" This, despite the fact that Joey was possibly the only kid in the entire Dominion of Canada who didn't even own a pair of ice skates and a hockey stick.

"I *can't* eat, Heschy! I just don't want it. Here, you eat it for me so Mamma won't get mad."

"We'll take turns, Joey." He took a forkful, then gave Joey a forkful. "Man, this pot roast is great! And Mamma's *luxion kugel* — how can you not eat? Please, Joey, for me. One more bite." Little by little, he managed to get as much food as possible into his brother.

Joey never left his bed anymore. Malka would come into the room waving a bedpan, and Herschel would explode. "He doesn't need that, Mamma! Now will you please go downstairs? He doesn't like you to see he can't walk so good." When Malka had left, he would pick up Joey in his arms and carry him to the bathroom.

Then one day Herschel came home and Joey wasn't there. His father was home from work.

"We had to put him in the hospital, Heschy. He needs round-the-clock care."

Herschel pounded his fist on the table. "Can't they find out what's wrong with him, for gosh sake? Are they just going to let him die?"

"They're doing everything they can. It isn't cancer, it isn't leukemia, it isn't pernicious anemia. Dr. Chaikoff says he's just a kid who doesn't have the strength to live."

"What the hell does that *alteh kocker* know? Can't you get him some decent Gentile doctors?"

"Our own doctors are the best, son," said David. "You know that. Just to get to be a Jewish doctor in this country you have to be twice as good." Then he added gently, "Why don't you go visit him now?"

Herschel ran out of the house and caught the streetcar to Mount Sinai Hospital. His brother was lying in bed, an intravenous tube in his arm.

"I'm glad you came, Heschy," said Joey weakly. He clung to Herschel's hand. "Please stay with me as long as you can."

Herschel was on the verge of tears. "You can't do this to me, Joey! You're all I've got! You've got to get strong again."

"You've got Mamma and Pop. You're strong. You'll be okay. Just sit with me a while and I'll try not to doze off."

"How about a game of cards, Joey? Or maybe some chess?"

The boy shook his head weakly. "I can't, Heschy. I don't feel up to it. I just want to rest, okay?"

One week later, he died in his brother's arms. David and Malka had just taken a brief respite from their ceaseless vigil to go to the coffee shop, and it was as though Joey had waited until he and Herschel could be alone at the end. When the parents returned a few minutes later, they found Herschel rocking Joey's body in his arms, tears streaming down his face. Yussel Cohen would never again have to be afraid of nightmares, traffic, stray dogs, or Gentile kids.

3

From that moment on, Herschel threw himself into his activities with a feverish intensity. His grades were straight A's, as though he had to achieve now for both Joey and himself. He was also an all-city athlete. Always politically aware, he now joined the Young Pioneers, a Zionist youth organization, and, with the mixed blessings and misgivings of his parents, spent the summers of his fourteenth and fifteenth years in Palestine, working in a kibbutz.

For the Canadian kids in his group, it was a superb education paid for at the cost of some hard physical labor during the day. They met other Jewish kids of their own age group from all over North and South America and Europe. Yiddish was the common tongue at first, but they quickly learned Hebrew, that ancient Biblical language which had been revived as the official language of the new Jewish homeland.

In the evenings, the kids sat around a campfire singing folk songs to the accompaniment of a guitar, banjo or mandolin. Despite the fact that they were strictly chaperoned, illicit romances inevitably sprang up. Herschel, with his curly-headed dark good looks, attracted every other adolescent in the kibbutz. He made love to the local girls, to the local boys, to the Pioneer girls, to the Pioneer boys, and, for the first time, discovered the delights of Arab boys from the nearby settlements. When they weren't shooting at each other, they were making love.

At this time, Palestine was under the British Mandate, as it had been since the collapse of the Turkish Ottoman Empire following World War One; but under the terms of the Balfour Declaration: "His Majesty's Government views with favour the establishment of a Jewish national homeland in Palestine," there flourished the Pioneer movement which was later to culminate in the State of Israel. The Arabs, obviously, did *not* look with favor upon the enormous influx of Jewish pioneers and settlers.

The kibbutz, frequently under attack, had a defense perimeter and guards were posted all night. Although the Young Pioneers were supposed to be kept safe and guarded, Herschel broke the rules and volunteered for defense duties. He learned to ride a horse and to shoot a rifle.

Back in Toronto for the fall semester, Herschel realized sadly that the Cohen home was no longer a happy place. The spirit of their departed Joey weighed heavily upon them all. David Cohen moped around the house when he wasn't working long hours, trying to immerse himself in his books. Malka read novels and magazines and sewed and cooked, but without enthusiasm. Herschel came home only to do his homework and to sleep.

In 1936, the Spanish Civil War broke out. The rebel forces of the Falangist general, Francisco Franco, aided by planes, tanks and arms supplied by Nazi Germany and Fascist Italy, were determined to overthrow the Loyalist forces of the Republican government, which appealed to the Western powers for help but received in return an embargo and a blockade. From Europe and the Americas, some of the children of the Great Depression, unable to find work, or else fired by the idealism of the cause, saw a chance to fight abroad for the social justice they had not been able to attain at home. The legendary International Brigade was formed; from the United States came the Abraham Lincoln Battalion; from Canada, the Mackenzie-Papineau Battalion. The battle lines of World War Two had already been drawn.

To the dismay of Malka and David, Herschel Cohen announced that he intended to join the International Brigade and ship out to Spain to fight fascism.

"You're crazy," said his father. "Not only you're crazy, also you're only sixteen years old. Go do your homework."

"And not one more word about Spain," added Malka, "or I'll give you such a *shlog in kopp* you'll have a sore head for a week." She was always threatening to hit him, but never had.

"Please," said Herschel. "Just one more word."

"We're listening," said David.

"Mamma, Pop, you *know* what's going on over there! If we don't win, if the Loyalists don't win, you know we're going to be fighting Hitler and Mussolini in Europe in another two years! It's not just a civil war, for gosh sakes! It's our war, too!"

"Nobody's questioning that, son," replied David. "What you say is absolutely right. And I'll support the Loyalists, Heschy! I'll write them a check every week, and you can watch me sign it! But I'm not giving them the only son I got left!"

The next day after school, Herschel made contact, through

one of his political youth groups, with the local recruiter for the International Brigade. The office was in a dingy, smoked-filled union hall. The recruiter was a young Spanish officer who had already lost one arm in the earlier fighting in Zaragoza.

"You look too young, *joven*," said the officer. "How old are you?"

Herschel had never grown as tall as his brother. He would never grow taller than five feet, nine inches, but he was strong and very husky, with a football player's build.

"I'm eighteen," he lied. "And I've already fought in Palestine. I can drive a truck, ride a horse, and shoot a rifle."

"Any languages besides English?"

"Yiddish, Hebrew, and high school French. My parents taught me a little Russian, but I'm not fluent."

"Fill out this form and sign it, *por favor*. Be at Union Station tomorrow morning at eight o'clock. Your group will meet near the newsstand at the east end of the concourse. And *buena suerte, joven*."

In Spain, Herschel learned both guerrilla and convential warfare, using both Spanish and Russian-supplied equipment. He became fluent in Spanish. He learned to fly a light reconnaissance plane. He watched in horror as the dreaded German Stuka dive-bombers machine-gunned the civilian refugees who sometimes clogged the roads. To the German pilots, it was just target practice for World War Two.

In 1938, even before the fall of Barcelona, there was no longer any question that the war was lost. Many of the Loyalist forces fled into France, and the International Brigade was disbanded.

There was a huge rally in Toronto's Union Station the night the surviving Mac-Paps returned from Spain. Malka and David were there to help give their son and his comrades a hero's welcome. Once they had gotten over their shock at finding his note the morning he left, their feelings of dismay had gradually given way to pride. Malka had spent two years one-upping her Hadassah ladies and her B'nai B'rith friends. "So? Your husband gave five hundred dollars to the Loyalists? Big deal! I've got a son fighting in Spain!" There was no way anyone could top that.

Most of the returning veterans had no homes, no jobs, and no money. Herschel, after their tearful and joyous family reunion, introduced his parents to three of his combat buddies whom he'd invited to stay with the Cohens for a week, until they could make their own arrangements. To Malka and David's dismay, they weren't even Jewish; one was Ukrainian, a wheat farmer from Saskatchewan; one was Italian, a coal miner from Sudbury; and one, a lumberjack from British Columbia, was Anglo-Saxon. They were all much older than Herschel.

"Please, Mamma, it's just for a few days, okay?"

They all looked gaunt and hollow-eyed, more from their war experiences than from lack of food. One could read death in all their faces, especially in their eyes. Malka fed them lavishly, of course. By the time they left to go their separate ways, they all looked less gaunt and tired, and were a little less prone to dive under the nearest table and grab for an imaginary rifle if there was a thunderstorm or they heard the siren of an ambulance or police car.

"So, what now?" David Cohen asked his son when they were once again alone. "You've missed two years of school. I needed you in the business and you weren't there. Was it worth it?"

"It was a tragic waste, Pop. If Britain and the States had backed the Loyalists, we could have won. Instead, it was all for nothing."

"And you're still glad you went?"

"I'm still your son, Pop. You and Mamma are the ones who made me political. You're the ones who made me read books and learn the kind of history they don't teach in school."

"So what are you going to do now, Herschel?"

"Rest and take it easy until the next one. The big one."

"The *next one?* The *big one?* You're that sure?"

"I'm that sure, Pop. It's too late to stop them now. We could have stopped them in Spain, if we'd had the support. Now the Germans have marched into Austria, and even while we were fighting and dying in Spain, Neville Chamberlain gave away Czechoslovakia without even asking the Czechs about it."

Indeed, the Man With the Umbrella had returned from Munich, after making huge concessions to Adolph Hitler, proclaiming triumphantly, "Peace In Our Time," believing that appeasement could stop the Nazi juggernaut.

"You're not gonna be a *soldier* again?" demanded David Cohen. " A smart, educated Jewish boy like you?"

"I'm gonna be a fighter pilot, Pop."

"*Oy, veh is mir!* For God's sake don't tell your mother."

On September 1, 1939, the day the German armies marched into Poland, Herschel left again. He had very little money of his own, and was too proud to ask his parents for any, so he started hitch-hiking eastward. There were no freeways in those days, so it took him a day and a half of long waits and short local rides to reach the Ontario-Quebec provincial border, the boundary of French Canada.

The French-Canadians, who were anti-British, anti-war and notoriously anti-Semitic, were not likely to help a Jewish boy from Toronto make his way to England. Throughout the duration of World War Two, they continued to oppose the Canadian war effort. Although their young men were subject to conscription just like everybody else, they could be sent into combat only on a volunteer basis. Relatively few of the French-Canadian soldiers volunteered. The rest of the country referred contemptuously to these non-combat troops as "Zombies."

Using his excellent high school and International Brigade French, plus the little bit of Quebec patois he'd picked up over the years, Herschel was able to make his way. Arriving in Montreal on a rainy evening, he found a pool hall on Sherbrooke Street where he successfully hustled a few games of snooker, which bought him a great dinner and a room at the Y.M.C.A.

On September third, he was in a lower-working-class tavern in Quebec City when the news came over the radio that England and Germany had declared war against each other. The tavern went wild.

"*Vive les Boches!*" the men screamed. "*A bas les Anglais!*" It took all of Herschel's self-control not to start a brawl, but he wanted to smash every one of those smug Gallic faces. He would have been happy to walk out of Quebec Province to the New Brunswick border, but on the Trans-Canada Highway once again, a friendly truck driver from home gave him a ride.

When he finally arrived in Halifax, Nova Scotia, he looked up the local Jewish Community Center, which referred him to a kindly rabbi who took him into his home for the night. The rabbi's wife fed him a dinner that tasted almost as good as his mother's, and he told them about his adventures in Palestine and in Spain.

The rabbi said, "We have an emergency fund, you know. I can pay your way to Sydney so you won't have to hitchhike. No, no, *shemtzach-nisht!* Don't be ashamed! To help a good Jewish boy like you go fight Hitler, you'd deny me the privilege?"

So Herschel caught the train the next morning to Sydney, and from there took the ferry to Newfoundland and the bus to the Royal Canadian Air Force base at Gander. This was the staging depot for all eastbound military flights. He was promptly taken into custody by the military police, who thought he might be a spy. After questioning, he was taken in front of the base security officer.

"We caught him trying to sneak onto the base, Sir. Says he's trying to get to England."

"Is this right, eh?" Squadron-Leader Hamilton looked Herschel over and was impressed by what he saw. He ordered the guards to leave them alone, and poured Herschel a cup of coffee.

"Where are you from, son?"

"Toronto."

"Where did you go to school?"

"Harbord Collegiate."

"That's nice. I'm also from Toronto, but I went to Jarvis Collegiate."

"With all due respect, sir," said Herschel, "Harbord could kick Jarvis' ass at football any day of the week."

"You think so, eh?"

"I *know* so, sir. I played on the team."

They chatted amicably for a while, reminiscing about Toronto, talking about the war situation and about politics. Trying not to sound too doctrinaire, Herschel made known the intensity of his feelings. Finally, Squadron-Leader Hamilton picked up his phone and called Operations.

"Flight-Lieutenant Rogers, please. Tommy? George Hamilton here. Listen, I've got a crazy Jewish kid here from Toronto in my office who's so anxious to start killing Jerries that he can't even wait until our own people get over there. No, he's not a spy,

Tommy; I've never heard of a German spy who knew all the Toronto intercollegiate football scores for 1934 and 1935. Tommy, I'm giving you a direct order. I don't care how you do it, and I don't even want to know about it, but I want this lad on the next plane out, do you hear? Thanks, Tommy."

A day later, Herschel was in England, where he enlisted in the R.A.F. By the early months of 1940, he was flying a Spitfire. With his height of five feet, nine inches, he was just the right size.

4

Sergeant-Pilot Herschel Cohen's twentieth birthday was also memorable for two other events that marked the day. It was the day he made his first aerial kill, the first of thirty-three to follow; and it was the day he met Aaron Ten Eyck.

They were flying a Friday afternoon patrol over the English Channel, when Herschel's Spitfire squadron engaged a squadron of Messerschmidt ME-109's. The German Luftwaffe fighter planes were more heavily armed, and the pilots much more experienced and better-trained; after all, they'd been working at it since 1936. However, the Spitfires, with their wide, stubby wings, were incredibly maneuverable.

Herschel felt a pulsing in his loins and a salty taste in his mouth as the adrenalin of combat poured into him. Just as in baseball, football and hockey, he never had to think his moves in advance. His body was a perfect, finely-honed machine, exultant in battle.

The two opposing squadrons had broken up into individual dog-fights, and Herschel maneuvered until his opponent was facing into the afternoon sun. Then, a swift, looping, barrel-roll climb and he was bearing down on the Jerry from above. A hail of bullets tore into the Messerschmidt, and as Herschel swooped past, he caught a split-second glimpse of the startled young pilot's face as blood and oil spurted all over the cockpit. Then the Messerschmidt was out of control, tail-spinning into the Channel with thick black smoke and bursts of flame pouring out of it. There was an explosion when it hit the surface of the water.

He had killed men before, of course, Falangist soldiers in

Spain; but he had killed them cleanly, with a well-placed shot to the heart or the head. Even a Fascist deserved a clean death. But somehow this was different. He found himself mumbling in Hebrew:

"*Yisgadal vi Yisgadash* — What am I doing? Why in the hell am I saying Kiddush for a fucking Nazi, for gosh sake?" But he could not help thinking, what if the other pilot hadn't been Nazi, just a nice German boy who'd been brainwashed into doing his job? What if he'd had a brother like Joey?

The squadron regrouped and the leader waggled his wings, then broke radio silence. "All right, men, petrol's running dry. Let's head for home. Congratulations, Cohen, bloody good show!"

When they landed, the whole squadron was buzzing. "The Jewboy got one! Cohen got his first Jerry!" Two of the men in his squadron hoisted Herschel to their shoulders and carried him across the tarmac amid cheering and back-slapping. The loudspeaker crackled, "Sgt.-Pilot Cohen! Report to Squadron-Leader Bradshaw's office!"

Herschel knocked on the door, entered, and snapped off a smart British salute which Bradshaw, his commanding officer, returned. Then he clasped Herschel's hand warmly. "Bloody good show, Cohen! Keep up the good work, and we'll see what we can do about getting you that commission!"

"Thank you, Sir."

"The Jewboy," as he was affectionately known to his mates, was once again a Big Man On Campus. He hadn't felt this good since the last time he'd scored a game-winning touchdown against Jarvis just as the clock ran out.

That night, much to his own surprise, he went to religious services.

A huge Quonset hut served as ecumenical chapel for Church of England, Roman Catholic, and on Friday night, Jewish services. Herschel was still thinking about the German pilot when suddenly, to his astonishment, his brother Joey entered the sanctuary.

It wasn't the Joey he had known, of course, the Joey he remembered and thought about when he slept with his pillow cradled in his arms. This was the Joey-who-might-have-been, now grown up very tall, healthy and robust. This Joey also had golden blond hair, but his cheeks, instead of being pale and hollow, were full and rosy. This Joey carried himself not with diffidence and timidity, but very straight and proud, as though wherever he was originally from, his family had owned half of it. And yet, the resemblance was almost uncanny. Throughout services, Herschel could not take his eyes off the young man.

At the Oneg Shabbat following services, the Sisterhood of the local synagogue served wine and raisin cake. Carrying his wine and his cake, he walked over to the young blond Pilot-Officer.

"Shalom Shabbat," said Herschel, offering his hand.

"Shalom Shabbat," replied the young man. They shook hands warmly.

"My name's Herschel Cohen."

"I'm Aaron Ten Eyck. How do you do." He regarded the handsome, dark, curly-haired Sergeant-Pilot with interest. "You're not British, are you?" It was a statement rather than a question.

"No," he grinned. "Take a guess."

"American, of course."

"Very close. I'm Canadian."

"Oh, I adore Canadians! They talk exactly like Americans — well, not quite, perhaps, although my European ear cannot distinguish the accent — but even so, they still remember how to think British when the need arises! How come you're not in the R.C.A.F.?"

"Couldn't wait for them to get here. Killing Fascists is what I do."

"Oh, dear, we *are* a bit bloodthirsty, aren't we? Well, I daresay we could all use a taste of revenge. I'm from Amsterdam, you see."

"Never been there. Heard it's a great town, though."

"I'll invite you there after the war."

"Thanks, Dutchie. Hey, wanna go have a beer?"

"I'd love one. I believe the canteen on the north side of the station serves mixed ranks."

"Nah, I've got a better idea; let's go into town. I found a pub that serves Canadian beer. O'Keefes, Moulson's, Labatt's, you name it. The landlord's Canadian."

"Sounds enchanting. Let's go." Arms linked in wartime comradeship, they left the chapel.

From that moment on, they were inseparable, or at least as inseparable as their respective duties would permit. The fighter planes operated mostly in the daytime, as the technology of night-fighting was still in its infancy. The bombers operated mostly at night, but occasionally with fighter cover as far as the French coast whenever they left before dusk.

"It's a hell of a note," Herschel complained to Aaron. "I finally meet a real buddy, and wouldn't you know, we work different shifts."

"Better than not to have met at all," said Aaron, himself bewildered by his strange attraction to the Canadian boy. Apart from the fact that they both happened to be Jewish, their backgrounds could not possibly have been more different.

"Well, at least we can spend our off-duty time together," said Herschel. "I have a weekend leave coming up. Want to go up to London together?"

"Need you ask?" replied Aaron, flinging an arm around him and squeezing his shoulder. Herschel felt the masculine strength of the other young man and could not help thinking, I'd never have to kick ass for him; he'd kick ass for me!

That Friday evening, they skipped services and caught a jam-packed train for the tedious, halting journey into blacked-out London, where they looked for lodgings. There were military hostels, of course, where they could have stayed, but by mutual agreement they both wanted to get away from the military. Near the Earl's Court tube station, they found a bed-and-breakfast.

"Pilot-Officer Ten Eyck and Sergeant-Pilot Cohen," said the frowsy old slattern of a landlady as she signed them in. "I've just the one room left, very nice and clean it is, and the bath just down the hall. I hope you gentlemen don't mind sharing a bed?"

They both shrugged, never having dared even to consider the possibility, except, perhaps, in the innermost recesses of their minds.

"It'll do just fine, Ma'am," said Herschel.

"Right, then! Down there's the cellar, by the way, in case Jerry comes over tonight. And make sure you don't open the blackout curtains."

In the privacy of their room, they unpacked their kit bags. Herschel had a bottle of real Canadian whiskey that a ferry pilot had smuggled over for him. He poured them each a whiskey-and-water. "Alone at last," he said, as they stripped off their Air Force tunics.

"That's the worst thing about wartime," said Aaron. "No bloody privacy."

"None at all. Well, here's mud in your eye."

"L'chayim."

"L'chayim."

"Do we have time for a pub?" asked Aaron.

"Not a chance. It's about 'Time, Gentlemen, Time,' right now."

"We can do the pubs tomorrow, then. If Jerry doesn't come over."

"He won't," said Herschel. On a sudden impulse he tousled Aaron's hair vigorously. "I've given the Luftwaffe weekend leave."

Aaron grabbed him and tousled Hershel's hair in turn. "Bloody bastard!" They fell on the bed, wrestling affectionately.

"Fucking Dutch asshole!" Herschel tried to pin Aaron's arm behind him.

"Bloody cheeky Canuck!" Aaron, larger and heavier, fell on top of Herschel, pinning him. Suddenly they stopped. Their faces were close to each other.

"Hey, Aaron," he said very quietly.

"Herschel." He rested his face against Herschel's.

Then their arms were around each other.

"Herschel, what is happening? I've never before. . . ."

"I have," said Herschel. "It's wartime, Dutchie. You don't pass up a goddamn thing. If it's there, enjoy it."

"I'm embarrassed, Herschel. Shy. I never even did it with a girl before."

"No shit!" exclaimed the Canadian. "A fucking virgin! Well, we'll take care of that damn quick! Let's get these goddamn uniforms off, right now!"

They got into bed and lay naked together under the covers. When they reached to embrace each other, Aaron felt confused, overwhelmed by sensations he had never felt before, or at least never recognized; certainly, he had never had feelings like this with Rebecca Cardozo. And yet, it just felt so appropriate, so *right* to be held in Herschel's strong arms.

He was making love to him now, running his lips over Aaron's forehead, his eyes, his strong, firm jaw, and then their mouths were firmly planted on each other, Herschel forcing his tongue into Aaron's mouth as they clung to each other. Their cocks were stiff and raging.

"I'm gonna fuck you first, Dutchie," said Herschel, "just to show you how it works. After that, we can do anything we like."

After twenty years of denial, Aaron received a full-fledged sex education that night. It was the most beautiful and sublime experience he would ever remember.

In the morning they awoke snuggled securely in each other's arms. Herschel was close to tears. "It's almost like having my Joey back," he thought, "except that this one's so big and strong." He got up and drew back the blackout curtains, and then returned to bed. In the dim, foggy, London morning light, they made morning love together before they got up, dressed, and went down to breakfast.

Over porridge and tea, they could hardly take their eyes off each other.

"It's all right, luvs," said the kindly old frump of a landlady. "It happens like that sometimes, in a war. Now, you lads just feel at home here, and for tonight there's a nice little pub around the corner in Old Brompton Road where some of the service chaps like to go. Some very *special* chaps, if you catch my meaning."

"But I'm not — we're not—" Aaron started to protest.

"Yes, we are," said Herschel, gently but firmly.

That day they took a walking tour of the city. There were vast areas that had escaped almost unscathed, and there were entire blocks that had been bombed into rubble. There were anti-aircraft batteries and barrage balloon implacements wherever room could be found for them. Harrod's was still open, however, although the legendary Food Halls were sadly depleted. At Fortnum and Mason's, Aaron even found still in stock a few of the Indonesian specialties so dear to the Dutch palate.

In the evening they looked in at the pub in Old Brompton Road that their landlady had recommended.

Neither of them had any experience in socializing in a gay environment. Although they tried to keep an open mind, what they found was simply not to their taste. A few of the service personnel drinking there were men who acted just as masculine as they did, but the majority screamed and shrieked and twittered and called each other by women's names. It was crowded and smoky.

On the stage, a soldier made up as Gracie Fields was singing that entertainer's famous wartime song, "The Biggest Aspidistra in The World," accompanied by a beefy sergeant at an out-of-tune piano. He was followed by three Royal Fusiliers in improvised drag giving their impression of the Andrews Sisters singing, "Don't Sit Under The Apple Tree With Anyone Else But Me."

"Oooh, look, Madge," screamed a tall, willowy subaltern as he spotted Aaron and Herschel. "Here come a couple of butch ones! And airmen, too! Now, tell me that's not dead butch!"

"Not as butch as tanks, Stella," replied a bearded Royal Navy submariner. "Anyway, fat lot of bloody good it'll do you, bitch. Can't you see they're lovers?"

"Well, it's certainly very gay in here," commented Aaron. He'd managed somehow to get close enough to the bar to get them a couple of gin-and-tonics. "I'm not prejudiced, mind you, but they're very definitely not my sort. Our sort, I should say."

"They make me want to puke," said Herschel.

"There, there," soothed Aaron. "Let's not be too judgemental, shall we? Anyway, we'd best bash off to our hotel before somebody lusts after you and you start a bloody brawl."

Lying in bed after their first round of lovemaking, Aaron said, "I'm afraid I'm an incurable romantic, Herschel. I'd never thought about male love in physical terms until now, only in the abstract. Yet even so I'd always felt instinctively that it should be — well, like ours. The Greek ideal — warrior-lovers, that sort of thing."

"You can intellectualize about it all you want, Dutchie," replied Herschel. "But what it boils down to is this: when I want a man, I want to make love to a real man. If I wanted a woman, I could sure get one easily enough; I don't need a man that tries to act like one."

Later, in the dark, Herschel held Aaron in his arms and whispered in his ear, "I never thought I could ever love anyone again, Dutchie, not after my brother Joey died. But you're everything I would have wanted him to be if he'd lived to grow up.

Everything." They kissed, holding onto each other, as the air raid sirens started to wail.

"Cellar?" suggested Aaron.

"Fuck it. If Jerry gets us, let it be right here in bed, making love."

But it was not their night for Jerry to get them. In a few minutes they heard the chattering ack-ack fire from the nearby batteries, and then shortly after that, the all-clear sounded.

During the ensuing months, they took several more leaves together. A walking tour of the Lakes District. A visit to the Yorkshire moors — "Wuthering Heights Country," Herschel called it. Another walking tour out of Inverness, Scotland, where they visited Loch Ness, but did not see the Monster — "I'm afraid it's the wee beastie's day off," said Aaron.

Wherever they traveled on leave, the trains were packed to bursting and the service was sometimes uncertain, sometimes delayed due to air raids, but everyone, everywhere, gave the two R.A.F. pilots royal treatment; they were, after all, the men who had saved England in her direst hour.

They had been together a whole year, and were still totally enraptured with each other. Herschel admired Aaron for his poise and formal education and aristocratic bearing; Aaron worshipped Herschel for his travels and experiences and facility with languages. Sometimes as they lay in bed at night, they would gaze at each other without saying a word, and perhaps run their fingertips gently over each other's bodies, absorbing the physical perfection of each other. Although the initial thrill of sexual novelty had long since worn off, their lovemaking continued to get better and better as they learned each other's little nuances, each wanting to bring the ultimate gratification and pleasure to the other.

It was, as Aaron Ten Eyck was later to recall, the happiest and most sublime period of his life, even though they were both flying combat missions almost every day. Never had he felt so fulfilled, so *complete*. He was a part of another human being who was also a part of him. Intellectually, he was well aware of the possibly tragic consequences of wartime romance, but what soldier, going into battle, does not believe implicitly that if only one member of his platoon survives, he will be that man?

They talked about what they would do after the war. Aaron had assumed that he would some day return to Amsterdam and re-establish the family diamond business. Herschel had similarly taken for granted that he would one day return to Toronto and take over his father's garment factory. They decided they would visit both places before making their decision.

"We could always go to New York," said Herschel. "You could be in diamonds, and I could be in *shmattehs*. They do both there."

"It would be an excellent place for us to be able to live together," said Aaron. "I've always had fantasies about Greenwich Village."

"Well," Herschel finally shrugged, "I guess lots of people are making plans for after the war. Maybe we better just try to survive it, first."

Aaron had begun to nurture so strongly the hope that they might both survive the war together that he had even begun to discount the possibility that they might not. Walking happily across the tarmac one afternoon to check out his plane for that night's mission, he suddenly became aware that the loudspeaker was calling his name.

"Pilot-Officer Ten Eyck, please report to the Squadron Commander's office." He had absolutely no sense of foreboding as he responded; all he could think of was himself and Herschel making love the night before in a meadow just outside the base. Tonight they were scheduled to meet at the all-night canteen as soon as Aaron got back from his bombing run and before Herschel left to fly dawn patrol. No thought was given to, or mention made of, the fact that each night, not all of the bombers returned.

Squadron-Leader Carringdon returned his salute and then invited him to sit down. "Tea?" he asked.

"No, thank you, sir. Is anything wrong?"

"Ten Eyck, I don't quite know how to bring this up, but I've just had a call from Squadron-Leader Bradshaw in the Fighter section."

Suddenly there was a great hollow space in Aaron's chest where his heart had been a moment before.

"It's your mate, I'm afraid. The Canadian chap." In wartime, the institution of male bonding was deeply respected. The sexual aspect, if there happened to be one, was simply not mentioned.

Aaron looked at his commanding officer pleadingly. Injured, hopefully? Taken prisoner?

"I deeply regret having to tell you that Pilot-Officer Herschel Cohen was shot down this afternoon over the Channel."

Aaron was silent for a very long moment while his mind tried to digest this. "Sir, is there any chance he was captured?"

"Sorry, old man. He didn't have time to ditch. I'm afraid there's no mistake."

"I see, sir. Very kind of you to call me in to tell me yourself."

"Not at all."

"And thank Squadron-Leader Bradshaw for me, too, sir, if you would."

"Yes, of course. Quite so. Well, there it is, lad."

"May I be dismissed, sir? I'm flying a mission tonight."

"I'd really rather you didn't," his senior officer replied. "A man's mate gets shot down, it affects his judgment and we wind up losing two instead of one. You wouldn't be at your best tonight anyway, Ten Eyck, now would you?"

"I daresay not."

"Strudwick will fly your plane. You take a couple of days off. Go out and get drunk or whatever you need to do. And, Ten Eyck, for whatever it's worth, I'm dreadfully sorry."

"Thank you, Sir."

In a daze, Aaron walked across the tarmac, not seeing anything around him. It was not until he reached his quarters, locked himself in the room he shared with another officer, who, thankfully, was away, and threw himself on the bunk, that the tears came; loud, wracking sobs that he did not even try to suppress.

There would be no meeting at the canteen tonight, or any other night; no more shared leaves, no long nights lying in each other's arms. Before him stretched a long, interminable vista of meaningless missions, decorations, promotions; of watching with an aching heart as other young men formed wartime attachments and went off to town together, two by two. He was to go it alone from now on.

After that, Aaron Ten Eyck went a little bit mad. His skill on bombing runs became legendary, but he also earned the nickname of "The Mad Dutch Butcher." No matter how important the military target, he usually managed to drop a couple of bombs on the nearest civilian area.

"Get ready to drop one," he would tell his bombardier.

"But, sir, we're still four minutes away from target! We're directly over a block of flats!"

"That never seems to bother Jerry, does it, Sergeant? We're just testing our new bomb-sight, then, aren't we? Drop one fragmentation and a couple of incendiaries."

"Yes, sir."

The gunners and the bombardier complained to him over an off-duty beer. "Aaron, we're the R.A.F., not the Luftwaffe. We're not beasts, you know, nor bloody butchers. It's been proven well enough that bombing civilians doesn't win a war."

"Don't give me that bloody rot," replied Aaron. "It's been proven only that bombing *British* civilians doesn't win a war. What it does to Jerry remains to be seen. So if any of you want to give me this Lord Haw-Haw line about 'Let's not be beastly to the Hun,' I'd suggest you find yourself another crew."

His men looked at each other in amazement. The gentle Dutchie had really gone around the bend since his mate was shot down. It was a tribute to the affection they felt for him that not one of them chose to transfer to another crew.

Eventually, he started drinking heavily and his nerves and his judgment began to go, which was certainly not uncommon. In recognition of his splendid record, they awarded him the D.F.C. and promoted him to Flight-Lieutenant. They also grounded him to a desk job for the duration. Later in the war, his savage bombing of civilians was to be far eclipsed by the Luftwaffe attack on Coventry, and by the Allied fire-bombing of the lovely old city of Dresden, not even a military target, in which almost the entire civilian population of the city was burned to death.

Aaron corresponded with Herschel's parents, David and Malka Cohen in Toronto. He told them glowingly of their son's exploits, and promised to visit them after the war.

But as far as he was concerned, the only real life he had ever known came to an end the day that Herschel Cohen's Spitfire, with thirty-three swastikas painted on the side, was shot down over the English Channel.

5

There were tears in Ashcroft's eyes as Ten Eyck finished his tale.

"You had it all, man," he said. "You really knew the real thing, for as long as it lasted."

Aaron walked over to a marquetry credenza and took out a photo album. In fascination, Aaron turned the pages, looking at the faded photographs of the tall, fair-haired Dutch pilot and the shorter, darker, curly-haired Canadian boy, their arms around each other, grinning into the camera. Ashcroft marveled at the World War Two Royal Air Force uniforms, and the aircraft in the background that appeared to have come straight out of an aviation museum.

"Aaron, you were one hell of a hot number! Talk about an awesome blond hunk, you could have given my lover Troy some competition!"

The old man smiled, pleased. "I daresay I could have passed in those days."

"Did you ever visit Herschel's parents?"

"Yes, I did, in 1950. I was in New York on diamond business, so I flew up to Toronto. It was quite bizarre. As soon as his mother answered the door, she screamed, 'My God! It's Joey!' before she realized who I was.

"They no longer lived in their old neighborhood. After the war, there was a vast influx of immigrants into Canada, and the ethnicity of Toronto's traditional Jewish neighborhoods gradually changed, becoming mostly Italian and West Indian. The Cohens took the money they'd put aside for the college education of their sons, and bought a condominium in North York, a high-rise Jewish suburb which was then just beginning to be developed.

"They were no longer alive, actually. They went through the motions of living, but they were hollow shells. Malka fixed me a traditional Jewish dinner, and David fed me schnapps, but I could see that my visit was disturbing them. Although they invited me to stay with them for as long as I wished, I told them that I had to rush back to New York on business. A few years later they died."

"And you, Aaron? Has there been absolutely *no one* in your life since then?"

"No, Stephen, there has been no one. After the sublime happiness I'd known with Herschel, the sheer perfection of him, the way we were attuned to each other, the way both our eyes would light up when we'd meet after a mission, even if it was only for a beer at the canteen — no, Stephen, I could not find it within myself to profane that memory, not even for physical release. I tell you this in all honesty. I have been completely celibate for over fifty years."

"My God, Aaron!"

"It is a tribute to the memory of Herschel Cohen. And some day I will find a way to repay him for the year of perfect happiness he gave me."

"But you already have, Aaron, with the happiness you gave him! You brought his beloved brother back for him, not as he was before, weak and sickly, but as Herschel had always wanted Joey to be! Aaron, you don't owe life or fate or Herschel Cohen a thing!"

"Well, old chap, you may be right. But that's not the way I felt about it. Yes, there is a debt, and I like to think that in some small measure my support of human rights causes has paid a few installments of it."

"It has, Aaron. Believe me, it has."

They drank a nightcap and said their goodnights. Then, as Ashcroft was leaving, he suddenly turned back to Ten Eyck.

"Aaron, there's just one thing that bothers me about what happened during the war. I probably don't even have the right to ask you about it."

"Don't be ridiculous. You may ask me anything you wish."

"Those savage bombing raids against civilians, Aaron. It's just so totally out of character for you! What were you thinking? How did you feel about it afterwards?"

"I can see why you're such a good journalist," said Ten Eyck, drily.

"You don't have to answer if you don't want to."

"I think I should prefer to answer, because there is a lesson in there somewhere about the ultimate horror of war." He poured them each a final shot of cognac and drank his down before answering Ashcroft's question.

"What was I thinking? I was thinking of some of the things the enemy had done. The slaughter of innocent civilians when the Nazi armies overran Europe. The concentration camps and the death camps: Auschwitz, Dachau, Bergen-Belsen and all the rest. I thought about Herschel when he was fighting in Spain, flying that tiny Lysander reconnaissance plane and dodging German Stukas amongst the tree-tops. I thought about what he must have felt the first time he watched the German dive-bomber pilots machine-gunning innocent civilians, including women and children, along the roadsides. I thought about Herschel's comrades in the Loyalist regular forces who were left behind when the International Brigade fled into France, and the ones who waited futilely on the docks at Alicante, waiting for the rescue ships that never came, until finally they were rounded up by the Falangist troops of Generalissimo Franco, who gave no amnesty or quarter. Those of Herschel's Spanish comrades who were not tortured to death or shot immediately were cast into prison camps, where many of them spent the rest of their lives.

"What did I think, afterwards, about what I had done? Stephen, I thought what any civilized man would have thought. Intellectually, I was shocked, horrified, appalled. I should not have thought, when I was a young boy, that Aaron Ten Eyck, of the Jewish diamond merchant Ten Eyck family of Amsterdam, whose roots go back to the sixteenth century, could ever have sunk to the level of a beast. I simply would not have accepted it.

"But what did I feel? Ah, dear boy, therein lies the true horror. Because what I felt inside myself — I believe the modern American expression is 'gut level' — what I felt, actually, was pride and glory and exultation! There was simply no greater pleasure for me than to kill as many Fascists as I could, for what they had done to me, and to so many others. I could have cheerfully killed a hundred — a thousand of the enemy, just for taking my Herschel from me! And never, Stephen, never as long as I live, can I truly feel the slightest regret or sorrow, only pride, happiness and satisfaction, for every single bomb I dropped on their civilian targets!"

VI

CHILDREN OF
THE BOILED FROG SYNDROME

That night at the Viking Bar, Kiki and Anton came over to him with exciting news.

"I've found our flat, Stephen!" said Kiki. "It overlooks Vondel Park, and it's only twelve hundred guilders a month, which is four hundred for each of us."

"Let me think about it, guys."

"But what is there to think about?" protested young Anton. "We can be a family to each other!"

"He needs to be convinced some more," Kiki said to him. "Let's stay at the Leather Eagle again tonight."

"Oh, good!" exclaimed Anton. "Can we maybe try out the sling that we didn't use last time?"

"Whatever for?" replied Ashcroft. "You're too young to get into that sort of thing."

"*Ach*, no, Mijnheer Stephen! My daddy used to spank me sometimes, when I'd been naughty. Once he caught me in the barn with one of his farm workers, and he beat me with his belt. I liked it!"

"You're a kinky little kid," said Ashcroft, hugging and kissing both of them. Still brooding over Ten Eyck's strange and haunting tale, he felt the need of sexual release. He went to the phone and called Hartt at the hotel to make sure the VIP room would be available. "And this time we'll pay for it," he added. "The boys had a very good gig tonight."

"Oh, lovely," said Hartt. "Shall I remove the sling and put in a bloody rocking horse? And perhaps a playpen, in case you want to try on some confinement fantasies."

"Oh, fuck off," said Ashcroft.

"I'll also put fresh bedding in the perambulator, just for diaper fetishes, eh? Is it true, Ashcroft, that paedophiles like you get turned on by the smell of soiled nappies?"

"You're a bloody swine, you Limey fuck," laughed Ashcroft.

When they got back to the hotel, Hartt, with a prurient grin, once again handed Ashcroft the keys to the VIP room. This time the dim lights had been turned on, the bed turned down, and there was a bucket of inexpensive champagne, the house special, with a card that read, "Compliments of the House." Next to it was a baby's pacifier and a rattle.

"I'll kill him," said Ashcroft.

They uncorked the champagne and sipped a couple of glasses each. Anton complained that the bubbles went up his nose and made him giggle. After they had showered, Anton whispered in Ashcroft's ear,

"May I show you please, how my father used to beat me?"

"Well, sure," said the older man, not suspecting anything.

Anton and Kiki fastened a pair of leather restraints around Ashcroft's wrists, then led him over to the wall where they secured the restraints to the wall hooks. Kiki handed Anton the studded leather belt that he loved to wear to the disco.

"This is how he used to hit me," said Anton innocently, "like *this*, and like *this*, and like *this!*" Ashcroft could not suppress a howl of pain as the lash of the belt caught him by suprise.

"Boy, did I get suckered into this!" he thought, as the blows of the belt came down on his back, his legs and his buttocks again and again.

When the boy had tired of beating him with the belt, Kiki tied his feet with a length of rope and Anton secured the wrist restraints together as though Ashcroft had been handcuffed. Then they lifted him into the sling. His wrists and ankles were secured to the four chains that supported the sling.

Anton straddled the sling and put his cock next to Ashcroft's face. "You think I have a nice one, *ja*, for a boy my age?"

"You sure do, kid. One hell of a nice one."

"That's good, Mijnheer Stephen, because I'm going to fuck you with it." He slipped on the condom that Kiki handed him.

"Kiki, are you just going to *let* him do this to me?"

The Indonesian boy was cracking up laughing. "But Stephen," he pointed out, "you *told* me that we could be all things to each other, and that you had no hangups. Did you not say that?"

"Well, sure, but. . ."

"But what?" asked Kiki as he helpfully lubricated Stephen's rear end for his young lover's pleasure.

"It just seems to me," said Ashcroft, "that for an old leather Daddy, I've been spending a lot of time lately getting beaten and fucked by goddamn *children!*"

"Yes!" exclaimed Kiki delightedly. "And for free, too! Do you not realize that we would charge anyone else three hundred guilders for this scene?"

"A bargain," said Ashcroft, as the cherubic blond boy slid into him. Then he lay back in the sling and abandoned himself to ecstasy as Anton pounded him with youthful vigor. This time it was Kiki who fondled and stroked him when he sensed the younger boy approaching completion.

When Anton had pumped himself dry, the boys released Ashcroft from restraint and helped him out of the sling. Anton leaped into his arms, his legs wrapped around Ashcroft's waist, and kissed him passionately.

"Now I can be your little boy again!" he squealed.

The three of them slept peacefully in each other's arms, with no sense of foreboding or menace about what might happen the next day. Ashcroft, not wishing to alarm them, had told them nothing of the danger he was in. Perhaps, he thought later, I should have warned them, just to put them on their guard.

In the morning they made love once again, then Ashcroft sent Kiki down to the bar to order a breakfast tray. The boys had orange juice, *uitsmijter* and milk; Ashcroft had orange juice and coffee.

"Can we go look at the flat this morning?" asked Kiki.

"Oh, I suppose so," replied Ashcroft unenthusiastically. "We can look, but both of you know I'm not in a position to make any sort of commitment."

"It's only a flat, Stephen," said Kiki. "If your situation should change, we won't insist that you stay. Anton and I can manage the rent by ourselves, if we have to."

"Well, in that case," Stephen finally agreed, "I guess it won't hurt to look at it."

"*Verrukkelijk!*" exclaimed Anton, giving him hugs and kisses. Quickly they dressed and left the hotel.

They stood on the bank of the canal, arms around each other, inhaling the promise of spring in the air.

"*Ach*, Stephen," said Kiki, "what a wonderful day to go look at our new home!"

Those were very nearly the last words he ever spoke.

Suddenly, his eyes grew wide with terror as he saw something in a window of one of the tall narrow houses across the canal. His

206 The Boiled Frog Syndrome

mouth dropped open, and began to emit the beginning of a shrill, ululating scream as he shoved Ashcroft very hard into the young boy Anton, knocking both of them over. Simultaneously, three shots were fired, very close together, and Kiki fell to the ground clutching his chest.

Knowing reflexively that he should have rolled on the ground for the cover of the nearest parked car, but heedless of the danger from across the canal, Ashcroft instead crawled to Kiki's side. The boy lay crumpled on the ground, but jerked convulsively as Ashcroft gently turned him over onto his back. Blood was flowing from three separate wounds, staining his clothing bright red. His eyes were open, but he could not speak.

Ashcroft had always heard it said that the fastest way to draw a crowd in Holland was to stop a stranger and ask him for directions. In a moment, the whole village would have gathered, all arguing good-naturedly with each other and trying to be of help. It was not surprising, therefore, that at the sound of the shots, doors and windows in the immediate vicinity flew open and people came running — the people of the neighborhood: housewives, businessmen, merchants, prostitutes, leather dudes, foreign visitors, all talking volubly and trying to find out what had happened. At the same time, hastily-torn shirts and undershirts, and then at last clean towels, were being proffered to Ashcroft.

He had Kiki's windbreaker open and the boy's shirt ripped down the front. There were three bullet wounds — one on the left side, too near the heart, and two more on the right side. Anton was crying hysterically, clutching Kiki's hand. Ashcroft slapped him hard across the face.

"Sorry about that, kid," he said. "Now just get hold of yourself and hold these towels against the bullet holes. Firm steady pressure. That's it. Good boy!" With one arm, he cradled Kiki's head, and with his free hand, he held a towel firmly against the bullet wound nearest the heart.

By this time, the foot constables had arrived on the scene. In the background he heard the shrill warble of the police sirens and the ambulance. Although it seemed to take forever, it was probably no more than two minutes before the ambulance and the paramedics were there, along with the police cruisers. Hans, the young gay cop, was there too. He squeezed Ashcroft's shoulder sympathetically.

"You were very lucky this time, my friend," he said. "Your young friend was not so lucky. We've sealed off the neighborhood, but I doubt we'll find anybody. They'll have gotten rid of their weapons, left through the basement of another house, and mixed with the people on the street. But we'll keep trying."

"Thank you, Hans."

Hartt came running out of the hotel, dangling Dirk's car keys. "Get in, you two," he commanded Ashcroft and young Anton. "I'll follow the ambulance to the hospital." When they were inside the car, he said, "Your people never let up, do they, Ashcroft? Bloody beasts!"

But Ashcroft knew perfectly well what not only the bartender but Hans and the rest of the police had not even dared to think. This was no miscalculation, no shoddy marksmanship. They had not hit the wrong target. They could have shot him just as easily as they had shot Kiki. Indeed, they could have killed him, if they had really wanted to. For that matter, they could have killed Kiki. Instead, they had shot and seriously wounded the boy, for the sole purpose of sending Ashcroft a message. Yes, they were bloody beasts, although Ashcroft would have used much stronger American terminology.

Ashcroft and the boy waited for six hours until Kiki finally came out of surgery. There was not much that could be said to comfort each other. Ashcroft paced the hall, drank endless cups of coffee, and tried to read a magazine in Dutch. Finally, a doctor spoke with them.

"There's nothing more we can do," he said. "He's in intensive care, and with luck he'll survive, but he's lost a lot of blood. I'm sorry, but I can't let you visit him yet. Perhaps tomorrow."

"Thank you, Doctor." He gave the man his name and the phone number of his hotel. "What are *you* going to do?" he asked Anton. "If you don't feel like being on your own at a time like this, you're welcome to come back to the hotel with me."

"Thank you, Mijnheer Stephen, but no, I will wait right here. My place is here in the hospital, with Kiki."

"That's fair," said Ashcroft. "Call me at once if there's any change." He took a cab back to the Leather Eagle.

Dirk, a man who seldom, if ever, drank, was sitting at the bar with three shots of *oude genever* in front of him.

"Don't go up to your room, Ashcroft."

There was a long, significant moment of silence.

"I have to," said Ashcroft, finally. "They'll kill you if I don't."

"They'll kill you if you do," replied Dirk.

"No, they won't. That's not what they're here for." If they had wanted, they could have killed him that morning.

The door of his room was ajar. He kicked it open and stood to one side. "I'm coming in," he said, loudly and clearly. "I'm not armed."

"Oh, come in and sit down, Ashcroft," came an American voice. "Don't be so melodramatic; we just want to talk."

There were two of them, one white, one black, just like in all the spy movies. They were impeccably dressed, each wearing about six hundred Standard New Dollars worth of American tailoring. Even their shirts and ties looked custom made. A Washington tailor had once told Ashcroft during an interview, "Our intelligence agents may be among the dirtiest operators in the world, but they're also the best-dressed."

They didn't stand up when Ashcroft entered the room, just sat in their chairs with their hands at the ready. They even introduced themselves. The black one was McPheeters, the white one Richardson.

"Looks like we fucked up, Ashcroft," said Richardson.

"Yeah, well, sometimes they just fall through the cracks," said McPheeters.

"Sometimes it takes awhile to match them up on the computer," said Richardson.

Ashcroft was silent, wondering what they were getting at.

"We didn't know until recently," explained McPheeters, "that Troy Anderson was your little fuck-buddy."

"Well, don't feel too bad about it, partner," said Richardson to McPheeters. "You can't expect us to know which cock every faggot in America is sucking."

Ashcroft's eyes were narrowed with hatred. He felt his fists clenching and unclenching.

"Why in the hell did you have to shoot a goddamn innocent nineteen-year-old kid?" he demanded.

"Just so you'd shut up and listen to us," said Richardson. "Besides, he's just a queer. Next time we'll nail the little blond one."

"We'd really like to nail you, Ashcroft," said McPheeters. "Messing around with kids! You know damn well what we'd do to you at home."

"Yeah," said Richardson. "America's a pretty decent place, now that we've gotten rid of your kind."

"You call that decent?" said Ashcroft quietly. "A great big prison camp where everyone does as they're told?"

"Oh, you'd suprised," said McPheeters. "See, that's where you stupid perverts and liberal Commie sympathizers all have your heads up your ass. You'd really be surprised at how much better the quality of life is in the United States these days."

"Yes," agreed Ashcroft. "I really would be surprised."

"When," asked Richardson, "was the last time you can remember being able to walk anywhere in America at any hour of the day or night in perfect safety?"

"You can now," said McPheeters. "The streets are finally safe again."

"How did you accomplish that?" asked Ashcroft. "How many people did you have to kill?"

"Oh, lots," said Richardson. "Lots and lots and lots. But it was worth it." He paused and then recited as though quoting from a text that he had learned by rote. "Anybody who chooses to break their compact with society, the written and unwritten contract of laws and ordinances and courtesies that embody the rules that society lives by and that govern society, is very simply removed from that society."

"We give every first offender a prison sentence and one more chance," said McPheeters. "The second time . . ." He drew his finger across his throat.

"Don't look so shocked, Ashcroft," said Richardson. "You'll have to admit that the death penalty has its advantages. For one thing, the recidivism rate is absolutely zero. No one who has ever been executed has ever come back to commit another violent crime. It's just like shooting a mad dog before he bites any more people. Not to mention all the money it saves the taxpayers."

"I can take my white friends anywhere in Harlem late at night," said McPheeters, "just like sixty years ago, and not even have to worry about it."

"We took a poll," said Richardson. "We take lots of polls, but this one was almost like a referendum. Do you know how many people are very happy with the way Reverend President Wickerly is running the country? About eighty percent."

"And the other twenty percent," said McPheeters, "aren't making any waves. They know better."

"It's a whole different country from the one you left," said Richardson. "Peaceful, quiet, prosperous and stable."

"The national I.D. cards and the border checks at all airports and state lines really helped a lot," said McPheeters. "No more illegal aliens, no more interstate crime."

"Why don't you tell me all about your concentration camps?" demanded Ashcroft. "Like the one Troy Anderson is in."

"Those aren't concentration camps," said Richardson. "Those are country clubs."

"Then why are so many men dying in them? What happens to the ones who go to the camp hospitals and never come back?"

McPheeters chuckled. "What makes you think that all of them really go to the hospitals? Oh, some do, of course, and some die. That happens even in the best of detention camps. But not all."

"All right, then, what do you do with the rest of them?"

"I thought you'd never ask," said Richardson. "That's actually what we came to see you about. Tell him, partner."

"We sell them," said McPheeters.

"*Sell* them?" echoed Ashcroft in amazement.

"Sure," said McPheeters. "It's a form of revenue enhancement. You'd be amazed at how much money our beloved Reverend President Wickerly can get toward running the country debt-free, just from the ransom we get for some of you faggots."

"Even the poorest ones," said Richardson. "Usually there's a mother or father somewhere with a house that can be mortgaged. Or some rich old closet case that we don't arrest, just so we can bleed him for ransom money."

"And these are just the ordinary faggots. People like your ass-hole buddy bring a very special price."

"Show him the picture, partner."

The black agent opened an attaché case that had been leaning against his chair, and extracted a small color photograph.

I must keep control, thought Ashcroft. I mustn't go for their throats. But I just can't handle this!

The picture they handed him was undoubtly, although barely recognizably, that of his lover, Troy. He was gaunt, hollow-eyed and hollow-cheeked, skeletal to the point of emaciation.

"What have you done to him?" said Ashcroft in a low voice. "Why are you starving him to death?"

"Oh, we're not, we're not, said Richardson. "We've just moved him to a different camp, and he gets four huge meals a day."

"The problem is," said McPheeters, "that we also give him a little enzyme in his food that fucks up his metabolism so that nothing he eats does him any good. Just sort of passes right through. How much would you say that queer weighs right now, partner?"

"About one-twenty," said Richardson. "Down from one-eighty in just a few weeks. Poor bastard doesn't even have the strength to do his exercises anymore. And in another few weeks, he'll be down to about ninety pounds."

"If he lives," said McPheeters. "But that's not up to us, Ash-croft, that's up to you."

Ashcroft stared at the picture in horror. Nobody could do something like that to a fellow human being — but he knew from long experience that they could, and did, and throughout history had frequently done so, and much worse.

"How much?" he asked quietly.

"Tell him, partner," said Richardson.

"One million Standard New Dollars."

"Or its equivalent in any negotiable currency. Sorry, no checks or credit cards."

"You're crazy," said Ashcroft. "I've never had more than a couple of thousand to my name at any one time in my entire life."

"We know that. But you can get it."

"Where the hell would I get a million bones?" demanded Ashcroft.

"Oh, come on," said McPheeters. "A famous writer like you! Political aide to the late lamented boss faggot, Douglas McKittrick! Make your underground organizations cough it up, Ashcroft. Like, some of the money they've stolen from our banks."

Ashcroft was silent for a moment, staring at the picture. "How long do I have?" he finally asked.

"You're looking at the picture, Ashcroft. You tell us."

"And if I were to find the money? What happens then?"

"We take him off the enzyme immediately," said McPheeters. "It'll take a while for his metabolism to get back to normal, but at least he'll stop losing weight. Then we give him a new passport and deliver him anywhere outside of the United States. On condition that he never comes back, of course."

"How do I know you'll deliver?"

"We've never burnt anyone yet for ransom money," said Richardson. "Not that we wouldn't like to, but we can't. If we did, the word would get out and it would dry up damn quick, so we have to keep our word."

"Tell you what we'll do, Ashcroft," said McPheeters. "We'll take him off the enzyme for ten days, commencing right now. At the end of ten days, you hand over the million bones, and we deliver your lover boy within seventy-two hours."

"And if I can't come up with the money?"

"Then we put Anderson back on the enzyme, and also we shoot the young blond kid. Then the staff of the hotel, one by one."

"I'd like to see them shoot your lesbian mother," said Ashcroft.

The two men stiffened. "Don't push, Ashcroft," said Richardson. "We're doing you a real big favor. Think about it."

They rose in unison. "We'll be in touch, Ashcroft," said McPheeters. "Have a nice day."

2

For ten days, Kiki hovered between life and death, and for ten days, Anton never left his side at the hospital. A sympathetic staff set up a cot for him alongside Kiki's bed, and, impressed by the younger boy's devotion to his friend, brought him his meals and coaxed him to eat whenever the trays came around.

Throughout the ten days, between visits to the hospital, Ashcroft scurried back and forth trying to meet the deadline that the two agents had set for his lover's life and freedom. With increasing desperation, he sounded out his underground contacts.

His unit leader, Arguello, was sympathetic but not encouraging. At a meeting in a small tavern off the Amstel canal, the big, tough former paratrooper revealed the reason behind the hatred and the sadness in his eyes.

"A million bones, Ashcroft? Come on! You gotta be crazy!"

"Is it crazy for me to want to save my lover's life? Hey, I thought that kind of brotherhood was what this movement was all about! Have you ever had a lover, Arguello?" The moment he said it, he was sorry he'd asked. The big man's eyes became suddenly hard and cold, yet somehow void and empty.

"Yeah, I had a lover once," Arguello replied.

"I'm sorry," said Ashcroft. "I shouldn't have asked."

"That's okay. I'm glad you did." He fished out his wallet and extracted a photo which he handed to Ashcroft. The picture showed a lovely young Puerto Rican boy of about Kiki's age, with soft, Latino skin and clean, well-cut features.

"He was from my home village on the Island," said Arguello. "From the day I went in the service, we kept in touch. We spent every one of my leaves together. Between times, he never once went out with nobody else, and I'll kill the son-of-a-bitch that says he did. We was gonna move to New York after I finished my hitch."

"What happened to him?" inquired Ashcroft, almost not daring to ask.

Arguello shrugged. "What do you think? He went into San Juan one weekend, just 'cause he liked to dance at the discos. They picked him up on the Condado late at night — they said he was hustling; I know that's bullshit. This was after the take-over, so Wickerly's Warriors had him put right into the camps. They found my picture, too; he always carried it. They made him tell them who I was. After I got busted out of the service, they were gonna put me in the camps, too, but I killed a guard and got away. Later I found out through my relatives in the village that he died in the camps. I been working in the Resistance ever since."

"Oh, my god," said Ashcroft. He'd heard so many similar horror stories. Sometimes he felt as though he had no tears left.

"A million bones would of got him out, too," said Arguello, "plus about twenty or thirty others. Just what makes your lover more special than anybody else's?"

How do you answer a question like that? thought Ashcroft.

"Something else," said Arguello. "I've seen your Resistance dossier. As your unit leader, they made me read it; me, I don't like to be nosy. But isn't it true that your lover was rich?"

Ashcroft nodded.

"He could of kept his money off-shore. He could of bought his own way out. He could of left with you. As far as I'm concerned, Ashcroft, your lover boy put himself into the camps."

"What can I say?" replied Ashcroft. "We can't all have a crystal ball. He did what he thought was right."

"Look," said Arguello, "I didn't mean to bust your chops. I know how you feel. The most I can authorize from the funds of this unit is five thousand bones. Maybe you can make a deal."

"They won't deal," said Ashcroft. "They know who Troy is and they know who I am. The price comes high."

"Then there's nothing more I can do. I'm sorry, Ashcroft. I hope you come up with the bread someplace."

"Maybe if I talk to the man higher up?"

"The man higher up don't talk to nobody lower down. It's for our own security. You know how the unit system works."

"I don't want to know who he is. I just want to try to convince him. Please, Arguello?"

The big man drank most of a half-liter of pilsner almost at a gulp. "I'll see what I can do."

The man higher up was sympathetic, but did not want to meet with Ashcroft because there was nothing he could do, either. He ordered Arguello to send Ashcroft directly to the Finance Committee, which operated in Switzerland where the money was fairly safe.

Ashcroft caught the TGV to Zurich. The Finance Committee had a dummy holding company with a flock of subsidiary corporations, all operating out of an attorney's office off the Bahnhofstrasse, near the Jelmoli department store. The receptionist quickly passed him through to the inner office of a kindly, white-haired American who, Ashcroft had been forewarned, had been a successful banker back home.

"I've been a fan of yours for many years, Ashcroft," the older man said. "I wish more people had listened to you."

"So do I," replied Ashcroft. "Should I know you from home?"

The man smiled. "No names, please, I'm sorry. But if you used to watch Rukeyser on Wall Street Week, back when they still had Public Television, you might have heard my name mentioned once or twice. But as I said, I used to read your articles avidly."

Ashcroft asked, "Does that mean you're going to help me?"

The white-haired man shook his head sadly. "I'm afraid not. I've already pleaded your case with the Finance Committee, of which I happen to be the chairman. They were sympathetic, of course, but they overruled me."

"But why? Somehow, some day, I'd find some way to pay you back."

"I'm sure you would, Ashcroft. But right now it's a matter of priorities. Do you have any idea how many grenades, how many Uzi submachine guns, how many Kalashnikov rifles for our field operations a million dollars would buy? Do you know how much money I can make for the Resistance whenever they give me a million to use as leverage? I'm sorry, Ashcroft. You'll have to find some other way."

"Thanks a lot," said Ashcroft bitterly. "Tell me something. Did you have any trouble getting *your* lover out?"

"None whatsoever," replied the banker. "When the DIVAF program started, my lover was skiing in Gstaad. Thanks in part to being a reader of yours, I had my passport ready. We already had a Swiss bank account. Why didn't you?"

"Because I never made enough money in my life to put into a Swiss bank account. You say you're a fan of mine; well, then, you know the kind of writer I am. Nobody ever got rich from it. I didn't write trashy novels that made a million bones just from the movie rights."

"Console yourself with all the good that you accomplished. I'm truly sorry about your lover, Ashcroft. But if you can make a deal with them, I'll lend you twenty thousand myself."

"I appreciate that," said Ashcroft, "but their price was firm."

Back in Amsterdam, he sat despondently in Aaron Ten Eyck's living room, drinking the diamond merchant's best cognac. He had never felt worse in his life.

"The Finance Committee just turned me down," said Ashcroft. "They were very sorry about it, but they felt it would be unfair to all the other detainees to expend that much money just to ransom one man's lover, even mine."

"I'm sorry, Stephen," replied Ten Eyck. "I'm afraid I have to tell you that the Documentation Committee has decided likewise. I'd already asked them on your behalf." He squeezed the American's shoulder in sympathy.

"It's not fair!" protested Ashcroft. "I've paid my goddamn dues to the Movement! For God knows how many years I've paid my dues! Now all I want in return is my lover's life. Is that so much to ask?"

"It is," replied Ten Eyck, "when the same money could buy ten or twenty other lives. Who is to say which one is more valuable? If we did that, we'd be making the same judgmental decisions that our enemies do."

"You're right, Aaron. Intellectually, I know you're right. But what am I supposed to do? Just sit here and let my lover die? What would you have done if the Jerries had captured Herschel Cohen and held him for ransom?"

"My dear Stephen, I daresay you know how much I wish they had!"

"And if they had, Aaron? How would you have handled it?"

The old man looked very pensive. "I've been thinking about that," he said. "All right, Stephen, I'll show you what I would have done, and what I am going to do."

Walking very slowly, as though burdened with a great world-weariness, he opened the cabinet that contained his computer console. He flipped it awake and waited for the screen to light up.

"What are you doing, Aaron?" asked Ashcroft.

"You may stand right here by me and watch, if you'd like."

From his disk file, Aaron took a program disk and inserted it into one of the disk drives. When the menu came up, he selected the "Certified Value" program, and initialized. When the screen flashed, "Program Ready," he inserted a "Selected Inventory" disk in the other drive and gave the machine a "Define Search" command. Ashcroft noted that the search command read, "$10,000 Standard New Dollars or More."

"We use Eurodollars here," Aaron explained, "rather than marks or francs or guilders."

The machine began to scroll through the inventory. Every few seconds the cursor would stop, and Aaron would hit the "Printout" key. The printer which stood alongside the console would clatter for a few dozen strokes, and then the machine would re-commence scrolling. Finally it stopped. Aaron tore off the printout sheet.

"Please excuse me for just a few moments," said the old man. "I shan't be long."

Ashcroft sat and sipped the liqueur that Aaron had given him. From the next room, he heard the beeping of an electronic safe, and then a heavily-armored door sliding open, followed by the sound of metal drawers being pulled back and forth. In a few minutes, Aaron returned, bearing a small velvet bag.

"One million dollars, Stephen. Certified value on any diamond exchange in the world."

"Oh, God," said Ashcroft. "Aaron, I can't let you do this."

"And why not?"

"Aaron, I know you're well off, but do you mean to tell me you can turn over the very cream of your inventory without suffering an irreparable loss?"

"Of course the loss will be irreparable. But believe me, I will have more than enough left to live in comfort the rest of my days. And I assure you, they will be much happier days knowing that I have used my wherewithal to do something to repay — well, you remember what we talked about the last time you were here."

"Aaron, I can't tell you. . ."

"Then please don't, my boy. Let's just call it the Herschel Cohen Memorial Fund. Now, let's get down to practicalities. How do you propose to make the exchange?"

"Well, I suppose at the American Embassy or whatever."

"No!" exclaimed Ten Eyck. "That's just what they'll be expecting you to do! I daresay they probably wouldn't double-cross you for the ransom money, but these are, after all, my stones, and I'd feel very ill at ease about trusting your American friends."

"Whatever you say, Aaron. What would you suggest?"

"Why not right here? I am, after all, a member of the Royal Dutch Parliament. I shall send Her Royal Highness a request that one of her secretaries be present as a witness to the exchange — sworn to secrecy, of course. Even your Reverend President Wickerly feels constrained to honor diplomatic protocol. Does that meet with your complete approval?"

"Of course," said Ashcroft. "It's the best possible arrangement I could have hoped for." He took the old man in his arms in a warm embrace. "Aaron, I don't know how I can ever..."

"Oh, my dear chap, how can I ever thank *you*! It's a debt I've waited for over half a century to repay!"

On his way home from Aaron's apartment, he stopped at the hospital. Kiki was sitting up in bed, and Anton was feeding him soup. He kissed Kiki and hugged him.

"Stephen, I shall be well again in a few days. But I know that the bullets they removed from my body were meant for you. Are we still in danger, Stephen? Must we continue to run and hide?"

"You don't," replied Ashcroft. "I probably still do. We'll know very shortly."

When he returned to the Leather Eagle Hotel, he found the two American agents, McPheeters and Richardson, waiting outside for him. They were in an inconspicuous rented car.

"Last day, faggot. Does your fuck-buddy live or die?"

Ashcroft smiled sweetly at them. "You have one million dollars in certified diamonds waiting for you when you deliver the goods. Present at the exchange will be a member of the Royal Dutch Parliament and a representative from the Queen herself. Just to make sure nothing goes wrong." He gave them Aaron's address and telephone number.

"We wouldn't have burned you, Ashcroft," said Richardson. "Not right now, anyway. Not for the ransom. But since you're so paranoid about dealing with your fellow-countrymen, we'll go along with your arrangement."

"Sure we will, partner," said McPheeters. "For now, that is. But let me tell you something, Ashcroft."

"I'm listening."

"Okay, then, it's up to you to make sure nothing goes wrong at your end. None of your smart-ass faggot reporter games. No press or television. Nobody from the World Court or the United Nations. And those stones better be worth at least one million Standard New Dollars, or you and everyone else you know in 'Dam is in a world of very deep shit. You do still understand American, don't you?"

"He understands, partner," said Richardson. "Let's go."

I wish, thought Ashcroft as they drove away, that I could run into those two some day during a field operation.

He sat at the bar drinking *oude genever* with beer chasers, not wanting to be too far from the phone. Each time it rang, he tried to be calm and not show his anxiety. Fortunately, he did not have too long to wait. About an hour and a half after McPheeters and Richardson had left, Aaron Ten Eyck phoned him.

"My word, old chap, you do have some very charming American friends, don't you?"

Despite the gravity of the situation, Ashcroft could not help but smile. "They really are something else, aren't they?" Actually, just the sound of Aaron's calm, self-assured voice had told him what he needed to know; that the arrangements had gone smoothly.

"I shouldn't ever try to double-cross those two," said the old man. "However, in this case both sides seem to be negotiating in good faith. Or at least enlightened self-interest, which is usually just as good. I suppose you want to know about your shipment, right?"

"Yes, for god's sake! When and how?"

"The 'how' they wouldn't tell me but one may reasonably conjecture a military aircraft, probably an air ambulance. As to the 'when,' I would suggest you be prepared to accept the merchandise here at my home at precisely noon, three days hence. In other words, two days from noon tomorrow."

Suddenly Ashcroft found himself shedding real tears, very copiously, as he sat at the bar clutching the telephone.

"Stephen!" he heard Ten Eyck's voice. "Are you all right, my boy?"

"Hell, yes, Aaron!" he exclaimed into the phone, composing his voice. "Absolutely super! I mean, wow! It's great! I mean, hey, I never even dared to hope, you know? I mean. . ." He realized he was blubbering and talking somewhat less than coherently.

"Stephen," said Ashcroft severely, "you're talking exactly like an American! Now really, lad, if you can no longer speak to me in complete sentences, I shall have no choice but to ring off!" Ashcroft could tell that the old man was proud and happy and pleased.

"Aaron," he said, "thanks for everything. I'll see you in three days." If I can live that long, he thought.

3

The next three days were passed in an agony of anticipation and suspense. Ashcroft prowled the streets of Amsterdam, trying to make time pass. The milder weather had brought out every hustler and drug peddler in town from wherever they had burrowed in to hibernate for the coldest months of winter. On the Damrak, he was offered drugs in infinite variety, and sex in even greater variety. Many of these pushers and hustlers were American. Sometimes he thought the Dutch were a little *too* easy-going and lenient about granting sanctuary to all who claimed political necessity, but he supposed it was better to err on the side of compassion.

"Hey, American bro," said one typical piece of human flotsam who accosted him. He was a bearded, shabbily-clad black dude, with hard, street-smart eyes. "How about some North African *kif?* Primo shit, man, I guarantee it."

"Sorry," replied Ashcroft, and added truthfully, "I get everything I need right where I'm staying."

The man looked over Ashcroft's boots, levis and leather vest. "Yeah," he said. "I guess you do. Well, hey, bro, if you don't wanna buy nothin', how about a couple of bones so I can eat?"

Ashcroft gave him a few guilders. The man shook his hand.

"Hey, you're a real American bro, man. Some day we goin' back, right?" He gave a clenched fist salute. "Kill the Preacher!"

Ashcroft returned the salute. "Kill the Preacher," he responded automatically.

The storefront that had once housed a famous cut-rate American travel agency was now a porn shop, both hard and soft core. On an impulse, Ashcroft stepped inside.

"Do you have anything by an American writer by the name of Greasy Grossberg?" he inquired.

"*Ach, ja,*" said the good-looking young clerk, beaming. "He is a very big seller all over Europe now. Ever since your country fell, they buy his books so we can hardly keep them in stock. I have one copy left of his latest. It's called *Luxembourg Loving.* Would you like to have it, sir?"

"How much?"

"Only forty guilders."

"I'm sorry," said Ashcroft. "Some other time." He left the shop thinking that a paperback edition of Dickens or Proust would have been less than ten guilders. Well, he thought, as the cliché goes, it's an ill wind that doesn't blow somebody some good.

That night as he sat at the hotel bar, Hans von Broecklen came in and sat next to him. He had a pleased smile on his face.

"Would champagne be in order, by way of congratulations?" he asked.

"Hans, I don't know what the hell you're talking about."

"Stephen, please. I am a policeman, after all. We have been asked to assign an inconspicuous plain-clothes detail to Aaron Ten Eyck's house on the day after tomorrow. A source at the palace informs us that a representative of the Court will also be there. A couple of well-dressed but very unsavory characters have been observed here at this hotel. All of this following upon the awful shooting of your friend Kiki. Now really, my friend, does one have to be a Sherlock Holmes?"

"Why don't you just run a news bulletin on television and let the whole country know?"

"*Ach,* Stephen, give us some credit for discretion! This conversation is strictly between friends. Believe me, not for all the world would any decent Dutchman do anything to — shall we say

— compromise the outcome of the, ah, transaction." Suddenly he grabbed Stephen, right at the bar, and gave him a huge, warm hug. "I am so happy for you, my friend," he said.

"I'll feel much better after it's all over," said Ashcroft. "Then we can have that champagne."

"I know what you must be going through right now. May I offer you a suggestion?"

"Let's hear it."

"Why don't we go upstairs to your room for a while? It will help make the time pass."

"Hans, I couldn't," protested Ashcroft. "Not with my lover due to arrive day after tomorrow. It just wouldn't be right."

Hans lowered his eyes and looked up at Ashcroft. "You can do anything you want to me," he said, and then, when the older man did not respond, he added, "Look, you are wound up so tight like a violin string. At least let me massage your shoulders and back a little so that you can relax."

Ashcroft shrugged. "I guess that'd be okay," he agreed. The blond young cop called Hartt over and ordered a round of drinks to take upstairs.

"Oh, my," said Hartt. "And this one's even old enough so he doesn't drink formula! Will wonders never cease!"

"One of these days, Hartt," said Ashcroft, "one of these days. And we'll see who gets spanked next time."

"Promises, ruddy promises," said Hartt, as he rang up the round of drinks.

In Ashcroft's room, Hans put his arms around the American and kissed him fondly on the lips. In a moment they had slipped into an embrace and then, despite his former resolution, the older man was roughly tearing off Hans' shirt. His fingers fastened on the boy's nipples, inflicting pain. Hans sighed with satisfaction and sank down onto the bed, pulling Ashcroft on top of him.

It was a long, hot, very rough session. Thinking of the two American agents and what they had done to Kiki, and of what had been done to his lover Troy, Ashcroft had a lot of hostility to let out of his system, and Hans did not seem to mind being on the receiving end. Ordinarily, although he enjoyed some good recreational leathersex, Ashcroft's prime directive would never let him actually harm anyone. This time, however, he had to focus all his awareness and sensitivity to keep himself from going beyond the blond boy's limits. At long last, with Hans almost in tears from his ordeal, they lay in each other's arms in a brotherly embrace.

"You see, Stephen? What did I tell you? Do you not feel much better now?"

Ashcroft had to admit that he did.

At the appointed hour, he took a taxi to Aaron Ten Eyck's apartment, one of the stipulations having been that he must not arrive until after the exchange had been completed. Apparently they had been afraid that he might lose control when he saw what had been done to Troy, or perhaps they had simply preferred not to have to deal with the wrath of an angry man.

A private ambulance was just pulling away, along with a large black unmarked American sedan that might have been an American Embassy staff car. A nearby limousine was probably from the Royal Palace, and there were a couple of unmarked police cars. A plainclothes constable recognized him and greeted him amiably.

"We have been waiting for you, Mijneer Ashcroft," he said. "Allow me to escort you upstairs." In the elevator, he smiled sympathetically. "Relax, my American friend," he said. "All is going to be well."

Aaron Ten Eyck greeted Ashcroft at the door of his apartment. They shook hands very warmly, and then the old man clasped him in an embrace.

"He's here, Stephen," he said. "He's free and he's safe. But — he is not at all well. Please prepare yourself for a severe shock."

Troy Anderson had been placed on a couch in the drawing room, where Aaron had tenderly covered him with a light blanket. The word horror would have been inadequate to describe what Ashcroft felt when he first saw his lover.

Troy was gaunt and emaciated beyond belief. His arms, which rested on top of the blanket, were like matchsticks. His face was skeletal, the skin dry and translucent like old parchment. He looked like the photographs Ashcroft had seen of concentration camp victims liberated after World War Two. Troy's eyes brimmed with tears as his lover knelt at his side.

Ashcroft did not see the gaunt, wasted figure. Once again, he was transported to Fort Lauderdale, and the house in which they had spent five happy years. He smelled the orange and hibiscus flowers in bloom; saw once again the bougainvillea. He saw the tall, hunky well-muscled blond, the all-American fantasy dripping in leather, whom he had first met so long ago at the Glory Hole in Miami. Very gently because Troy now looked so fragile, he took his lover in his arms, holding him tightly and rocking him back and forth. At last, they kissed.

"I never dared to hope," said Troy. His voice, which had once matched his stalward physique, now came out faint and raspy, almost a croak.

"Neither did I," said Ashcroft.

"If my parents could see me now," said Troy.

"Don't tell me," said Ashcroft, recalling the night of the Jefferson-Jackson Day Dinner at which Douglas McKittrick had first announced his campaign, and at which Troy Anderson had first knowingly broken bread with overt Democrats. "They'd not only be spinning in their graves, they'd have to install a rotisserie."

"You got that right," said Troy. He was crying, in spite of his efforts at self-control. So was Ashcroft.

So were Ten Eyck and the man from the Palace.

"How my Herschel would have cherished this moment," he said, as Ashcroft cradled his lover in his arms.

"I wish he had been captured," said Ashcroft. "I wish you two could have had a moment like this."

The man from the Palace said something to Aaron in Dutch, and then they shook hands. To Ashcroft and Troy, he said in English, "I am happy for both of you and I wish you the best of luck." He wiped his eyes.

"Thank you very much," said Ashcroft, as he departed.

Ten Eyck's maid served hot chocolate and biscuits. Troy sipped his very slowly, almost as though he were still apprehensive as to what might be in it.

"Aren't you going to ask me if I had a nice flight?" he said.

"All right," Ashcroft responded. "Did you have a nice flight?"

"It was different," replied Troy. "You know how these cheap discount fares work. I'll give you a hint, though; don't ever fly military if you can help it."

"I promise," said Ashcroft. "Believe me, I promise."

They finished their cocoa and biscuits.

"I think we'd better get on our way home," said Ashcroft.

"You surely can't mean you're taking him back to your digs at the Leather Eagle," said Ten Eyck in surprise. "He'd be much more comfortable here, until he recovers. He'd be most welcome, and I assure you he'd receive the best of food and care."

"I know he would, Aaron. Thank you very much for the offer. But the Leather Eagle is where I live. Dirk said we could have the VIP room for as long as we need it."

"All right, then," said Ten Eyck. "If you absolutely insist. I'll have one of my chaps go scrounge up a wheelchair someplace."

"That won't be necessary," said Ashcroft. "I'd appreciate a ride home in your car, but I can take care of my lover."

"It's yours, dear lad," said Ten Eyck, handing him the keys to his Volvo. "You can fetch it back later, after you've gotten Troy all settled in."

Ashcroft wrapped Troy tightly in the blanket. Before, he would have had difficulty in hoisting the big, hunky blond over his shoulder. Now, he picked Troy up in his arms with ease. Troy clung to him, his arms around Ashcroft's neck.

"Been kind of overdoing it on the dieting, haven't you?" said Ashcroft.

"Yes, well, you know, it's this fitness craze. You can never can be too rich or too thin." His voice was hollow and weak, but the old bravado, the insouciance was still there.

"Wait until you taste the food at the hotel," said Ashcroft, as he carried Troy to the elevator. "We'll get you back in shape damn quick. Have you ever eaten Dutch *fricadellen* with noodles and gravy?"

"Sounds fattening as hell. Can you get a McGreaseburger in this town? With American style french fries?"

"Unfortunately," said Ashcroft, "yes."

4

The celebration party and the strategy session which followed it were held one week later in the VIP room of the Leather Eagle Hotel. The celebration was for Kiki's release from the hospital, and Troy's release from the American detention camp. They were both still weak and emaciated from their respective ordeals, but gaining weight and strength every day.

The travel season had commenced, and the hotel was almost full. There were leather brothers and bike club members from most of the neighboring countries, and they all looked in to have a drink and to wish good luck to Kiki and Anton and to Ashcroft and Troy.

Dirk had gone all out on the food, champagne, beer, whiskey, and *oude genever*. In addition to the hotel guests, the entire staff of the hotel was present, replenishing food and drink and taking turns to watch the front counter and the lobby bar. Hans von Broeklen was resplendent in his police uniform, much to the envy of some of the bikers. Even Aaron Ten Eyck was present, ensconced in the very best chair and being treated much more deferentially than he would have wished.

Eventually, even Dirk's lavish collation had been consumed, the liquor and beer was almost gone. The guests drifted off, leaving the principals to hold their strategy conference. Hans was the first to discuss the bad news.

"I have spoken to the chief of my section, but his orders are very firm. I'm afraid Stephen will have to go."

"That's a bloody shame," said Ten Eyck. "A disgrace to the city of Anne Frank! I can see I shall have to bring some influence to bear in the right places."

"No!" said Ashcroft emphatically. "I appreciate it very much, Aaron, but please don't do anything of the sort."

"But why not?" demanded Dirk. "I thought you liked it here."

"I do," replied Ashcroft, "very much, and if I felt I had any right to stay, I would have asked Mijnheer Ten Eyck to use his influence. But the fact is that their reasons for wanting me to leave are perfectly reasonable and valid. We've got two that we know of — more likely a dozen — cold-blooded, ruthless professional killers out there, operating with impunity from behind a diplomatic cover."

"He's right, I'm sorry to say," said Hans. "As much as we would all love to have Stephen and Troy stay with us forever and ever, we just can't have our own people being shot and killed."

"Hans," asked Ashcroft, "would your chief let us stay at least until my lover is well enough to travel?"

"Well, of course," said Hans. "That was never even a matter of discussion! Take as long as you need, Troy; three weeks, a month, whatever. We'll keep a police guard on the hotel until then."

"But what are you two going to do when you leave?" asked Dirk.

"I plan to go on with my work for the Documentation Committee," said Ashcroft. "And the Resistance. The only thing is, we'll just have to keep on traveling, until we can find a safe haven we can call our home."

"Any ideas about that?" asked Troy. "It sure would be nice if we had a home of our own again, eventually."

"Well, we can make our first stop in Luxembourg and visit Greasy Grossberg and his *ménage*. You might like it there. After that, who knows? Maybe Vienna."

"Why Vienna?" Troy wanted to know. "That's pretty close to the wrong side of the Danube, isn't it?"

"Yes, that's the whole point. Hungary and Czechoslovakia have both been making overtures toward the expatriates and refugees. It would be one hell of a propaganda coup for the other side."

"You can't really be serious," said Troy.

"Why not?" said Ashcroft. "Actually, neither of those two countries would be *too* awful. At least they have great food and lots of it, and Czech beer is outstanding."

"Forget it!" said Troy, very firmly. "Our present situation is bad enough, but that's where I draw the line! I know you've always quoted Voltaire to me about patriotism being the last refuge of scoundrels, but no matter how bad things are back home, I'm not going to defect to the other side, and that's final!"

"The High Command has just spoken," said Ashcroft. "There goes my fantasy of endless streams of slivovitz and Pilsner Urquell."

"How about Australia?" asked Troy. "You've always liked it tremendously. Great leather scene, you told me. And at least they do speak English — well, sort of."

"Australia's a great country," said Ashcroft, "but the government is homophobic as hell. Of course they'd accept us in a minute, just on humanitarian grounds, but I wouldn't be allowed to do any Resistance work or Resistance writing."

Aaron Ten Eyck spoke up. "Let me suggest that you shouldn't make any firm decisions right now," he said. "For the present, just keep on traveling and doing your work and your writing. Allow me, however, to make one small contribution, if I may."

"You've done so much already," said Troy. "I owe you my life."

"Now, now," said the old man. "We shan't dwell on that. But it has occured to me that there is a better alternative to knocking about on trains and buses and sleeping in railway stations and the like. I happen to have a rather large delivery van that I've used for years for courier work simply because it looks the very last piece of transport on earth that one would use for carrying precious gems. Like myself, it's ancient, but still very travelworthy. What I propose is to turn this vehicle over to you two lads to use as your traveling home on wheels for as long as you need it. And since you're working for the Documentation Committee, I shall also provide a credit card for the petrol and maintenance."

"Wow!" exclaimed Ashcroft. "Aaron, I don't know what to say!"

"Then it's settled. Troy, does that meet with your approval?"

"It sure does, Mr. Ten Eyck! I've seen some awesome delivery van conversions. I'll bet I could fix it up just like *La Belle Hélène!* Stephen, do you remember our wonderful cross-country trip, way back before all this happened?"

"I remember every single moment of it," replied Stephen, squeezing his lover's hand.

"Right, then!" said Aaron. "Well, at least that's settled."

Little Anton, who had been standing by Kiki's chair with his arm around his lover's shoulders, spoke up. They had been whispering to each other briefly.

"Stephen, Kiki and I have just made a great decision," he announced. "We have decided that we are coming with you. If you and Troy will have us, that is."

"I'd love to have you," replied Ashcroft, "and I'm sure Troy would, too." His lover nodded assent. "But why on earth would you want to leave this lovely, comfortable city to live on the road?

And in constant danger, too; let's not forget that to my country's government, I'm a marked and wanted man."

Kiki spoke up, weakly but determinedly. "After what has happened to me, Stephen, I'm sure you'll have to admit that we have a right from now on to share in your work. And besides, wouldn't a *ménage à quatre* be even more fun than a *ménage à trois!*"

Ashcroft put his arm around Troy. "I should have warned you," he said. "They're a couple of *very* kinky little kids. Do you think you can handle it?"

Troy grinned. "I can now," he replied. "Hey, Stephen, I think you'll find me a hell of a lot less doctrinaire about a lot of things after what we've both been through. I know, I used to be pretty uptight about monogamy as well as politics."

"But not anymore?"

"I sure hope not. It's not that I don't love you more than ever, and I always will. But hey, I just don't see anything wrong anymore with having a little brother or two helping to keep our bed warm. As long as we all love each other, that is."

"Watch out, Stephen," said Aaron Ten Eyck, winking at him. "I think Troy is becoming more European every day." He rose from his chair. "Well, it's past my bedtime. I'll bid all you beautiful young people a goodnight."

"Me, too," said Dirk. "Stephen, I'm sorry we never did get to..." He suddenly remembered that Troy was present. "Well, anyway."

"After all you've done for me," said Ashcroft, "and for the Resistance, I would have been proud, Dirk. An act of brotherhood." He gave the hotel owner a warm and brotherly embrace.

When everyone else had left the room except Kiki and Anton, Troy suddenly asked,

"Are there any good discos and leather bars in this town?"

"In *Amsterdam!*" exclaimed Ashcroft. "You've got to be kidding! The best in all of Europe!"

"Okay, then, as soon as I feel strong enough, the four of us are taking the Grand Tour. We're going to hit every good bar and disco in town." Then his face suddenly fell. "Oh, my god, I just remembered! I don't have any money." He looked up at his lover grimly.

"That's going to be the hardest thing to get used to," he said disconsolately.

"Oh, nonsense," said Ashcroft. "You'll find out how unimportant it is. Besides, we won't starve. We'll have Resistance salary, local refugee relief, and I still do some writing that earns a Eurodollar or two. Not much compared to what you used to have, but did we ever really need all that?"

"It's different for you," said Troy. "You've never had any."

"That's okay," said Ashcroft. "You'll learn. And besides, since when did you suddenly develop a thirst for the bars? You used to say, and I quote you verbatim, 'Why should anyone have to buy high-priced drinks in order to endure a physical environment that would be totally unacceptable in a concentration camp?' Is this one of the things about which you've now become less doctrinaire?"

"You're damn right," said Troy. "That was before I saw the inside of a *real* concentration camp. Hey, guys, I don't *care* about the noise and the crowds and the smoke! I just want to be on my own turf again, with gay brothers and lesbian sisters and leather brothers all around me, even if they do get a bit rowdy at times!"

Kiki hugged Anton and said, "I'll see that he gets a hero's welcome at the Viking. Stephen, you'll have to make your own arrangements at the leather bars."

"No special treatment," said Troy firmly. "Just the Grand Tour."

They drank and relaxed in the warmth of each other's company. Anton's eyes filled with tears.

"I think," he said, "that I have found my real family at last."

"I think I have, too," said Troy. "Maybe this is the kind of life I should have had all along, instead of being a prostitute for the advertising business." And then, very sadly, he asked, "Do you think we'll ever be able to go back to the United States?"

Ashcroft thought for a moment. "I rather doubt it." He had never really admitted that to himself before.

"All gone, huh?"

"It ended the night Doug McKittrick was assassinated."

"But, Stephen, how — why — did we let it happen?"

"There's an old saying," said Ashcroft. "It's been repeated so often it's trite, but it's true. It goes like this: 'In order for evil to triumph, it requires only that men of good will remain silent and do nothing.' I'm sorry, Troy. We had it all in America, and we blew it."

"And I was one of the ones who said nothing. Hell, I even denied it was happening!"

"Well," said Ashcroft gently, "let's just put it down to the Boiled Frog Syndrome."

"*Ach*, Troy," exclaimed Anton, rushing over to him and hugging him, "stop this talk at once! You also had in your country years ago the most wonderful folk-singer in the world, a chap by the name of Bob Dylan. Over here we still play his records very often. And did he not say, *Don't Look Back!*"

"You're right, little brother," said Troy, who had become very fond of the younger boy. He liked Kiki, too, but Anton was something very special: the kid brother he had always wanted and never had. "You make good sense, Anton. From now on, it's just the four of us. We'll travel light and we won't ever look back."

"*Ja*, I know," said Kiki solemnly. "Right now it looks very uncertain, our future. But as long as we are all four of us together, and we keep up our strength and our courage, we will be just fine, *neen!*"

"We'll be just fine," said Ashcroft reassuringly, even though the spectre of Richardson and McPheeters still hovered at the edge of his awareness. "We'll all be just fine."

"I'll tell you something else," said Troy. "If we ever do find some nice, safe little country where we can settle down, I promise you one thing. No matter what happens politically, there'll be no more kidding ourselves that it can't happen here. I've learned my lesson about that, okay?"

Kiki raised his glass. "The four of us. Here's to the future!"
They drank.

Other books of interest from
ALYSON PUBLICATIONS

Don't miss our FREE BOOK offer at the end of this section.

☐ **HOT LIVING: Erotic stories about safer sex,** edited by John Preston, $8.00. The AIDS crisis has encouraged gay men to look for new and safer forms of sexual activity; here, over a dozen of today's most popular gay writers erotically portray those new possibilities.

☐ **MEDITERRANEO,** by Tony Patrioli, $12.50. Through exquisite photos, Italian photographer Tony Patrioli explores the homo-erotic territory in which, since the beginning of time, adolescent boys have discovered sex. (Oversized paperback)

☐ **IN THE TENT,** by David Rees, $6.00. Seventeen-year-old Tim realizes that he is attracted to his classmate Aaron, but, still caught up in the guilt of a Catholic upbringing, he has no idea what to do about it until a camping trip results in unexpected closeness.

☐ **THE HUSTLER,** by John Henry Mackay; trans. by Hubert Kennedy, $8.00. Gunther is fifteen when he arrives alone in the Berlin of the 1920s. There he is soon spotted by Hermann Graff, a sensitive and naive young man who becomes hopelessly enamored with Gunther. But love does not fit neatly into Gunther's new life ... *The Hustler* was first published in 1926. For today's reader, it combines a poignant love story with a colorful portrayal of the gay subculture that thrived in Berlin a half-century ago.

☐ **ALL-AMERICAN BOYS,** by Frank Mosca, $5.00. "I've known that I was gay since I was thirteen. Does that surprise you? It didn't me..." So begins *All-American Boys,* the story of a teenage love affair that should have been simple — but wasn't.

☐ **I ONCE HAD A MASTER and other tales of erotic love,** by John Preston, $8.00. One of this country's best-known writers of erotic gay male fiction here tells the story of a man's journey through the S/M world, beginning with another man as his master and ending in that role himself.

□ **A HISTORY OF SHADOWS,** by Robert C. Reinhart, $7.00. A fascinating look at gay life during the Depression, the war years, the McCarthy witchhunts, and the sixties — through the eyes of four men who were friends during those forty years.

□ **THE MEN WITH THE PINK TRIANGLE,** by Heinz Heger, $6.00. In a chapter of gay history that is only recently coming to light, thousands of homosexuals were thrown into the Nazi concentration camps along with Jews and others who failed to fit the Aryan ideal. There they were forced to wear a pink triangle so that they could be singled out for special abuse. Most perished. Heger is the only one ever to have told his full story.

□ **SAFESTUD: The safesex chronicles of Max Exander,** by Max Exander, $7.00. "Does this mean I'm not going to have fun anymore?" is Max Exander's first reaction to the AIDS epidemic. But then he discovers that safesex is really just a license for new kinds of creativity. Soon he finds himself wondering things like, "What kind of homework gets assigned at a SafeSex SlaveSchool?"

□ **ENTERTAINMENT FOR A MASTER,** by John Preston, $8.00. When a Master plans a party, it's no small undertaking. Here — in the long-awaited sequel to Preston's *I Once Had a Master,* you'll follow the planning, the testing of applicants, and the execution of one of the most outrageous parties of all time.

□ **TALK BACK! A gay person's guide to media action,** $4.00. When were you last outraged by prejudiced media coverage of gay people? Chances are it hasn't been long. This short, highly readable book tells how you, in surprisingly little time, can do something about it.

□ **THE LAW OF RETURN,** by Alice Bloch, $8.00. The widely-praised novel of a woman who, returning to Israel, regains her Jewish heritage while also claiming her voice as a woman and as a lesbian. "Clear, warm, haunting and inspired" writes Phyllis Chesler. "I want to read everything Alice Bloch writes," adds Grace Paley.

☐ **QUATREFOIL,** by James Barr, introduction by Samuel M. Steward, $8.00. Originally published in 1950, this book marks a milestone in gay writing: it introduced two of the first non-stereotyped gay characters to appear in American fiction. For today's reader, it remains an engrossing love story, while giving a vivid picture of gay life a generation ago.

☐ **GAY AND GRAY,** by Raymond M. Berger, $8.00. Working from questionnaires and case histories, Berger has provided the closest look ever at what it is like to be an older gay man. For some, he finds, age has brought burdens; for others, it has brought increased freedom and happiness.

☐ **IN THE LIFE: A Black Gay Anthology,** edited by Joseph Beam, $8.00. When Joseph Beam became frustrated that so little gay male literature spoke to him as a black man, he decided to do something about it. The result is this anthology, in which 29 contributors, through stories, essays, verse and artwork, have made heard the voice of a too-often silent minority.

☐ **LONG TIME PASSING: Lives of Older Lesbians,** edited by Marcy Adelman, $8.00. Here, in their own words, women talk about age-related concerns: the fear of losing a lover; the experiences of being a lesbian in the 1940s and 1950s; and issues of loneliness and community.

☐ **CODY,** by Keith Hale, $7.00. What happens when strangers meet and feel they have known one another before? When Cody and Trotsky meet in high school, they feel that closeness that goes beyond ordinary friendship — but one is straight and the other gay. Does that really matter?

☐ **THE LOVE OF A MASTER,** by John Preston, $8.00. After the successful S&M party that was the subject of *Entertainment for a Master,* what more could the Master desire? Well, certainly not a return to the quiet life. Perhaps one of the hunky young men around him in the mountains of New England needs *The Love of a Master.*

THE ALEX KANE BOOKS:

☐ No. 1: **SWEET DREAMS,** by John Preston, $5.00. In this, the first book of the series, Alex Kane travels to Boston when he hears of a ruthless gang preying on gay teenagers; in so doing he meets his future partner, Danny Fortelli.

☐ No. 2: **GOLDEN YEARS,** by John Preston, $5.00. Operators of a shady nursing home think they can make a profit by exploiting the dreams of older gay men — but they haven't reckoned with the Alex Kane factor.

☐ No. 3: **DEADLY LIES,** by John Preston, $5.00. Kane goes after a politician who's using homophobia to advance his own political career.

☐ No. 4: **STOLEN MOMENTS,** by John Preston, $5.00. Kane takes on a tabloid publisher in Texas, who has decided that he can take advantage of homophobia to increase his paper's circulation.

☐ No. 5: **SECRET DANGERS,** by John Preston, $5.00. Kane and his partner battle a world-wide terrorist ring that has made a specific target of gay tour groups.

☐ **WORLDS APART,** edited by Camilla Decarnin, Eric Garber and Lyn Paleo, $8.00. Today's generation of science fiction writers has created a wide array of futuristic gay characters. The s-f stories collected here present adventure, romance, and excitement; and maybe some genuine alternatives for our future.

☐ **ONE TEENAGER IN TEN: Writings by gay and lesbian youth,** edited by Ann Heron, $4.00. One teenager in ten is gay; here, twenty-six young people tell their stories: of coming to terms with being different, of the decision how — and whether — to tell friends and parents, and what the consequences were.

☐ **WANDERGROUND,** by Sally Miller Gearhart, $7.00. Here are stories of the hill women, who combine the control of mind and matter with a sensuous adherence to women's realities and history. A lesbian classic.

☐ **BETTER ANGEL,** by Richard Meeker, $6.00. For readers fifty years ago, *Better Angel* was one of the few positive images available of gay life. Today, it remains a touching, well-written story of a young man's gay awakening in the years between the World Wars.

☐ **WE CAN ALWAYS CALL THEM BULGARIANS: The Emergence of Lesbians and Gay Men on the American Stage,** by Kaier Curtin, $19.00. Despite police raids and censorship laws, many plays with gay or lesbian roles met with success on Broadway during the first half of this century. Here, Kaier Curtin documents the reactions of theatergoers, critics, clergymen, politicians and law officers to the appearance of these characters. Illustrated with photos from actual performances. (Clothbound)

Get this book FREE!

Personal classifieds are an increasingly popular way to meet people these days. In their book *Classified Affairs*, John Preston and Frederick Brandt take a look at the gay male personals. Here's everything you need to know about how to write a personal that really attracts attention, and what to expect when you place, or answer, an ad. Interspersed with the text are dozens of the most memorable classifieds you'll ever read.

CLASSIFIED AFFAIRS

A Gay Man's Guide to the Personal Ads

John Preston & Frederick Brandt

Normally $7.00, *Classified Affairs* is yours **free** when you order any three other books described here. Just check the box at the bottom of the order form on the next page.

To get these books:

Ask at your favorite bookstore for the books listed here. You may also order by mail. Just fill out the coupon below, or use your own paper if you prefer not to cut up this book.

GET A FREE BOOK! When you order any three books listed here at the regular price, you may request a *free* copy of *Classified Affairs*

— — — — — — — — — — — — — — — — — —

Enclosed is $_____ for the following books. (Add $1.00 postage when ordering just one book; if you order two or more, we'll pay the postage.)

1. _____
2. _____
3. _____
4. _____
5. _____

☐ Send a free copy of *Classified Affairs* as offered above. I have ordered at least three other books.

name: _____

address: _____

city: _____ state: _____ zip: _____

ALYSON PUBLICATIONS
Dept. H-8, 40 Plympton St., Boston, Mass. 02118

This offer expires Dec. 31, 1989. After that date, please write for current catalog.